PRAISE FOR CAROLYN BROWN

Hummingbird Lane

"Brown's (*The Daydream Cabin*) gentle story of a woman finding strength within a tight-knit community has just a touch of romance at the end. Recommended for readers who enjoy heartwarming stories about women overcoming obstacles."

—*Library Journal*

Miss Janie's Girls

"[A] heartfelt tale of familial love and self-acceptance."

—*Publishers Weekly*

"Heartfelt moments and family drama collide in this saga about sisters."

—*Woman's World*

The Banty House

"Brown throws together a colorful cast of characters to excellent effect and maximum charm in this small-town contemporary romance . . . This first-rate romance will delight readers young and old."

—*Publishers Weekly*

T0262434

The Family Journal

HOLT Medallion Finalist

"Reading a Carolyn Brown book is like coming home again."

—*Harlequin Junkie* (top pick)

The Empty Nesters

"A delightful journey of hope and healing."

—*Woman's World*

"The story is full of emotion . . . and the joy of friendship and family. Carolyn Brown is known for her strong, loving characters, and this book is full of them."

—*Harlequin Junkie*

"Carolyn Brown takes us back to small-town Texas with a story about women, friendships, love, loss, and hope for the future."

—*Storeybook Reviews*

"Ms. Brown has fast become one of my favorite authors!"

—*Romance Junkies*

The Perfect Dress

"Fans of Brown will swoon for this sweet contemporary, which skillfully pairs a shy small-town bridal shop owner and a softhearted car dealership owner . . . The expected but welcomed happily ever after for all involved will make readers of all ages sigh with satisfaction."

—*Publishers Weekly*

"Carolyn Brown writes the best comfort-for-the-soul, heartwarming stories, and she never disappoints . . . You won't go wrong with *The Perfect Dress*!"

—*Harlequin Junkie*

The Magnolia Inn

"The author does a first-rate job of depicting the devastating stages of grief, provides a simple but appealing plot with a sympathetic hero and heroine and a cast of lovable supporting characters, and wraps it all up with a happily ever after to cheer for."

—*Publishers Weekly*

"*The Magnolia Inn* by Carolyn Brown is a feel-good story about friendship, fighting your demons, and finding love, and maybe just a little bit of magic."

—*Harlequin Junkie*

"Chock-full of Carolyn Brown's signature country charm, *The Magnolia Inn* is a sweet and heartwarming story of two people trying to make the most of their lives, even when they have no idea what exactly is at stake."

—*Fresh Fiction*

Small Town Rumors

"Carolyn Brown is a master at writing warm, complex characters who find their way into your heart."

—*Harlequin Junkie*

The Sometimes Sisters

"Carolyn Brown continues her streak of winning, heartfelt novels with *The Sometimes Sisters*, a story of estranged sisters and frustrated romance."

—All About Romance

"This is an amazing feel-good story that will make you wish you were a part of this amazing family."

—*Harlequin Junkie* (top pick)

The Party Line

ALSO BY CAROLYN BROWN

Contemporary Romances

The Sawmill Book Club

Meadow Falls

The Lucky Shamrock

The Devine Doughnut Shop

The Sandcastle Hurricane

Riverbend Reunion

The Bluebonnet Battle

The Sunshine Club

The Hope Chest

Hummingbird Lane

The Daydream Cabin

Miss Janie's Girls

The Banty House

The Family Journal

The Empty Nesters

The Perfect Dress

The Magnolia Inn

Small Town Rumors

The Party Line

CAROLYN BROWN

Published by Montlake, Seattle

www.apub.com

Amazon, the Amazon logo, and Montlake are trademarks of Amazon.com, Inc., or its affiliates.

ISBN-13: 9781662514357 (paperback)
ISBN-13: 9781662514364 (digital)

Cover design by Lesley Worrell
Cover image: © Jasmin Sander / Plainpicture

Printed in the United States of America

To Janice (Davis) Pendley,
for all the good memories

Chapter One

Aunt Gracie wasn't afraid of spiders, mice, or snakes, and there was no doubt in my mind that she would face off with the devil himself without blinking. Just that look she could give when she was angry would have him whimpering and running away with his forked little tail tucked between his legs. She taught me fearlessness, so why were my hands shaking and every hair on my head feeling like I'd just gotten hit by a lightning bolt?

As a child I had hunted ghosts in Aunt Gracie's old two-story house lots of times—under the beds, where all I found was dust bunnies the size of baby elephants, and in closets where musty old clothing that had been stored for at least a hundred years made me sneeze. So why was this so different?

You are dreaming, an eerie voice whispered in my head. Holy smokin' hell! I had finally located a ghost, even if it was in a nightmare. I opened my mouth to ask who was talking to me, but no words would come out. The thought went through my head that someone had drugged and kidnapped me, and this was one of those crazy reactions to whatever potion they had given me.

A loud noise brought me somewhere between sleep and fully awake. Was that chains I heard rattling in the attic? I blinked a couple of times, and a strange scent wafted across the room. Had whoever drugged me done so by putting something in the air vent? I shook my head and glanced over at the open window. Fresh morning air carried the aroma of a skunk somewhere in the neighborhood, or maybe someone was smoking weed in my yard.

I scanned the room, moving only my eyes. The door was open, so I hadn't been kidnapped, but I was not in my apartment in Austin. I was in my bedroom in Aunt Gracie's house, the one with the yellow floral wallpaper and the antique furniture. I sat up slowly and reached for my cell phone to see what time it was, only to find the bedside table bare of everything. Evidently, I had swiped it clean when I was dreaming about the ghosts that might know whatever secret Aunt Gracie had taken with her to the grave a couple of weeks before.

All the folks in Atascosa County had wondered about that secret for more than eighty years, and still today I didn't know what it was. Aunt Gracie had most likely hung on to it so tightly that the angels in heaven—or ghosts down here—couldn't pry it out of her hands.

The sheets were tangled up around me, holding me down tighter than if I'd been chained to the bed. Sweat popped out all over me as I fought my way free. When I was finally on my feet beside my bed, I tried to remove my ragged old sleep shirt, which was drenched with sticky moisture, but that was another fight. It was glued firmly to my body like it had taken up squatter's rights. By the time I freed myself from the thing, I felt as if I'd fought and barely won a battle. I waved my hand above my head until I found the wooden thread spool attached to the string that turned on the overhead light bulb. The brightness almost blinded me when it lit up the room.

A coyote howled, and for a minute I thought the critter was coming right into the house. I rushed over to close the window and realized I was wearing nothing but a pair of white cotton granny panties. If anyone had been standing outside staring up, they would have caught sight of me, but at least a coyote wouldn't crawl inside my bedroom. So it was a win.

When I moved to Austin to go to college, I had gotten so used to sirens going off every few minutes that I didn't even hear them after a few weeks. Ditto, Texas, population less than twenty-five, didn't have sirens, except when there was an ambulance arriving from Poteet to take someone to the hospital. The howling coyotes, barking dogs, and donkeys braying to celebrate the sunrise were something I would have to get used to.

"Coyotes cannot climb trees or sticky bushes to get into a second-story window," I assured myself.

I took a step toward the nightstand and tripped over the base of the old party line phone. I fell face forward over the bed and into a big feather pillow that did its best to smother me to death. Damn, did my toes hurt.

The sun wasn't even up and my day was already crappy. I rolled over on my back and stared at the ceiling until that bare light bulb put red dots in front of my eyes. Finally, I got up, picked up the base of the phone, and slammed it down on the nightstand with enough force to rattle the pictures on the walls. The receiver swung back and forth like a pendulum, barely touching the floor. My sweat-dampened hair hung in limp strands and kept getting in my eyes when I dropped down on my knees to search for my cell phone. It had skittered halfway under the bed and was lying in a pile of dust bunnies.

"I hope y'all don't bite," I whispered as I reached as far as I could and still couldn't put my hands on the phone. Then the dang thing lit up and started ringing—startled me so badly that I jumped and hit my back on the bottom of the bed.

After several words that almost wilted the yellow roses right off the wallpaper, I finally freed myself and stormed out into the hallway, still wearing nothing but my sweaty granny panties. I forgot all about my phone and headed to the bathroom. The old pipes squealed like baby piglets when I turned the knobs and sent the water up to the shower-head. After what seemed like half an hour later, the water was finally warm enough for me to step around the end of the curtain into the claw-foot tub that probably was put into the house when it was built a hundred years before. I thought the disastrous morning was over when I'd finished washing my hair and started to step over the edge of the tub.

I was wrong.

I did not inherit Aunt Gracie's fearlessness when it came to spiders, and one was sitting on the braided rug where I was about to plant my foot. I didn't squeal or scream. What came out of my mouth sounded more like a screech—maybe from a two-hundred-pound owl from pre-historic times. The spider stared up at me with pure unadulterated evil in his beady little eyes. In that moment I was ready to move back to Austin even if the rent on my apartment doubled. The eight-legged critter pranced across the rug like he was the king of the house, and just to show me what he could do, he jumped on top of my towel, which was lying on an old ladder-back chair.

I didn't care if he was one of those wolf spiders that could win a pole-vaulting contest. In my mind the only good spider was a dead one, so I grabbed a bottle of shampoo from the little shelf above the tub and, with one blast, sent him to that great spiderweb in the sky. I got another towel, because I wasn't about to use the towel he had touched to dry my body.

I did not tempt fate by thinking nothing else could possibly go wrong that morning, just marched out of the bathroom with a towel around my body and another one wrapped turban-style around my head. I went to my room and dressed in a pair of faded jeans and a T-shirt that had George Strait's picture on the front of it—Mama brought it to me when she and her boss, Madge, had attended a concert.

The door to Aunt Gracie's bedroom was open when I walked past, so I peeked inside. There was another of those black party line phones on her bedside table. When I asked her why the phones didn't have a dial or push buttons on them, and why she kept something that didn't even work, she explained the process to me. Seems like way before my time, back before Aunt Gracie was even a teenager, whoever wanted to make a call picked up the receiver, and the operator said, "Number, please." The caller gave her three or four digits—Aunt Gracie's line was 298—and the operator plugged in a cord on the other end that rang that person's phone.

"And sometimes folks like us here in Ditto had to share lines. Our phone rang three short times when the call was for us, but we shared with two other folks. One of them got a long ring, the other got a short followed by a long one," she had told me.

"But now you have a working phone in the kitchen, so why don't you throw these away?" I asked.

She said that she kept them as a reminder of a very bad time in her life. Her expression when she thought about that experience was one I figured she used to freeze mice, spiders, and the devil's horns. She had kept me from the time I was an infant so my mother could work at one of the cafés in Poteet, and I liked staying with her, so I didn't pry any further.

A memory surfaced, and I tried to give that black phone the same look she did when she told me about it. I was a little girl back then, and overheard Mama telling Madge, who was her boss at the café where she had cooked and waitressed since before I was even born, that she didn't understand how anyone could live in a house full of ghosts and secrets.

I thought it would be great to find a real ghost, so for a whole year, I prowled through all the nooks and crannies in the whole two-story house, looking for one. I'm not sure what I would have done if an eerie figure had popped out from behind a dresser or even from behind a door—probably turned tail and run, screeching like I did when the spider showed up in the bathroom.

I also never did find what the big secret was; it was only whispered about behind those fans at church with Jesus on one side and a big bowl of strawberries on the other. That morning, almost two decades later, I wondered if somewhere, hidden away safely, there might be a diary or a journal, or maybe even a piece of paper with SECRET written in big letters on the front and an explanation on the back.

"I think the secret is that there is no secret," I said out loud as I walked down the stairs and into the foyer and the kitchen. The plastic strawberry slapped me right in the forehead as I crossed the floor. The thing was about the size of a golf ball and was attached to the chain that turned on the lights. I grabbed it on the second swing and pulled so hard that it came off in my hand.

"*Why* didn't you have the electricity updated?" I groaned as I searched for the chain. I'd just found it and given it a tug when Mama came in, carrying a take-out container of soup.

She set it on the counter and headed across the floor. "The breakfast crew will be waiting at the café door to come in for their morning gossip session, but I saved you back some soup from yesterday."

"Do you know what this big secret is about this house?" I asked. "I was having a nightmare and . . ." I went on to tell her about my morning. "I figure it's that there is no secret at all. That someone made up a rumor and it's hung on all these years, like Bigfoot, Santa Claus, or that monster in the ocean."

"Oh, there's a secret, all right. Aunt Gracie knew what it was, but she didn't tell anyone."

"Then how did anyone even know there *was* one?" I asked.

"Something happened when she was a teenager that upset her so badly that she wouldn't come out of her room for a week," Mama answered. "When anyone asked about it, like I did years later, she would get this look on her face that was frightening. I only asked one time because her expression scared the bejesus right out of me."

"The look that would terrify the horns off Lucifer?" I asked.

"That's the one," Mama said with a nod and a shiver. "Rumor has it that when she came out of her room, she had words with her parents, but whatever was said stayed between the walls of this house. That's when the gossip started about the secret. Poteet was already known for being the birthplace of George Strait and the best strawberries in the state, but they added the secret to the list."

"She never told anyone?" I asked. "Not even Jasper?"

Mama shook her head. "Not sure, but if she told him, he's never said a word, either. That would have been more than eighty years ago, and no one knows to this day what it is. How can you spend any nights in this haunted house? It's not easy for me to be here in the daylight." Mama crossed the room and put her hand on the doorknob.

"The sun is coming up and ghosts don't like daylight, so you are safe," I told her.

She shook her finger at me. "Don't tease me about something this serious."

I outgrew my mother in height when I was in the fifth grade. That old adage about dynamite coming in small packages was what came to mind that morning. She had been a young mother at eighteen and raised me by herself, with help from Aunt Gracie. Mama's dark hair didn't have a gray streak anywhere, and she had that peaches-and-cream complexion that movie stars would die for. That was the good DNA from Aunt Gracie's side of the family. The Evanses were known for never having gray hair and always having lovely skin. But she was Mama's first cousin—three times removed—and by the time the Matthews' DNA tainted what came from Aunt Gracie's family, I didn't get any of their good looks.

People often said I didn't look a thing like her, and they were right. I am a tall redhead with pale skin that burns and freckles but never tans, and I have a curvy body that could weather an F5 tornado without needing even so much as a breath mint in my pocket much less a rock or two.

"Evidently, the superstition gene wore plumb out when it got to me, because I don't believe in spirits and ghosts." I opened the container and ate several bites of the cold vegetable soup as I carried it to the table.

"That's cold, and it's not a breakfast food," Mama scolded me.

"Tastes good to me, but if you insist." I put it in the microwave and hit the two-minute button. "There. It'll be hot pretty soon, and you need to get to work. Those old coffee-drinking guys will be banging on the door for you and Madge to let them inside. Thank you for the breakfast. I could eat your soup three times a day and not get tired of it."

Mama opened the door and took a step out onto the back porch. I could feel her relief when she was officially out of the house. She waved from the other side of the old screen door. "You are welcome. Now that you are living close by, you can reap the benefits of your mother working in a café. You want to come watch a movie with me tonight?"

"Thanks, but no thanks." I took the soup from the microwave and set it on the table. "I'll be chained to the computer all day, so I'm going to take some time to sit on the porch, breathe in the fresh night air, and watch the sun go down. Want to come down here and have a beer with me?"

"Thanks, but no thanks," she repeated. "You know how I feel about this place. I'll be here at ten thirty in the morning to pick you up for church."

"Call me when you get here, and I'll come right out," I told her.

She waved again, and then I heard the crunching sound of tires on gravel as she drove away.

Since I had searched diligently for the ghosts when I was a little girl and never found even a single one, I didn't believe the house was haunted. The secret folks still talked about and had become as important as strawberries and George Strait—now that was a whole different matter. If it concerned Aunt Gracie, I wanted to know all about it.

I opened the drawer where Aunt Gracie had always kept the cutlery, grabbed a spoon, and had a nice hot breakfast. When the bowl was empty, I got a piece of bread and sopped up what juice was left. I tossed the container in the trash, washed the spoon, made a cup of coffee in the new one-cup-at-a-time machine I had given Aunt Gracie for Christmas, and headed to the back porch.

Jasper, Aunt Gracie's lifetime friend, was sitting in an old wooden rocker on his porch, only twenty yards from mine. He waved and motioned me over. I held up my coffee, and he held up his to show me he had a full mug. I crossed the yard and set my mug on the tree stump that had been between the two rocking chairs for as long as I could remember and took a seat.

"Beginning of a brand-new day. It's time to sit a spell to let the peace settle around you and reflect on life before you dive into your work," he said.

"Amen to that," I told him. "I've got a full load waiting for me today."

He took a long drink and then said, "You shouldn't work on Saturday. You need some time for the body to rest. Even God needed some downtime."

"I'm still playing catchup from the days I used to live in Austin," I said. "But this is the last Saturday I'll have to put in hours."

"That's good," Jasper said with a curt nod. He had aged well and could have easily passed for eighty instead of ninety-six. I used to try to count the freckles on his face, but after I got to a hundred, I gave up. One thing for sure, he had more than I did. His hair was once a dark chestnut brown, but now it was as white as Aunt Gracie's bedsheets. When I was a little girl he had a beard and mustache that he kept expertly trimmed, but these days he was clean shaven.

"Gracie has been on my mind a lot lately. I sure do miss her. I figured I'd go before she did," he said.

"Y'all were friends for a long time, so it would be normal for you to miss her." I took a drink of coffee and set the chair to rocking.

"I can't remember a time when we wasn't friends," he said with a long sigh. "Davis and me and Gracie were inseparable as little kids." He stopped talking and rocked awhile before he continued. "Every day after school, we'd meet up right here in this yard and play all kinds of games. Davis and his mama lived in this house back then, and me and my grandma lived on the back of the property. Granny and Davis's mama, Rita, both helped the missus with cooking, cleaning, and taking care of Gracie. When we was in high school, Davis and his mama moved to Poteet, and my grandma and I moved into this house. Gracie and I saw Davis at school every day, but things wasn't the same after that."

"How were they different?" I asked.

He just shrugged and changed the subject. "A tornado demolished our old house in 1950 while I was still in the army. Nobody had lived in it for years, but it was my childhood home, and I missed it when I got back from the army. I moved in here with Granny and never did get around to finding my own place. Mr. Evans hired me to help him with his oil well business. He sold off all that just before he died. My granny still cleaned the house until Gracie made her retire. She died a year after that. Gracie kept me on the payroll, and I helped her out with yard work and whatever else she needed done until we were both sixty-five."

That didn't sound like it could be connected to the secret, but I filed it all away to think about later.

"Why did they move? Did Davis's mama get a better job?" I wondered if leaving Ditto had something to do with the secret.

"Granny didn't know, but it wasn't long after that when the missus left Mr. Evans and went to live with her friend up in Oklahoma. When I asked Granny about it, she just told me to mind my own business," Jasper said.

"Did you?"

"Yes, ma'am. I still don't poke around in other people's business," Jasper said with a smile and pointed up to the sky. "Look at that beautiful sunrise with all the pretty colors. It comes up in the east just like it does every morning. That's one thing we can depend on that never changes. It'll never disappoint us, and it'll come up in the mornin' and go down in the evenin' sure as shootin'. You goin' to church with your mama tomorrow?"

"I guess I am," I said with a sigh.

Aunt Gracie had taken me to church every Sunday morning until I graduated from high school and went to Austin. Mama worked the morning shift in those days, but she always went to the evening church service. That meant I had to sit on a hard oak pew twice on most Sundays. After I left, Mama had Sundays and Mondays off, so she and Aunt Gracie went to the morning services and seldom attended in the evening. And me? Well, Sunday became the day for doing my laundry and catching up on sleep.

"You do know that God don't live in a church house building?" Jasper's statement came out more like a question. "If we look at nature, we can see him."

"But *you* go to church," I reminded him.

"Yes, ma'am, I do," Jasper said in a serious tone. "I like the singin' and the fellowship. I'd be glad for you to go with me if you want. You might even drive me into Poteet for a hamburger afterwards."

"What time?" I asked.

"It starts at eleven, so we need to leave about a quarter till. I go to the little church only a couple of miles down the road." He motioned to his left with a wave of his hand.

"Then I'll pick you up at that time," I told him.

"That'll be good. I don't drive anymore. I had one fender bender too many, and Gracie wouldn't let me get my license when it came up for renewal. She drove both of us until the day she went on to heaven to meet up with Davis."

"When did Davis die?" I asked.

"We both enlisted right out of high school. Four years later I came home, but he didn't." His voice quivered, so I didn't ask any more questions.

He stood up, picked up his cane, and headed across the porch. "Have a good day, Lila."

I pushed up out of the chair and took a step toward the house. "You, too, Jasper."

"I'm glad you decided to live in Gracie's house. Seems fittin'," he said before he disappeared inside.

I kicked off my flip-flops so I could feel the soft green grass beneath my feet—something I hadn't done since I was a child—sucked in the cool morning breeze, and enjoyed the smell of spring that filled the air as I crossed the yard from the little house to the big one. I exhaled and then took another deep breath, and that time I got a whiff of ripe strawberries. "Bless the Broken Road," an old song by Rascal Flatts, popped into my mind. I sang the lyrics off-key and out of tune as I made my way to the back door, leaving the cool grass behind for the wooden porch. The lead singer said that he blessed the broken road that led him home. Of course, it was a love song, and he was glad that all the roads he had traveled had brought him home to his soulmate. I wasn't sure the universe had a person like that in store for me, but I was glad for the peace that washed over me that Saturday morning.

I left my flip-flops on the back porch and went upstairs to my new office, and when I reached the foyer, I could have sworn that I heard Aunt Gracie say, "Turn off the kitchen light. Electricity ain't free, my child."

With a smile, I turned around and went back to obey her. At least it was daylight and I didn't have to grope around for the wooden spool on the end of the cord. I was crossing the foyer when I noticed the arrangement above the credenza. I stopped and studied the collage Aunt Gracie had made of my school pictures, from kindergarten all the way through my senior year. It had hung there in the foyer for more than a decade, but that morning I really looked at the photographs.

"Hmmm . . ." I studied each of the twelve pictures lined up around the one in the center, which had been taken my senior year. "I wonder if there's a picture of my father hidden away somewhere. I must look like him because I certainly do not look like Mama or Aunt Gracie." I giggled out loud at the crazy thought that went through my mind. "And I dang sure don't look like George Strait."

I have to admit that in the past I did wonder if my birth father—maybe George Strait—was the third thing, but then I remembered that party lines were done away with years and years before my mama was even born. I still had hopes that a file with CLASSIFIED written in red letters was hiding somewhere in the house, and maybe when I found the thing, there would also be something about my father in it. Mama said that he left town before I was even born. She had looked so sad that I was afraid she would cry if I asked about a picture, so I didn't.

Maybe the file is hidden behind something, I thought as I continued to stare at the picture. Something that was out in plain sight all the time—like the photograph right there before me. I removed the frame from the wall and turned it over. Nothing there, and the only thing behind where it had been hanging was a perfect rectangle of Wedgwood blue wallpaper sprigged with tiny white flowers, which had not faded like the rest of the foyer walls. There wasn't a piece of paper, a file, or even a safe hiding behind the picture with a secret combination, like maybe the numbers in Aunt Gracie's birthday. Not even a tiny cabinet that I could open and find a journal inside.

"It's got to be here somewhere," I muttered as I hung the picture back where it belonged and went on up to my office.

Aunt Gracie's gravelly voice popped into my head. *Three people can keep a secret if two of them are dead.*

"Does that mean that one person still knows?" I asked out loud.

She didn't answer, so I had no clue. I glanced over at a stack of mail on the credenza and promised that I would go through it the next day after church. Since we had a Poteet address, went to church in Poteet, and I'd ridden the bus for thirteen years to Poteet schools, I figured that gave me bragging rights to say I was from Poteet when anyone asked. That sounded better than telling folks I was from Ditto.

I went on up to my office, which was really the fourth bedroom. I stood at the double doors that opened out onto the balcony and stared out across the land. Only a few houses remained in the community of Ditto—now barely even a community, much less a town. Aunt Gracie's two-story place—with four bedrooms upstairs and a living room, kitchen, and dining room on the first floor—was the biggest house in the area. Mama's small place was down the road a quarter of a mile, and Jasper's was in the backyard. A couple or three more were scattered between our little part of the community and Poteet, but not many. The last time a census was taken in Ditto, the population was somewhere around twenty.

That evening, when I had finished my work, I went out to the back porch expecting to see Jasper. His front door was open, and I could see the blue light from his television. A loud voice was announcing an upcoming ball game. I didn't want to disturb him, so I went back inside, grabbed a beer from the refrigerator, and carried it to the front porch. By the time I finished it, I had had my fill of crickets and tree frogs announcing that it was now spring and strawberry season was about to be in full swing. I went inside and had a long bath, read several chapters of a book, and went to sleep earlier than usual.

That night I dreamed that I was riding the bus home from school, and we passed the sign at the edge of town that read WELCOME TO POTEET, BIRTHPLACE OF GEORGE STRAIT. Mama loved his music and played it so much that I used to tell myself that the man was really my father, that Mama had just made up the story about my dad not sticking around. In my dream, the King—that's what Mama called him—was waiting for me when I got off the bus at Aunt Gracie's house, and he held my hand all the way from the end of the lane back to her house. He called me *Princess* and then disappeared.

I woke myself up giggling. If there was ever a princess in Ditto, Texas, it dang sure wasn't Lila Matthews. I got out of bed thirty minutes before my alarm went off and headed down to the kitchen for my first cup of coffee.

I popped a couple of breakfast pastries in the toaster and wished for a bowl of Mama's soup or maybe even some cold lasagna. When the cinnamon-flavored carbs popped up, I carried them and my cup of coffee to the back porch and sat down on the top step. Jasper looked up from his Bible and waved, but he didn't motion me over. I waved but didn't intrude on his meditation.

The fields to the west of the house were red with strawberries. My first good, solid memory was a beautiful spring day when Aunt Gracie and Jasper took me out to the edge of the twenty acres to pick the first big, ripe ones. They let me eat half a dozen or more right off the plants before we carried a full basket back to the house to make a strawberry shortcake.

Way back before I was born, Aunt Gracie had leased the final twenty acres of what she had inherited to Otis Thurman. He had always let her gather what she wanted for her own use, so she made strawberry jam with some of them and froze several bags to put on the top of ice cream or to eat for dessert.

Like most small towns or communities, everyone knew everyone, and the family history that went with each person. Take the strawberry field, for instance: When Otis died, the lease was passed down to his son, Everett. He and his wife had one son, who hated the ranching business and instead chose the military life. Everett's wife died a while back, and his only grandchild, Connor, had come home last fall, according to Aunt Gracie. Everett had always reminded me of a scarecrow—tall, lanky, with a crop of unruly hair, and he always wore bibbed overalls. A person would never guess that he owned most of the town of Ditto and had more money than a mile of the golden streets of heaven.

I swatted flies, ate my breakfast, and drank my coffee in peace and quiet—something I had missed in the city. I noticed a streak in the sky and almost made a wish on it, but then I realized that stars falling out of the sky didn't show up in the daylight. What I had seen was the trail of an airplane, most likely flying south out of San Antonio.

The few times I had seen a falling star, I wished that party lines were still around so I could listen in on other people's conversations and learn their secrets—maybe I would even hear what Mama called "the big secret of Ditto."

Aunt Gracie was old when I was a little girl, and she wasn't really my aunt—but in the south, the word *aunt* is kind of an honorary title given to a kinswoman who is elderly. I could never figure all that cousin-so-many-times-removed stuff out, either, so in my mind, she was my aunt, my surrogate grandmother, and my friend.

A picture of the three people—my mother, Jasper, and me—gathered around Gracie's wooden casket the afternoon of Valentine's Day came to my mind. The preacher had read Psalm 23, said a quick prayer, and then each one of us put a rose on her casket. I had always given her a homemade valentine—complete with lots of hearts decorated with glitter—and a lollipop on the holiday, so I put the one I had ready to give her on the casket with the roses. We had followed her directions to the letter, except for the valentine. There was to be no big funeral at the church, where she had gone her whole life. No family dinner afterward. She wanted the three of us to be there, and the preacher to do exactly what she had written down. Then we were to go back to her house and hear her lawyer read her will.

We had done just that. I had been shocked to learn that she'd left everything—house, bank accounts, and her stock portfolio—to me and not my mother or Jasper. I signed papers for the better part of an hour. She had left Mama a nice big sum of money, and, according to the will, Jasper had the right to live in the little house for as long as he wanted or until he died. Mama was glad she didn't have to deal with Gracie's house or all its contents. Two weeks later, I had moved into the house and set up an office in one of the bedrooms.

The old golden housephone that hung on the kitchen wall startled me when it rang. I grabbed it and said, "Hello?"

"I'm not going to church this morning," Mama said and then sneezed. "I think I've just got hay fever, but it could be a summer cold. I don't want to spread it."

"Why didn't you call my cell phone?" I asked.

She coughed. "Sorry about that. I did try your cell, but it went straight to voicemail."

"It's under my bed, and I can't reach it. I'll have to take a broom up there and fight the dust bunnies to get it," I explained. "I should have called you last night. I promised Jasper I would go with him this morning and then take him on into Poteet for a hamburger afterwards."

"Aunt Gracie gave him rides to and from church all the time," Mama said and sneezed again. "They were a strange pair, but they'd been best friends since . . . well, way back when."

"Did Jasper ever work anywhere else?" I asked.

"If he did, Gracie didn't mention it," Mama said. "Before Gracie's daddy, Clarence, died, he sold off all his oil business and land to Otis Thurman . . ."

I jumped in. I didn't have all that much time—coffee was waiting. "Aunt Gracie filled me in on all that news, and I've always known that they were good friends." I took a couple of steps and figured out that the phone cord did not reach to the coffeepot.

"Are you sure you don't want to just drop him off and go on to our church?" Mama asked.

"No, I think I'll stay with him."

Mama sneezed a third time. "I've got to go find a box of tissues. The one beside the sofa is empty. Don't come down here until I figure out if I'm contagious."

"Want me to leave some chicken soup on your porch?" I asked.

"I've got a can or two in the pantry." She sneezed again. "Bye, now. If I get to feeling better, I may have you pick up a pizza—but don't get it until I call you."

"Will do, and if you need anything, I'm right here," I told her.

I was dressed and waiting in my SUV when Jasper made his way slowly around the house. His black suit hung on his frail body, and he leaned on his cane more than I remembered from the funeral, but he had a smile on his face and his Bible tucked under his arm.

"Let's go get some Holy Spirit," he grinned.

"I probably need a double dose this morning," I told him as I opened the passenger door for him.

He raised an eyebrow. "Front seat?"

"Of course," I said. "Why do you ask?"

"Me and Gracie thought it best not to rock the boat, so I rode in the back seat. She was one to keep things proper so rumors wouldn't get started."

"Well"—I patted him on his bony shoulder—"let's rock the boat this morning."

Chapter Two

*M*y old bones will hurt tonight, but they feel pretty good right now." Jasper eased into the front seat of my SUV after the Sunday-morning service, but he seemed to have a little more spring in his step than he had had earlier.

I closed the door for him, rounded the back end of the vehicle, and slid in behind the steering wheel. "That was a really uplifting service, but why do you expect your bones to feel bad tonight?"

"I smell rain in the air. Good for the earth. Good for the strawberries. Bad for the old bones," he answered.

"That sounds like something Aunt Gracie used to say."

"Yep, it does," he grinned. "She always loved spring. Declared that it took ten years off her age."

The mention of her name brought back so many memories of spring when I was a little girl. How we would sit on the porch swing and she would tell me stories. I could feel my brow drawing down. In all those wonderful days, why hadn't she ever told me a single thing about the secret?

"Do you know what Gracie's big secret is that folks have talked about all these years?" I blurted out. He'd know.

"Your aunt would have told you if she'd wanted you to know," he declared and cut his eyes around at me. *Foiled again!* "Let's go get a hamburger and maybe a slice of chocolate cream pie if there's some left at the café. It goes fast on Sundays. It's a big treat for me to get to go to the café. Gracie wouldn't let me renew my license because I had trouble getting my foot from the gas over to the brake . . ."

I shook my finger at him. "You are changing the subject."

"Yes, ma'am, I surely am, and I will every time you ask me that question about the secret," he said with a curt nod. "Someday that's not even going to be something that folks remember to tell their kids about, and it will die."

The café parking lot was full, so I let Jasper off right in front of the place. I made a couple of rounds and finally snagged a spot between two pickup trucks. Big white fluffy clouds floating lazily in the sky sent my thoughts back to a time when Aunt Gracie and I lay flat on our backs in the yard. We would take turns telling each other what kind of animal the clouds were shaped like. Mine were always puppies or kittens. Hers were teddy bears, church steeples, and sometimes even cowboy hats.

I stepped inside expecting to find Jasper waiting to be seated, but he waved from a booth back in the corner. I made a beeline toward it, grateful he hadn't had to stand for a long time. A couple of times I noticed folks whispering behind their hands, as usual with Aunt Gracie. I was halfway across the floor when an elderly lady reached out and touched my arm.

"You are Sarah Evans's daughter and Gracie Evans's kin, aren't you?" she asked.

"Yes, ma'am, I am," I said with a nod. "Were you a friend of hers?"

"Not really, but my grandmother knew her, and when I was a teen-ager, we picked strawberries on her place a few times. Poor old darlin' was such a recluse after she sold her dress shop, but she seemed to enjoy folks coming out to Ditto to gather berries," she replied.

I stuck out my hand and tried to control my anger. This woman was fishing for gossip—and how dare she call Aunt Gracie *old*. "I'm Lila Matthews, and yes, I'm kin to her."

"Edith Johnson," the woman said as she shook my hand. "Glad to meet you. I saw you and Jasper in church this morning."

"It was a very good service." I dropped her hand and hurried back to join Jasper at the booth.

"If you lie down with dogs, you might get up with fleas," he said under his breath.

"What does that mean?" I asked.

"There's some folks who like to spread rumors." He pulled the one-page menu out from between the napkin dispenser and the salt and pepper shakers, and shifted his eyes toward the table where Edith and her friends were whispering.

"Are you talking about . . ." I slid a sly glance their way, and felt I'd been right in my judgment of the woman.

He nodded. "Did you see any of them at the graveside service or bringing food to the house?"

"I understand, but her wishes were that only me and you and Mama attend the service." I kept my voice low. "Now, what's good in here these days besides their burgers?"

"Everything . . . But they still could have brought a covered dish to the house for you and Sarah." Jasper frowned, but his expression quickly changed to a more pleasant one. "All me and Granny could afford was the hamburgers back in the day, so I'll be ordering one of those, with french fries and a big old glass of sweet tea. And then some chocolate pie. I see a whole one up there under the dome on the counter, so I'm in luck."

I didn't even look at the second menu. "Then that's what I'll have, too, and dinner is on me today."

"I invited you to go to church and Sunday dinner, so I should pay," he argued.

I laid my hand on his and shook my head. "Let's just say that Aunt Gracie is paying for it. She left me well fixed, and she would love to know that we are having Sunday dinner together."

"In that case, I won't argue," Jasper agreed. "Reckon that we could make it a weekly thing?"

"I would love that."

"Then it's a done deal. I miss her the most on Sundays," he said with a long sigh. "Listen . . ." He cocked his head to one side.

"What?" I whispered and strained my ears to hear whatever it was that had gotten his attention.

"That's the sound of rain on the metal roof of this place. Our old house—the one where I grew up—had this kind of roof, and a good rain was like a lullaby that put me to sleep at night," he said.

I was surprised when I looked out the window to see that dark clouds had pushed their way past the pretty white ones.

"Mama's house has a metal roof, and I loved the sound of rain, too," I told him.

"Hello, Jasper," the waitress said. "Been a while since I've seen you."

"Yep, it sure has. You'll remember Annie, Lila. She's the great-grand-daughter of the folks who built this place."

"Of course I do," I said. "She's Mama's friend."

She was about Mama's height but had a stockier frame and build. Her brown hair had a few gray hairs starting to show, but her smile was genuine and reached her hazel eyes.

"You haven't changed since you were in high school." She pulled out an order pad.

"I can't believe you talked Jasper into actually coming into the café. He and Gracie usually order takeout," Annie said.

"It was my idea," Jasper admitted.

"Well, good for you," Annie said, then turned to me. "While y'all are eating, you should get him to tell you all about what's happened in Poteet and Ditto since you've been gone."

"He's pretty stingy with his stories," I said.

Annie air-slapped him on his thin shoulder. "Shame on you."

"Ouch!" He grabbed his shoulder. "I'm old and fragile."

"That's a load of BS." Annie chuckled and pointed at him with her pencil. "What'll it be today?"

"Burger with everything on it, fries, and a large sweet tea," Jasper answered.

"The special today is chicken and dressing and all the trimmings," she suggested.

"I'll take two of those to go," Jasper told her, "but today I want a big old greasy burger and fries."

"I'll have the same as Jasper, and I'll take a couple of those specials to go also," I told her.

"I'll put this order in and get it out to you real soon," Annie said. Her expression became serious as she turned to go. "I was real sorry to hear about Miz Gracie. I would have come to the funeral, but Sarah told me that Gracie left orders to only have y'all there."

"So will *she* tell me more stories?" I whispered when she had disappeared through swinging doors into the kitchen.

"Nope. Annie is rock solid. She probably hears a lot of gossip in this place, but she don't spread it," Jasper said out of the corner of his mouth.

Argh. "Good to know. I'm glad you thought to order some takeout for tomorrow. I'll take a dinner to Mama and keep one."

Annie brought out our glasses of tea and set them on the table, then hurried over to wait on another group that had come in out of the rain.

"The chicken and dressin' won't be as good as Granny's, but it will be my supper for a couple or three days," Jasper said. "We only had it on Thanksgiving and Christmas when I was a little kid. Granny made it for parties that Miz Betty and Clarence had up near the holidays. 'Course we always had plenty to eat because the missus did not eat leftovers."

"Why?" I wondered out loud.

"She had her own ways about things, but it was a good thing for us," Jasper replied.

The rain came down harder, and a flash of lightning zipped through the sky. Some folks hurried out of the café, but the smarter ones ordered dessert and stayed inside, probably hoping the storm would pass quickly.

Jasper tilted his head toward the window. "Looks like we got lucky."

"Because we got here before the rain started?" If he had tried to shuffle his way from the café to my vehicle, he would have been soaked to the skin.

"No, because it didn't hail. The strawberries will be fine with a good rain. Hail would have destroyed the crop."

"I would have whined until Christmas if I didn't get at least one strawberry shortcake," I told him.

"I'm putting those on the menu next Sunday," Annie said as she set a red plastic basket in front of each of us.

"We'll be here, good Lord willin' and the creek don't rise," Jasper chuckled.

"People are going to say that you're datin' a woman young enough to be your granddaughter," Annie teased in a low voice.

"Hmmph . . ." Jasper almost snorted. "Try young enough to be my great-great-granddaughter. And me and Lila don't pay no attention to rumors." He winked across the table at me. "Do we?"

"No, sir, we do not!" I exclaimed. "And we'll look forward to that shortcake next Sunday."

"If it gets low, I'll save back enough to make y'all each one," Annie said. "I'll have those to-go boxes ready by the time you leave."

"Thank you," Jasper said as he unwrapped the paper from his burger and took a bite.

"Just like you remembered?" I asked.

"Oh, yeah," he said with a smile. "You reckon we might go by the cemetery and see Gracie after we eat? If it's rainin', we wouldn't have to get out. She just needs to know that I ain't forgot her."

"We can do that," I agreed. "How about we go see her after Sunday dinner each week?"

His green eyes glazed over, and his chin quivered. "I'd like that very much."

Texans often tell folks that if they don't like the weather to stick around thirty minutes and watch it change. That's what happened that Sunday morning. One second, it was raining cats and dogs and baby elephants. The next, the sun was shining brightly, and a beautiful rainbow appeared in the sky.

The cemetery wasn't far from the café, but then Poteet only boasted a population of a little over three thousand people. Driving in a small town was nothing like going from one side of Austin to the other. I hated those years when the pandemic hit and I'd had to stay home, but I was more than glad to not have that hour-long commute to work every day. When things settled down, the folks decided that I could do my job from home permanently. That made it easy for me to move back to Ditto and set up an office in Aunt Gracie's house.

I drove slowly through the cemetery, and when I braked and pulled off to the side of the narrow road, Jasper threw the door open and grabbed his cane. He shuffled over to the tombstone with MARY GRACE EVANS engraved on it.

He pulled a bag from his pocket, removed a huge strawberry from it, and laid it on top of the stone. "This and the rainbow in the sky is for you. I'm right sorry I haven't been out here before now, but Lila says she'll bring me every Sunday from now on." He placed his hand on the top of the gray granite and didn't even try to hold back the tears. "Tell Davis hello for me," he said between sobs, "and y'all keep a watch on the gates. I'll be knockin' on them before too long."

His words brought tears to my eyes, and soon they were streaming down my cheeks and dripping onto my shirt. The memories of all the good times my aunt and I had during my growing-up years flooded my mind. He patted the stone, straightened his back, and walked on a few yards farther. A small headstone marked RITA POTEET was next to one engraved DAVIS POTEET. Jasper dropped to his knees right there in the wet grass and laid both hands on his old friend's name.

"She's with you now," he whispered. "I don't know why the good Lord ain't come for me. I know there's one more job I have to do, but

I'm not sure I can handle it all by myself. I'm stuck between a rock and a hard place, my friend. I want to run through heaven with y'all like we did when we had races to the old barn and back, but . . ." He paused and glanced over his shoulder at me and clamped his mouth shut.

He started to rise but stumbled. I grabbed him and hugged him close until he could get his balance. He wiped his eyes and chuckled. "Darlin', if folks see us like this, there *will* be rumors."

I took a step back. "I don't really care what people think or say. I'm not going to let you fall and hit your head on those tombstones."

He chuckled again. "Might be a good way to check out of this world," he said. "I'm ready to go home now."

"Which one?" I asked.

He straightened up to his full height and dried his eyes on a white handkerchief he pulled out of the pocket of his khaki dress pants. "I only got one home on this earth, and God ain't ready for me yet."

"Don't you usually use a red or blue bandanna?" I asked.

"This is my Sunday britches and hankie, and we need to get our takeout stuff put away. Be a shame for it to go bad after Gracie paid good money for it."

"She didn't like to waste anything, especially food," I agreed and remembered all the times that Gracie and I had made *gotta go*, which was simply getting all the leftovers out of the fridge and heating them up.

He nodded off a couple of times on the trip home, but when I pulled into the driveway, he awoke. "It's been a good day, Lila. I look forward to next Sunday."

"Me too," I told him. "I'll take your food to your house for you. Was your friend Davis related to the Poteets that the town was named for?"

"Most likely, but Rita's daddy was the black sheep of the family, and she kind of followed in his footsteps. Thank you for everything today, Lila. I'm needin' my Sunday-afternoon nap for sure." He covered a yawn with his hand.

"Why?" I asked.

"Why what?"

"What do you mean about Rita following in her daddy's footsteps?"

"Her daddy was the town drunk. Her poor mama had to scrape by doing ironing for other folks so she could feed their six kids. And then Rita wasn't married when she had Davis. You got to remember, that was almost a hundred years ago, and things were different then."

I picked up the bag with his food in it and followed him around the house and into the backyard. "I would have liked to have known them."

"They were good people. I'm glad I got to talk to Gracie and Davis. Me and Gracie went once a week to see Davis ever since he was brought home to be buried. I bet he didn't even know I missed a few weeks, since he's got his Gracie up there with him now. He's waited for her for a long, long time. Her daddy didn't like us going to the cemetery, but she never was one to take orders from him, not after . . . That's a story for later."

That was another little tidbit of information I filed away in my mind. Aunt Gracie seldom mentioned her father to me—or her mother, either, for that matter. Come to think of it, there were few pictures in the house of either of them. I couldn't imagine them not being good people, since Gracie was such a sweetheart to me and my mama. Gracie had no time for my biological grandmother—her cousin, twice removed—because she kicked her daughter, Sarah, out of the house when she got pregnant with me. That was when Aunt Gracie gave Mama the little house down the road, just plumb signed the deed over to her and told her cousin she wasn't welcome in her house anymore.

"Where is your mind, Lila?" Jasper asked.

His voice jerked me out of the past and into the present really fast, and I was surprised to see that we were standing on his porch. "Woolgathering," I said honestly. "What did you say?"

"I said that I could take my food from here," he told me. "I'd invite you in, but you need to get one of them boxes down to your mama."

"I really do." I refused to let the tears damming up behind my eyelids fall. Good memories seemed to pop up and hit me at the strangest times, like making *gotta go* soup or *gotta go* omelets with Aunt Gracie. "See you tomorrow sometime."

"I hope so," he said and slid a wink my way. "If I ain't out on the porch at dawn, just kick the door in and call the undertaker."

"Oh, no!" I shook my finger at him. "You've got more stories to tell me before we make that phone call."

"Gracie said you would keep me on my toes," he replied with a chuckle. "Tell Sarah hello for me, and to not be a stranger."

"I will," I agreed and headed back around the big house to my vehicle. A strong scent of chicken and dressing filled the SUV, making me really glad I'd brought home a for-later dinner for myself.

Just as I slid under the wheel, my phone rang. I tapped the front of the screen to answer my mother's FaceTime call, and her picture popped right up. "Hello, Mama. Are you feeling better?"

"Yes, I am. You know how allergic I am to cats? Well, a stray one left hair all over my porch swing. I didn't even notice it when I spent at least an hour out there last night. I've sprayed it down real good, and I've had some ginger tea and taken my allergy pill."

"That's great because I'm on the way to your house right now. We ate at Annie's Café today, and I'm bringing you a chicken-and-dressing dinner."

"That would be wonderful." Her voice sounded strained, but I attributed it to the allergy attack. "I was about to heat up chicken noodle soup from a can. Can you stay awhile? I've got some peach cobbler in the fridge, too, and there's always a beer if you want one."

"Of course—and, Mama, you don't have to entice me with pie and beer to get me to come spend time with you."

"Be aware that I'm weepy today," she said and then the screen went dark.

I started the engine and drove out of the circular driveway. I parked in the gravel driveway behind her ten-year-old pickup truck, grabbed the food from the back, and hurried inside the small house. I had only seen my mother cry a handful of times in my life—when she left me in the kindergarten room the first day, when I graduated from high school, and the day we buried Aunt Gracie came to mind. But she was sitting at the kitchen table with tears streaming down her face that afternoon.

I set the food on the counter and rushed over to wrap her up in my arms. "What's happened, Mama?"

"Thirty years of *happening* all hit me at once this morning," she said between sobs.

Evidently, she had been crying for hours, because an empty box of tissues was still in the middle of the table and the floor was covered with fluffy white wads.

I pulled one from a full box and gently wiped her tears away from her cheeks. "Talk to me and explain what has hit you. You are the strongest woman I know, and I can't stand to see you cry like this."

She took a deep breath, straightened her shoulders, and blew her nose. "Enough of this. I need to heat up the dinner you've brought me. Aunt Gracie always said that food heals a broken heart."

"It might not heal it, but it'll sure put a Band-Aid on it, and we both know the healing power of a Band-Aid and a kiss on the forehead." There was no way I could slap a Disney princess Band-Aid on her heart, but I could give her a kiss on the forehead, and I did. "Now, you sit right there while I warm up your food. Beer or sweet tea?"

"Tea for me." She wiped tears from her eyes. "I'm sorry that you are seeing me like this."

"Hey, I remember lots of times in the past when you helped me through a crying jag. And you also know that I never let anyone cry alone." I let the dammed-up tears stream down my cheeks. "What brought all this on, anyway?"

"Madge is selling the café. She called me today and offered it to me. I could use the money Gracie left me to put a down payment on it and borrow the rest from the bank, but . . ." She paused, took a deep breath, and finally went on. "I got to thinking back over all my past mistakes and how the consequences of them got me to this point in my life. I'm looking fifty right in the eye, and I'm still a waitress and cook at the same place where I went to work at sixteen. The same place where I met your father, and you know where that led. I'm not sure I'm capable of running a café. Madge is selling out because keeping help has become a major problem. I'd be inheriting that problem, plus having to learn about keeping books and all that."

I put her food on a plate and stuck it in the microwave. "You never talked about my father except to tell me that he took off when he learned you were pregnant, and—"

"I found him on the internet this week," she blurted out. "They say that bad news comes in threes, and I believe it. Aunt Gracie died suddenly. My job is in jeopardy. Your biological father died after a long bout with lung cancer six months ago. He was only fifty-one years old."

My mind went into overdrive so fast that I didn't hear the microwave ding. Did I have half siblings? Did I look like them? What was my father's name?

"I know you have questions," she finally said with a long sigh. "His name was Billy Grady. I was attracted to the bad boys, and he was the poster boy for that type."

"Do I have siblings?" I whispered.

"None were listed."

"Do I look like him?"

Mama shook her head. "Nope. You look like my grandmother. She was a tall redhead. Billy wasn't much taller than me and had dark hair and brown eyes. Anything else?"

"Not tonight," I answered, feeling a bit deflated. In my mind he had been a hero of some kind. A fireman who'd died rescuing a child from a burning building, a policeman who'd been killed by a fleeing bank robber, or even a movie star—and sometimes, in my dreams, he was George Strait.

"Good, because other than a few personal memories, that's all I know. His obituary was really sparse," Mama said.

"Let's talk about that café," I said when I finally got my mind to hop off the roller coaster and think about something else. "Do you want to own it? You don't have to go to the bank for a loan. You and I can buy the place for you with my inheritance, or you can retire and grow even more beautiful roses like the ones in the front yard."

Mama shook her head. "That money is yours, not mine."

I put her food on the table and sat down beside her. "No, Mama, it is not just mine. You sacrificed for me all those years and would have borrowed money for my college if Aunt Gracie hadn't insisted on paying. So if you want that café, we will buy it. If you want to retire, I'll put you on the estate payroll. Think about it a few days."

Mama raised an eyebrow. "She left me money, too, you know."

"I know, and neither of us ever need to work another day in our lives." I patted her on the shoulder. "I happen to like my job, and I'd go bananas if I didn't work. But after more than thirty years of waiting on people, I really think *you* should retire. Maybe you could do some traveling or upgrade your truck."

"Sweet Lord!" she said with a wave of her hand. "It's too much to think about today—but thank you, Lila, for giving me the gift of a choice."

I covered her free hand with mine. "I love you, Mama, and I appreciate everything you've ever done for me."

Chapter Three

Strawberry season had always been an exciting time of year for me. The berries ripened the first couple of weeks in March in our part of the state. Folks would come from miles around to pick their berries, and Aunt Gracie would let me sit behind the table with her and Mr. Thurman while she helped him with the sales. Everett would be setting up the canopy and tables nearly every morning once the berries began to really redden.

Before I started to school, we didn't see many people other than Jasper, the folks at church on Sundays, and, until they all passed away, maybe weekly visits from Gracie's poker friends. So strawberry season was the time when lots of folks came out to Ditto to gather what Gracie called the very best strawberries in Atascosa County. When folks asked Everett how he grew such juicy berries, he would tease and say that it was an old family secret. That morning, when I took my break and carried my glass of sweet tea out to the back porch, the idea of that secret hit me.

Was that little joke about whatever fertilizer or trick they had for strawberries been what had started the rumor that lasted for more than eighty years? I was pondering on that when I heard deep laughter and folks talking. What sounded like a dozen mice fighting over a chunk of cheese came from the hinges of Jasper's wooden screen door when he pushed it open. I reminded myself to take some oil out there and fix the squeak. Everett followed Jasper outside, both of them still chuckling.

They each claimed a rocking chair and set their mugs of coffee on the stump between them. I waved at the two old guys and peeked around the corner of the house to find a tall, dark-haired guy setting up a canopy not far from the house.

"That's Connor, my grandson," Everett yelled. "Go on out there and introduce yourself to him. He'll be taking over the strawberry business this week."

"He looks busy," I said, raising my voice. "Maybe some other time."

Jasper shook his head, frowned, and pointed at me, then swung his finger around toward the strawberry field. I bit back a giggle. There I was, almost thirty years old and still feeling like I had to obey my elders. Since I worked from home these days, I didn't bother with makeup or getting dressed in anything that resembled a power suit. That morning I was wearing an oversize T-shirt with a picture of Dolly Parton on the front, no shoes, and faded jeans—a step up from my usual pajama bottoms. A pretty stiff breeze sent strands of hair flying around my face. I was in no shape to meet anyone, but if Jasper wanted me to traipse out to where Connor was working, I would do just that.

He saw me coming and laid a wrench down on the long table. He wiped his right hand on the leg of his jeans and stuck it out. "You must be Lila. Grandpa has talked about you often. I'm Connor."

"I am, and I'm pleased to meet you, Connor." I looked him right in his mossy green eyes and shook hands with him. When Mama measured my height for my high school–graduation gown, I was just an inch shy of six feet tall. Connor towered over me and had to be at least six feet, three inches. His olive drab T-shirt—the same color as his eyes—stretched across his broad shoulders and did a poor job of covering his ripped abdomen.

"Since we're neighbors, I reckon it won't be long until we are friends," he said and dropped my hand.

"I hear you're retired from the army." My fingers still felt hot, as if I had held them up to Aunt Gracie's fireplace to warm them in the dead cold of winter.

"Not really retired. More like got booted out after sixteen years. The last mission got me this scar," he said, pointing to his cheek. "Right along with a worse one on my leg. The higher-ups determined that I couldn't do my job anymore, so they sent me packing with a medical discharge. Not to worry, though; Grandpa says that I'm capable of running a strawberry stand. If I do that well, then I get to sit on the board of directors at his oil company in San Antonio sometime in the future." He punctuated that with a chuckle.

I twisted my hair up and secured it with an elastic ponytail holder. "How does he determine if you did the job well?"

"I really don't know. I haven't ever had a list of what the criteria is for that particular job"—he shook his head with a smile—"and don't really care because I'm not so sure I want to wear a suit and drive to San Antonio every day, either." He waved over the canvas canopy he had already set up so the table would have some shade. "Come on into my parlor here and have a seat. I won't be leaving until Grandpa's done visiting Jasper. Those two old guys will talk for a while yet. I wouldn't be surprised if Grandpa doesn't come with me every day just to visit with Jasper. They do love to reminisce."

I rounded the end of the table and sat down in the nearest chair. "When I was home last year, there were only three chairs: one for Jasper, one for Everett, and one for Aunt Gracie."

"Yep, but Grandpa told me to set up four chairs, and the military taught me to obey orders." He handed me a basket full of ripe strawberries he must have picked that very day. "Have a snack while we visit. The new order of things is that there's a chair for me, one for each of the old guys, and one for you when you bring us sandwiches and tea for lunch."

I hadn't been aware that the job of providing sandwiches had come with my inheritance from Aunt Gracie, and I started to argue. But the pesky voice inside my head whispered softly, *This would be a great opportunity for you to hear their stories—and besides, that Connor is one good-looking fellow.*

"Thanks for the strawberries and for the chair." I used my thumbnail to remove the green leaves from the end of a plump red berry before I popped it into my mouth.

"You are welcome," Connor said. "I am sorry about Gracie. We would have been at the graveside service, but Grandpa said she told him that she wanted to go out of this world without any fanfare."

"Thank you for honoring her wishes. We tried to do things just like she wanted. Though you should hear Jasper be crabby about the lack of visitors."

Connor sat down in the chair at the far end of the table. "Grandpa told me that her passing made him get on the ball about making some new arrangements in his life. I don't know what they are, but he and his lawyer spent several hours in his office this past week."

"Aunt Gracie had everything written down—even to which hairdresser was to fix her hair and what red pantsuit we were to bury her in. I figured she would leave the house to my mother—but then, she knew how Mama felt about the place. I'm rambling on . . . ," I said and popped another strawberry in my mouth. I tended to talk too much when I was nervous, and a mouth full of food would keep me from doing that.

"You can ramble all you want. I love to hear you talk. Seems like I lost a lot of my accent while I was in the military," Connor said.

No one had ever told me that they liked my accent—but then, I'd lived in Texas my entire life and had only traveled to a couple of other states. "Thank you." I paused. "I think."

"It *was* a compliment," he said with a grin that deepened the scar on his cheek. "If you want to know for sure if I'm giving you a compliment, here's another one: you are a beautiful woman."

Blushing makes every freckle on my face stand out like Christmas lights, so I fought it, but the redness won the battle. "Thank you," I muttered as I stood up. "I really should be going now."

"You are blushing. I'll take my compliment back if you stay a while longer," he said.

"No, sir. It's mine and I'm not giving it back to you. I'm going to think about that the rest of the day. Not many folks outside of family has called me *beautiful* before." I liked the little tap dance of desire chasing through my body too much to give any of his words back to him.

He pushed back his chair and followed me across the lawn. "Then you've been around the wrong people."

I reached to open the gate, but he was faster. His hand brushed against mine, and there was that same little surge of heat again. I attributed it to not having had a date in a couple of years. Working from home certainly put a damper on any kind of social life. That, and the fact that most men even near my height ran toward short women who made them feel all macho.

He walked with me all the way to the porch steps and lingered there. "Did moving to Ditto give you a dose of culture shock?"

"A little," I admitted. "How about you?"

"Oh, yeah," he grinned. "But Poteet is only five minutes down the road, and it's got a little more to offer."

"And San Antonio isn't even half an hour away."

He nodded toward Jasper's place. "What do you think they're laughing about?"

"Jasper is older than Everett, but they've lived through a lot of the same eras. They've got a lot of memories to talk about—or old jokes that only they would think are still funny."

"You got that right. So, are you going to really live here, or is this just a stopover until you find out what you really want to do?"

"I have no idea." Where did that answer come from, the back corner of my mind? At this moment in time, I planned to live in Ditto forever. I noticed that he was waiting for me to say more, so I turned it back on him. "How about you? When do you get the fancy oil-business crown?"

"Very funny. I'm next in line to take over the business, but I need to learn everything I can from Grandpa," he answered. "I hope he lives to be a hundred or even beyond that. I figure it will take me that long to be ready to step into his old work boots."

"Starting tomorrow, you will likely know about the selling portion of the strawberry business," I said.

"More than that. I was here for the strawberry season last fall, and then I've been helping the crew take care of things since the spring season started."

"That's a step in the right direction." I put a foot on the lower porch step and tried to ignore the sparks dancing around like little fairies above my head. "Nice meeting you, Connor. My break time is over, so I've got to get back to work. I'll see you tomorrow at noon."

"I'll look forward to it," he said.

I worked on the files that had been sent to me the day before, but thoughts of Connor distracted me several times. He had liked my accent, and he'd said I was beautiful. I sure hoped he didn't think that a couple of compliments would cause me to lead him up to my bedroom. I'd played a similar game a few times before, and it had not ended well.

Because I had spent a few extra minutes on my break that morning, and time got away from me at noon, my workday didn't end until five thirty that evening. I was starving, so I heated up what was left of the takeout I had brought home on Sunday and ate it standing up by the counter. I had just finished off the last bite when Mama knocked on the back door and poked her head inside. "Hey, I'm going into town to get some groceries. Want to go with me?"

"Sure," I said with a nod, "and maybe we can get an ice cream cone afterwards?"

"Sounds good. Meet you in the car."

"Be there soon as I put on some shoes and grab my purse." I washed my plate and fork and put them in the dish drainer.

Hopefully, there would come a day when Mama would be comfortable in Aunt Gracie's house, but today wasn't that day. But whether she did or did not, she was still my mother, and it didn't matter if we spent time together in her house or in mine. Calling Aunt Gracie's place *mine* still seemed strange when the word came to my mind, and even stranger in my ears when I said it out loud.

Mama was listening to the playlist on her phone when I slid into the passenger's seat. George Strait was singing "Check Yes or No," and she was keeping time with her thumbs on the steering wheel.

"I went to see George three years ago," she said. "He and Chris Stapleton were touring together. They were both fabulous."

I set my purse on the floor and fastened my seat belt. "I remember how excited you were, and that you came home and started listening to Chris as well as George."

"Aside from having the blessings of you and Aunt Gracie, that was one of the highlights of my life," she said and then frowned.

"Whoa!" I said. "You were smiling one minute, and then it turned into a frown. What happened now?"

"Annie, my friend from Annie's Café, called me today and offered me a job," she blurted out.

"So now you have three options."

"Yes, I do, and I was struggling with two," she admitted. "But we'll think about that tomorrow. Today, we're going to talk about you and how you are adjusting to living in *that house*."

"Did Aunt Gracie's place always affect you this way?"

She started the engine and turned to face me. "Not as much as it has since Aunt Gracie died. There was a feeling in it when you were little, but not like now."

"What kind of feeling?" I bent forward and groped around in my purse until I found my sunglasses.

"I can't describe it. Just something unsettling, like that awkward feeling you get when you walk up on some folks having a conversation and they suddenly quit talking. You know they are talking about you, but you aren't sure how to handle it gracefully."

"Kind of like someone is pushing you out the door?" I asked.

"That's right!" She nodded as she released the parking brake. "Aunt Gracie wouldn't ever make me feel like that. But someone in that place doesn't want me there."

"But, Mama, I'm the only one there, and I would be happy if you moved in with me," I told her. "I get lonely rattling around in that place by myself."

"You've got Jasper, and you can always come to my house."

At that moment Connor and Everett came around the end of the house and got into a dark blue pickup truck. They both waved, and Mama stuck her arm out the open window on her side and waved back.

"That Connor is a good-lookin' guy. He and Everett always leave a good tip when they eat at my place." She put her vehicle in gear and drove down the lane.

"You are changing the subject," I said.

"Yes, I am, and I'm also telling you to be real careful of him, Lila."

"Why's that?" I enjoyed the fresh spring wind flowing through the truck, even if it was blowing my hair in my face.

"Since he moved back to this area, he approached Aunt Gracie several times with an offer to buy her house and land. Offered her more than it was worth, even." Mama fumbled around in the console and handed me a ponytail tie. She always seemed to have exactly what I needed, either in her purse, in the pocket of her jeans, or hidden away in the car. "I don't have a brush, so you'll have to just finger comb it up."

"I actually met Connor today, Mama. He's going to run the strawberry business this next week. I expect the folks who want to pick their own berries will keep the road hot and dusty until the plants are bare. He asked me if I planned to stay in the house or if I was just here until I could figure out if I wanted to stick around for the long haul. Maybe not in those words, but something similar."

"He's layin' the groundwork to sweet-talk you into selling out to him," Mama said. "It's your property, but you need to think long and hard before getting rid of it. It's been in the family for more than a hundred years. Gracie was born in that house."

I bit back a giggle. "You won't even come inside the house unless you have to. I'd think that you would be glad to see me sell it, take the money that's been left to me, and move far away from the eerie feeling you get in the place."

"Don't laugh at me." Her voice went into that scolding mode I recognized from my youth. "I grew up knowing when something wasn't right. If I had listened to my heart instead of my hormones, I would have known that your father was never going to be anything but a bad boy." She sighed and turned onto the road leading to the grocery store. "But then, things happen for a reason. If I hadn't had you in my life, then who knows what would have happened to me. You were the light in both mine and Aunt Gracie's world."

"Even if there were eerie feelings in her house?" I teased.

Mama pulled into a parking spot fairly close to the front of the grocery store. "Yep. She knew how I felt and said she understood, so we usually visited on the porch or else at my place. There at the end of her life, she had me bring her and Jasper takeout from the café several times a week. Rain or shine, she would meet me at the door because she knew how uncomfortable I was in the house, and it's worse now."

We got out of the truck at the same time and headed across the parking lot. I slowed my stride to match hers and asked, "Did anyone else feel like that about going in her house?"

"I wouldn't know," Mama said with a shrug. "Her Sunday school group came about once a year for the monthly meeting that rotated among them. Come to think of it, her turn to be the hostess was always in March—about this time of year. She always ordered food from the café and made strawberry shortcakes for dessert. After she retired, she and several of her friends got together to play poker on Friday nights.

That ended maybe ten years ago. She was the last one of her age group when she passed away, other than Jasper."

Mama grabbed a cart and pulled a list from her big black purse. "Let's meet back here when we are finished. I don't need a lot, so it won't take long."

"Yes, ma'am," I said and pushed my cart toward the deli. I needed to stock up on sandwich makings for the next week to ten days since I had been given the job of making lunch for "the strawberry crew," as Aunt Gracie used to call them. On the way to the back of the store where the deli market was located, I picked up a big box of tea bags, five loaves of bread, and two big containers of individually wrapped chips in various flavors. Cookies were on sale, so I added six packages to the cart.

Someone tapped me on the shoulder. "Lila Matthews, is that you?"

I whipped around to see a man who looked vaguely familiar. It seemed like I recognized the voice, but putting it with his face didn't work. Not one name surfaced.

"Richie Brewer," he finally said.

My mind felt like a hamster doing double time on a wheel. Where did Richie Brewer fit into my life? With that mop of gray hair hanging down to his shoulders, he looked too old to have gone to school with me.

"I worked at the café with your mama when we were both in high school. I remember when you were born," he explained. "I was real sorry to hear about your aunt passing away, but I understand you are back here to stay."

I smiled as if his explanation made all the sense in the world to me. "Yes, I am. It's good to see you again, Richie. Do you still live in this area?"

"I retired and moved back here six months ago. Lost my wife a couple of years back. Kids are all grown, have kids of their own, and are scattered seven ways to Sunday, as my granny used to say." He ran his fingers through his hair in a nervous gesture. For a minute, I wondered if he was about to ask my permission to go out with my mother.

"Well, it's good to see you again, all grown up. I heard that Gracie left her place to you. Wouldn't be interested in selling it, would you? A little strawberry farm might be just what I need to keep me busy on a part-time basis."

"Nope," I answered. "I plan on staying right out there in Ditto, and Everett Thurman still has the lease on the strawberry farm."

"If you change your mind, give me a call," Richie said and pushed his cart on around me.

I nodded but had no intentions of selling my newly acquired property. The warning Mama gave me about Connor popped into my head. Was he just another one in a line of folks who were coming out of the woodwork to get my house?

Mama said she felt an eerie presence in the place, but Jasper never mentioned anything like that. I personally felt a sense of peace there, but that didn't mean I wouldn't keep asking about the Poteet secret until I found an answer. She was already at the checkout counter when I pushed my cart to the front of the store. She went on ahead of me and had her full sacks in the back seat of her older model Chevy Silverado truck when I arrived.

"I'd have been here sooner, but I ran into Richie Brewer," I said.

"Gossip travels faster than the speed of light," she chuckled. "Gloria Sue and her sister, Tresia, asked me whether I was going to keep working at the café."

"Hey, Sarah!" A stout woman with salt-and-pepper hair got out of the car that had pulled in beside us. "Are you buying Madge out? I hear her café is up for sale."

"Not today, Melanie," Mama said.

While she visited with the lady, I loaded the groceries into the back seat and returned the carts to the front of the store. When I got back, she was behind the wheel and Chris Stapleton was singing "Millionaire."

"I always wanted that kind of relationship," she said with a long sigh.

The lyrics talked about having a woman whose love made him feel like a millionaire. Neither of my more serious relationships had ever made me feel like that. I wasn't even sure if such a thing existed. "If I can't have one like in the song, then I'll just be an old maid like Aunt Gracie," I declared.

Mama backed out of the parking spot, waved at a couple of folks who were walking toward the front of the store, and then pulled out onto the road heading toward town. "I want a strong, healthy, and happy relationship for you. I want grandbabies—and even more than that, I want you to have the joy of being a mother. But never settle for just anything, Lila. Be sure to listen to your heart. It won't ever lie to you."

The sound of her voice breaking when she spoke brought tears to my eyes. I'd been super emotional since Aunt Gracie's funeral, and crying snuck up on me at the strangest times. Like when I heard her voice in my head or when I started to get a coffee mug from the cabinet and saw her favorite one, with a long crack cutting through the words I LOVE MY AUNT. There was never any doubt in my mind that she loved me. But Mama's words about listening to my heart was the same advice she had given me the last time we visited.

"Why didn't you ever get married?" I asked.

"I had some trust issues, of course, and I was afraid to bring a step-father into our family. I'd seen what chaos that created in some of the regular customers at the café." She sighed. "I didn't want you to have to deal with someone new in our family."

"Not all of them were sorry excuses for fathers, though, right?"

"No, they weren't, but still . . ." She paused. "Some were good to the children they got with the marriage license, but it wasn't the norm. I'm changing the subject because something is making you all emotional. What did Richie Brewer have to say? He asked me out when he first came back to this area, but I turned him down."

"Why?" I asked.

"There's no spark, and without that, there's no passion. I had sparks with Billy, even if he wasn't a responsible man." She raised one shoulder in half a shrug.

I thought of the chemistry between Connor and me. Could there be responsibility and heat at the same time?

"Besides, Richie is dating Melanie, the woman that spoke to me back there," Mama was saying when I tuned back in to what she was saying. "I've decided that I don't want to buy the café. Finding dependable people is tough."

"Are you thinking about working for Annie, then?"

"I told her that I was weighing my options." Mama frowned. "That I didn't really want the responsibility of being an owner and doing all that paperwork, but I wasn't ready to have a full-time job. She said she would be glad to let me work a few days a week."

"Did Richie tell you that he wants to buy my house and strawberry field because he wants something to work at part-time?" I asked. "Why is everyone interested in a house that's over a hundred years old and is possibly haunted, if you are right? Do they think there's gold hidden in them there walls and under the strawberry fields?"

Mama giggled. "Maybe they want to turn Aunt Gracie's place into a bed-and-breakfast and bill it as haunted, or maybe they think there's more oil to be discovered on the acreage that Gracie's father kept when he sold the company. Or maybe Richie really just wants to have a hobby farm."

My mind was still trying to figure out why anyone would want to buy property in Ditto when my mother turned left off Highway 16 and onto West Ditto Road. She hadn't even gotten up to speed yet when she braked so hard that a bag of groceries flew off the back seat and landed upside down in the floor of her truck.

"What the . . . ?" I squealed and then saw the puppy sitting on the yellow line in the middle of the road.

"People who dump animals out on the road should be hung up by their toenails," Mama fumed.

"Even cats?" I opened the door and got out of the truck.

"Even cats. Just because I'm allergic to them . . . What are you doing?" she yelled out the open window.

"Rescuing a puppy and getting a free pet. We're going back to town to see the vet and get some food." I picked up the dog, carried it to the vehicle, and settled into the passenger seat with the pup in my lap.

"You're lucky I didn't buy any frozen food, what with this detour," Mama said. "That thing is going to grow up to be as big as a bear."

"Be a good guard dog, then—and the backyard is fenced, so he'll be safe until he gets used to the place. Look at his blue eyes. They are even lighter than mine and yours. I don't know much about dogs, but a friend of mine in Austin had a white dog with blue eyes just like this one, and he said it was part husky. If this feller grows up to be as big as my friend's dog was, he might scare away any of those weird feelings you get in the house."

Mama cut her eyes around at me as she pulled into the vet's parking lot. "Ain't dang likely."

Chapter Four

"How many sandwiches do three grown men need or even want for lunch?" I asked myself as I laid slices of bread on the counter and started to spread mayo on each piece. "No, that's not right," I whispered. I liked mustard on bologna but mayo on ham and cheese.

Running out and taking their orders, then coming back and making the sandwiches seemed like a lot of trouble. I didn't know how Aunt Gracie did the job, and she wasn't sitting on my shoulder whispering in my ear that day. I stared at the bread, but it didn't have any answers, so I didn't spread mustard or mayo on any of it.

I built a variety of sandwiches, put them on the largest cookie sheet I could find, and set the mayo and mustard off to the side. That way, the guys could use whichever one they wanted. I had done some relief waitress work for Madge when I was in high school, so I knew how to carry a tray. Still, it took two trips, but plenty of sandwiches, chips, chocolate chip cookies, and sweet tea was on the end of the table under the shelter by the time the grandfather clock in the foyer chimed twelve times.

"How's business?" I asked when I brought out disposable cups and ice for the tea.

Connor reached for a sandwich. "It's been steady—and thanks for not putting mayo on them. I like mustard better."

"Me too," Jasper added. "And where did the dog come from?"

"You are welcome, Connor." I reached for a sandwich and squirted mustard on it. "And, Jasper, I found the dog in the middle of the road on the way home from Poteet last night."

"Well, thank you for bringing her to me," Jasper said as he slathered a little mayo on his ham-and-cheese sandwich. "I've wanted a dog for years, but Gracie was terrified of them. Didn't matter if they were the size of a gigantic rat or as big as a small horse; she didn't want them around. One year, when she was a little girl during strawberry-pickin' season, a dog bit her on the leg, and ever since, she was afraid of all of them."

Another piece of the puzzle that was Aunt Gracie's life fell into place. Strange that I had always been so close to her and knew so little about her. I should probably start writing down the tidbits of information folks mentioned. Maybe then I would have a complete picture of the person who was the most influential in my life, other than my mother.

"So, what are you going to name him?" I didn't have the heart to tell him that I had actually thought the dog would be mine.

"I'm not naming *him* anything, but I'm calling *her* Sassy," he answered.

"Why did you pick that name?" I asked.

"Gracie and I watched *The Incredible Journey* together decades ago, and then we watched *Homeward Bound* a couple of dozen times through the years."

"I watched that movie with Aunt Gracie when I was a little girl. One of the dogs was Chance, and the other one was . . ." The name was right on the tip of my tongue, but I couldn't remember it.

Connor finished the sentence for me. "Shadow."

"You are right," Jasper replied with a nod. "I thought about naming her that, but it was a boy's name."

"Sassy fits her right well," Everett said. "She'll make a good guard dog, and I loved both of those movies, too. Still got *Homeward Bound* on a DVD but don't watch it since my wife passed away. She always laughed so hard at the cat. Makes me sad to see it without her."

"I got a sawed-off shotgun that's good as a guard dog," Jasper said between bites. "I want her to be a good pet, and she's already showing signs of that. She wiggled all over when I came outside this morning and rolled over on her back for me to scratch her belly."

Everett refilled his cup and took a sip. "She'll be loved, no matter if she's just a pet or a guard dog."

Connor finished off his sandwich and picked up another one. "Miz Gracie sure spoiled us by bringing out food during harvest season. I didn't think sandwiches could ever taste that good again, but they do today."

"Well, with this season, you'll have the full experience of both fall and spring," Everett said. "I reckon we'll be finished Friday at quittin' time. There'll be a few berries left, but between the bunch of us, we'll get them picked before the cleanup crew gets here."

"Then we wait six months and start all over again," Jasper said with a sigh.

"You've got a new dog, so you have to live that long," I told him. "Besides, we are planning a big party for you in November to celebrate your birthday."

"Well, in that case"—he grinned—"I wouldn't want to disappoint you or Sassy. She'd be sad if I died so soon after she came to live with me."

"Aren't you going to eat with us?" Connor asked.

"Of course she is. Gracie always ate with us, even after she leased the field to Everett's daddy. Lila will keep up with the tradition, won't you?"

I couldn't say no to eating with them since I was starving—or, for that matter, tell him I had actually planned on Sassy being my dog? That was certainly not the name I had thought about for hours before coming up with either Ghost, since he reminded me of something eerie with those blue eyes and white fur, or maybe Beau, just because I liked it. Then again, that was when he was a boy and not a girl.

"I've heard cars coming and going all morning," I said. "How many folks do you figure have been out here already?"

Everett nodded toward a notepad where he had made marks for each person who'd come through the line to pay for the baskets of strawberries they picked. "By my count, fifty since we got here."

"But this is the first day," Jasper said. "We'll see a big jump on Friday because everyone knows that is the last day we'll be open for business."

"I got a phone call early today saying that a jelly-making place up in San Antonio is sending pickers tomorrow for several gallons," Connor said, reaching for another of the individual bags of chips. "They said they'll be here every day until we close up shop on Friday, so we'll be lucky if there's a single berry left when we finish up."

His hand brushed against mine when we both reached for the tea at the same time, and a tiny jolt of electricity jabbed me. *No! No! No!* I told myself in the identical voice Mama used back when I was a little girl and got into trouble.

I chalked up the effect Connor had on me to the roller coaster of emotions that had happened in the past few weeks. Aunt Gracie had died suddenly. I'd made a major move from a big city to a tiny community. I hadn't dated in months. Meeting guys when I worked at home and hadn't even gone to church in Austin was not an easy thing. But I vowed that I would *not* be attracted to Connor, no matter how sexy he was. Mama could be right about him just buttering me up to get at the property.

And if he's not just interested in your house and land? the aggravating voice inside my head asked.

I'm not taking a chance. I could get hurt if he's only being nice to me so he can sweet-talk me into selling my house, I fired back.

"What kind of work do you do?" His deep drawl, those green eyes with yellow flecks in them, and his charm would make a saintly woman swoon, and the good Lord certainly knew that I did not have a halo—not even a tarnished one—or big white fluffy wings. But I was determined to resist everything He could throw at me.

"I'm an accountant, and I work for an insurance company," I told him. "When the pandemic hit, I worked from home, and still do."

"Want to work for me?" Everett asked from the other end of the table.

"You probably have a whole firm working for you."

"I do, but I can always use one more."

"Thanks for the offer, but I'll stay where I am," I said. "And speaking of that, I'd better get back to the house. I've got meetings all afternoon, starting in about "—I looked at my phone—"fifteen minutes."

"Thanks again for Sassy," Jasper said. "Let's have a beer while we watch the sunset this evening."

"Save me a chair and let me pet the puppy, and I'll bring the beer," I said as I stood up.

"Deal!" Jasper chuckled.

I wondered what was so funny, until I realized that he had pulled one over on me by getting me to bring the beer when I come over to pet what was supposed to be my dog.

"Sassy and I had our afternoon nap and ate our supper already," Jasper called out and motioned me over to his house that evening. Sassy was curled up in his lap, and he was rocking her like a baby. "I thought maybe you'd forgot about us."

I set an open bottle of beer on the stump and eased down into the other rocking chair. "Not a chance. I see you're already spoiling Sassy."

"Yep, I am." Jasper used one hand to hold on to the pup, who spilled out over the sides of his lap. "Right now, I'm rocking her to sleep. She ate supper with me and then went over to her dish on your back porch and ate some of her dog food. You'll have to wait until after her nap to hold her." He picked up the bottle of beer with his free hand and took a long drink. "I never did have any kids of my own—or even a pet—so I'm enjoying this."

A little bit of guilt washed over me for thinking he had duped me about the dog. His expression and the way he kept petting the dog so gently testified as to how much he already loved her. I wouldn't have had time to give her a lot of attention throughout the day, but he would dote on her. "I promised Mama I would come over to her house this evening, so if Sassy doesn't wake up, I may have to wait until tomorrow night to hold her. You do realize she's going to be a big dog."

He nodded and took another drink of his beer. "Yep, I do. That's why I didn't let her sleep with me when I found her. I gave her a blanket, and she curled up on it right beside my bed."

"You said that Aunt Gracie was afraid of dogs. What else was she afraid of?"

"Not a damn thing," he answered emphatically. "Before Miz Rita decided to move to Poteet, Gracie was a sweet girl. But . . ." He paused and grinned.

"But what? I just asked if she was afraid of anything else. Mama don't like to come into the house. She says there's something eerie, or maybe unsettling, in the place. Did Gracie ever mention that?"

"Honey, when she came out of her room after that week when she was so angry, she wasn't afraid of nothing. I reckon if she and the devil crossed horns, she would have taken his pitchfork away from him and killed him with it." Jasper chuckled. "I been in and out of that house my whole life, and I never felt anything strange. Your mama grew up around superstitious people. I bet if a black cat ran across the road in front of her between here and Poteet, she would drive all the way to San Antonio to keep from crossing that path."

"You knew my grandparents?" I asked and filed away another bit of information: Gracie wasn't sick when she went to her room; she was angry. Aunt Gracie had never told me anything about them other than they had treated my mother wrong.

"Yep, your mama's folks lived between here and Poteet, back in the woods a ways. They believed that kids were a blessing from God and had an even dozen. They had a double standard for the boys and girls. Maybe I ought to say *girl* since your mama was the only one in the family. Eleven ornery boys and one girl. Didn't your mama tell you about your kin? I might be overstepping, and I wouldn't want Sarah to be upset with me," Jasper said.

"Mama told me that she left home when she got pregnant with me and that Aunt Gracie took her in."

"That's right. Your mama was the oldest, and she came here when she was almost eighteen. Gracie didn't really take her in, though. At one time Gracie's father had owned several houses in Ditto, but he'd sold them all off but the one that his foreman lived in. After that guy passed away, Gracie rented it to folks. It hadn't been lived in in a while, so she gave it to Sarah and offered to keep you while she either worked or went to college. Your mama has worked her whole life and is a fine woman. If she's got a little tad of leftover superstition from her past, that's okay."

"She's always believed that hard work pays off," I said with a nod. "I've often wondered if my grandparents are still alive or if I might have cousins."

"Why don't you ask Sarah?"

"I don't want to upset her."

"Well, last I heard anything about them, they'd gone to Wyoming to live and work on a ranch, but that was before you even started to school," Jasper went on. "They up and moved after Gracie told them what she thought of the way they were treating their only daughter. They might've had more kids after that or stopped at a dozen. The youngest that they had back then would have been maybe a year or so older than you." He paused and cocked his head to one side. "That would be more'n twenty-five years ago. Time can sure get away from us. Sometimes I sit on this porch and remember when me and Davis and Gracie were young, and all the plans we made when we got to be adults."

"Such as?" I asked.

"Oh, they changed from one week to another, like most kids' plans do," he said. "Looks like Sassy is going to take a long nap. You ought to go visit with your mama and come back later to play with her. I made a toy for her by rolling up a couple of pairs of my old holey socks. We might teach her to fetch."

I finished off my beer and stood up. "Next time I'm in a store, I'll pick her up some chew toys. I hear puppies like to chew on shoes, so you might want to keep yours in the closet."

"She already taught me that," Jasper said with a grin.

The sun was a big orange ball sitting right above the trees on the horizon like a golf ball on a green tee. Another day finished—another one of the same-old, same-old. Nothing really new, just more of the old rut I had basically been living in for quite a while: Get up. Have coffee. Work until lunch. Eat a sandwich or maybe leftover pizza. Work until supper. Order out and have it delivered or else open a can of soup. Looking at the gorgeous sunset couldn't get rid of the restlessness in my heart, mind, and spirit as I drove to my mother's house that evening.

I needed *something*, but I had no idea what it was, where to get it, or how to even find it. I let out a sigh that was more like a plea for help when I parked beside a strange car at Mama's house. Maybe whoever the vehicle belonged to would bring some excitement to our lives.

Yeah, right, the aggravating voice in my head said. *How much excitement do you think you'll ever find in Ditto, Texas?*

Chapter Five

Mama met me at the door, stood up on her tiptoes to give me a quick hug, grabbed my hand, and dragged me back to the kitchen. "I've got some really exciting news to tell you about—or maybe I should say that *Annie* and I together have an idea to share with you."

You asked for something exciting, and here it is, the voice in my head whispered.

Annie waved from the yellow-topped chrome table set that had been in the house for as long as I could remember. "Lasagna was the special today at the restaurant, so I brought leftovers for supper. Sit down and have some while Sarah and I tell you about our idea for the future."

Mama placed a plate of food and a glass of sweet tea in front of me. "Neither of us want to retire altogether, but we want to be able to set our own hours. We thought about putting together a food truck of some kind."

"Maybe a sandwich one that only sets up three days a week," Annie said. "But that would still require a definite schedule."

"If it's finances—" I started.

"But we decided against the food wagon and decided to go with a catering service, and we want you to be our manager. We need someone who understands finances and taxes and all that stuff," Mama blurted out.

My first thought was to shake my head and remind them that I had a job, but something deep inside reminded me that only minutes before, I had wished for something to excite me. "Did y'all just hash this out this afternoon?"

"We've been talking on the phone since Sunday," Annie said. "Madge has a buyer for her café, and if the new owners don't kick all the employees out and bring in their own staff, Sarah might be able to work until she retires. The same guy that bought Madge's place came by mine and offered me a lot of money for my business. At first I said no way, but he gave me a week to think about it. Seems that his two granddaughters have been to a fancy cooking school back east. He lives in San Antonio, and if he has a café for each of them, they will live closer to him." She paused long enough to take a drink of tea and then went on. "Annie's has been in my family for generations, and I thought I couldn't possibly sell it. But then I got to thinking about the long hours I'm putting in and how tired I am at the end of the workday. I called Sarah and asked what she was going to do if the new owners wanted to make changes in both the menu and the staff."

"We started kicking around ideas for alternatives and came up with this one," Mama said. "I can use the money Aunt Gracie left me to have one of those metal buildings built on my property to use as a warehouse."

"And we'd like to put a commercial kitchen in one end," Annie added. "Can't you just see a wedding or any other event where *real* food is served? But you don't have to buy into the business, Lila. I'll have more than enough to build the warehouse with what I get from selling my café."

I put a forkful of lasagna in my mouth and held up a finger. I had less than a minute to think about how I was going to either back away or make these two women happy. I had always known I wanted to be an accountant, so this was the biggest decision I would ever have to make. So far.

The lasagna was wonderful, better than the hamburgers Jasper and I had had at Annie's Café. There was no doubt their catering business would take off like a Texas wildfire, and they would make a lot of money. I chewed slowly and then took a drink of tea. I didn't realize I was holding my breath until it came out in a whoosh. Aunt Gracie always said that when opportunity knocked to invite it in and feed it chocolate cake. Well, here was my chance to break out of the rut I'd been living in, so why was I hesitating?

You asked—no, you kind of begged—for excitement, and now it's right in front of you, Aunt Gracie's voice whispered in my head.

"But . . . ," I barely whispered back.

Never sit on a fence. It will make your butt flat, she said. *Either you are in or out.*

"I'm in," I finally said. In addition to the joy of doing something new, I would be helping my mother and Annie out. "Let's each put in one third of what it costs to start up the business. That way we are all full partners. I'm not much of a cook, but I can help with organizing, hiring help, and the paperwork for each job. I'm sure this project is going to require all of our time from the beginning, so I'll give my two-week notice tomorrow."

"Are you absolutely sure about this?" Mama asked. "Don't you want to think about it a few days?"

I shook my head. "Nope, I do not. Y'all's excitement has flowed over to me. Annie, when is your last day at the café?"

"I'll tell the buyer that I'm willing to sell to him, and I guess I'd need to give two weeks' notice, too."

"I'll let Madge know in the morning, myself." Mama's voice sounded like a little kid's who had found a brand-new bicycle under the Christmas tree.

My mind went into overdrive. "We can get a lot done in those two weeks. We'll get Aunt Gracie's lawyer to draw up papers for the business, get bank accounts started, and maybe even get in touch with a contractor for the building."

"Or at least think about the design," Annie suggested.

"We should have a rough idea of what we'll need before we decide on the size," Mama added.

Change had always terrified me. Leaving for college was as tough on me as it was on Mama. Graduating and taking a job with the insurance company meant living in my own place, and that was an adjustment. Moving from that tiny apartment into Aunt Gracie's big house was an even more giant step for me. But somehow, sitting there in Mama's little kitchen, the decision I had made on the spur of the moment seemed right and didn't send me running for the hills like finding a spider in the bathroom had done.

Mama and Annie were talking about what kind of commercial ovens they would need when I finally tuned back in to the conversation. A whole new vibe filled the house, and I could almost feel Aunt Gracie giving her blessing on the decision.

"Y'all do realize that it will most likely be fall before we'll be up and running?" I asked. "You could begin to put jobs on the calendar, but this project is going to take most of the summer. I can put all three of us on a payroll. It will drain some of the inheritance, and we will most likely run in the red for a few months. But after that, we'll probably be making money hand over fist when folks find out about the way y'all cook together."

"I'll have enough money to do me until we start getting some business," Annie said.

"I've got plenty with what Aunt Gracie left me that I'm good through the summer," Mama said.

"Okay, then . . ." I took my dirty dishes to the sink and rinsed them. I liked to bake, but cooking was not anywhere on my love-to-do list. Since Mama collected cookbooks, I'd grown up thumbing through them—mostly the dessert pages. That caused a memory to pop into my head. "While you are making up the recipes you can offer for the service, organize them by category—meats, desserts, salads—and we might have a cookbook published later."

"That's a great idea," Annie said with a wide smile.

The thrill of doing something new followed me out to my vehicle, and I wanted so badly to call someone to share the news of the new venture. But the few friends I had made at work had seemed to drift away after so many of us started working from home. Some of them were married and had started families. Others had moved on to new jobs in other parts of the country or world.

The excitement came to an abrupt halt when I got home, and doubts came crawling out of every nook and cranny in my head. I paced the living room floor for a while; then I wandered outside and saw Jasper sitting on his porch, trying to teach Sassy to fetch a pair of rolled-up socks. "She's brought this thing back to me three times this evening. We're getting some of her puppy energy run out before we go inside. Come sit on the porch with me."

Glad to have someone to talk to, I hurried across the grassy lawn and plopped down in the second rocking chair. "You'll have her bringing you a beer and opening it with her teeth by the time she's a year old."

"I hope so," he grinned.

"You'll never believe what I just did . . ." I blurted out, then went on to tell him about the catering business. "Now I'm thinking I should have thought about it a day or two before jumping in with both feet."

"Gracie would be proud," he said.

His words put an unexplainable lump in my throat. "Why would you say that?"

"She was always proud of you for making something out of yourself, but for you to take life by the horns and do something that will be a help to your mama . . ." He paused and smiled. "Honey, that means you and Sarah will be working together, and that would make the buttons pop off Gracie's best Sunday blouse. One regret she had was that she was afraid to take risks."

"Such as?" I asked.

He lowered his voice like he was telling me a secret. "Staying in that house, for one thing. She felt like since her grandparents built it, she couldn't sell it or leave, and when she got old, she wished she would have gone out and seen the world."

Sassy ran back to the porch and flopped down on her belly. Jasper picked her up and took a step toward the door. "Don't look back with regrets, Lila."

"But what if it's the wrong decision?" I asked.

"Could be." Jasper nodded. "But if you don't do this, you'll never know what it might have brought into your life. Good night, Lila. Sweet dreams."

Just minutes after he closed the door, the crunch of tires on gravel and headlights lighting up the area got my attention, and I tiptoed to the edge of the fence. We had had teenagers coming out to steal strawberries before, and Aunt Gracie usually put them on the run by firing her shotgun into the air.

The lights went out. A vehicle door slammed, and a dark figure headed toward the canopy where strawberries were sold. I opened the gate and slammed it shut, hoping to scare whoever was out there.

"Lila?" a deep voice asked.

The beam from a flashlight practically blinded me when it hit me in the eyes. "Put that thing down, Connor. What are you doing out here after dark?" I spluttered. It took a couple of minutes for me to focus again after the light went out.

"I forgot my favorite baseball hat," he said. "I didn't want a squirrel or a raccoon to carry it off. Got time to come on over and sit a spell?"

I swatted a mosquito the size of a Texas buzzard and shook my head. I held back a chuckle at that thought because Jasper had said the same thing many times. "No, thanks, but you are welcome to come in the house and have a beer or a glass of sweet tea."

"That would be great." He picked up his hat and took a step toward the gate. "Front door or back?"

"Back is quicker," I said and waited for him. "Have you been in Aunt Gracie's house?"

"Not since I was a little boy. She invited me and Jasper inside one day during the Christmas holiday to have a cup of hot chocolate and some cookies. Jasper had helped me build a snowman that day out there in the space between your house and his. We didn't get snow down in these parts very often, so Mr. Frosty wasn't very big," he explained.

This time I didn't hold back the giggle. "*Mr. Frosty* sounds like something you get at the Dairy Queen."

"Those are Blizzards, and I love them! Frosties come from Wendy's," he said. "But you are right. We'll have to try them both and see which one is better."

We walked up onto the porch together, and he opened the door for me. His mama had raised him right, or maybe it was the military that had trained him to be a gentleman. Since I'd been working from home for so long, I had forgotten that men could be so mannerly.

I stopped in the kitchen and opened the fridge. "Beer or tea?"

"Beer, please," he said. "I have to quit caffeine early in the day, or I can't sleep."

I twisted the tops off two bottles and handed one to him. He took a long drink and sat down at the kitchen table.

He seemed to take in the whole room with one glance. "This kitchen looks the same as it did when I was a kid. Same wallpaper and table and chairs."

"Yep," I agreed as I looked at the tiny daisies on the yellow-striped wallpaper. "How does it make you feel?"

He raised one shoulder in half a shrug. "Hard to explain. Kind of cozy, and like I stepped back into time where things were simpler and more peaceful."

Mama thought there were spirits in the house, and Connor called it *cozy*. What a contrast in opinions—but then, maybe he didn't know anything about the secret that haunted some folks.

"How does it make *you* feel?" he asked.

"The same as you do." I took a long drink of beer. "But folks talk about this house having some big secret. Do you know anything about that?"

"Sure. Grandpa says that this area is known for three things: Mr. George's birthplace, strawberries, and some big secret concerning this house. 'The three S's,' is what he calls them. I've listened to Strait's songs my whole life, and I sure know a lot about strawberries, and I'm learning even more. But that last *S* . . ." He paused and took a sip of beer. "Grandpa says that Gracie took it to her grave. No one knows if it was something to do with her folks or with her. Do you know what it is?"

"Nope, and probably never will." I didn't even speculate on whatever might have happened in the house. He thought it felt cozy, so maybe things couldn't be that bad. "You've been here a few months, and you said there was some culture shock at first. What do you miss the most?"

"My friends," he replied without hesitation. "How about you?"

"Most of my friends had already moved on with their lives. When we started working from home, we kind of lost track of each other. I've gotten over that issue. What I miss most is the little coffee shop across the street from my apartment building. They had the best orange-cranberry muffins, and I treated myself to one every Saturday morning."

His green eyes locked with mine. "If I brought you a muffin on Saturday morning, would you be my friend?"

I blinked first and then noticed he was smiling. "Is that your best pickup line?"

"It's not a line. I want a friend closer to my own age, and you want a muffin on Saturday. We can help each other out." He turned up his beer and finished it. "You don't have to decide tonight. Think about it until Friday—and then, if you agree, I will bring you a muffin bright and early on Saturday."

"Orange-cranberry?" I asked.

He nodded and grinned like a little boy bringing a bouquet of wildflowers to a girl. "Yes, ma'am, fresh from the kitchen at Grandpa's place."

"Well, then," I said, smiling. "Hello, my friend. I'll have the coffee made and ready to wash down some muffins with you on Saturday morning. Between now and then, I will bring you lunch each day at noon."

"I'll be lookin' forward to it," he said.

He's probably just wanting to be your friend so he can sweet-talk you into selling him this property, the pesky voice in my head said.

Maybe, but I'm sweet-talking him into bringing me a muffin. Or three, I countered.

Chapter Six

Surprises come in all shapes and forms. Like the day the lawyer told me I had inherited the bulk of Aunt Gracie's estate. But when I called my supervisor, Nadine, the next morning to tell her that I would be submitting my resignation and giving a two-week notice, her response was even bigger than the news the lawyer gave me.

"I will be more than glad to have you work for us another two weeks," she said, "but it would bother me if I didn't inform you of all your rights."

"And they are?" I asked.

"I'm pulling up your file on the computer right now," Nadine said. "You have forty sick-leave days built up and two weeks of vacation time. You will get paid for the latter, but the sick days will be lost."

"So what does that mean?" The possibility of being finished with my job that very day had not occurred to me.

"It means, if you want to take ten of those forty days of accumulated sick days and resign immediately, I will authorize it. In that case, you would finish whatever file you are working on this morning—"

"I'm completely caught up," I said before she could go any further.

"Well, then all we have to do is change your passwords and codes, and you are done if that is what you want. You have been such a loyal, dependable worker . . ." From there on for the next several minutes, all I heard was *yada, yada, yada.* Everything was happening so fast that my mind couldn't keep up with it all. I felt like I was on a roller coaster. Did I continue to work for two weeks and lose every one of those sick days I had built up over the years? Or did I simply say that I was done?

Aunt Gracie's voice was as clear as if she had been standing beside me. *Shut your eyes, think about what would make you happy, and don't look back.*

I closed my eyes, and the picture in my head showed me standing at a fork in the road. Every choice has a consequence; I knew that from the past. Which way did I go? What would my world be like with no job the next few days or weeks while Mama and Annie figured out how they wanted to run their catering service? What would life be like tomorrow morning, when I woke up with very little to do? I was trying to decide which path to take when the *yada, yada* stopped and the lady on the other end said, "Do you need some time to think about it?"

My eyelids popped open. "I would like to resign immediately," I said and then wondered if I'd really spoken the words out loud. Surprisingly enough, everything had stopped spinning, and quietness filled my heart.

"Like I said, we will miss you," she said in a business voice. "Your insurance will still be effective until the first of next month, and your next paycheck will show the two weeks' leave time you have accumulated. If you ever want to come back to us, the door is open."

"Thank you. It's been a pleasure working with you," I said.

"Same here. Bye, now." She ended the call.

I snapped my fingers, and the sound seemed to bounce off the walls. "Just like that," I said out loud. "I'm done with that job as of this very minute."

For the first time in many years, I had nothing that I *had* to do. The feeling was both terrifying and liberating at the same time. Aunt Gracie had popped into my head and told me to not look back. I tried, but it didn't work too well. Until it was time to take lunch out to the strawberry guys, I worried about whether this new venture that Mama and Annie had gotten me into would really make me happy. Or had that instant euphoria I'd experienced in the moment just been a passing thing? Money wasn't an issue, but would boredom set in after a while? I would only have one client—the new catering service. There was no way that would keep me busy.

At noon I got all the sandwich makings out of the refrigerator and pantry and laid them out on the counter. "I could have easily kept my job and done the work for Mama and Annie, too," I muttered.

I told you not to look back! For a second, it felt like Aunt Gracie was in the room with me.

The second that Connor saw the back door open, he jumped up and jogged over from the strawberry stand to the picket fence, hopped over it, and wasn't even breathing hard when he reached the porch. "Let me help you. No sense in you having to make two trips."

"Thank you," I said and handed him a gallon jug of cold sweet tea and a bowl full of ice. "I'll bring the sandwiches and—"

"We still have several of those little bags of chips left over from yesterday, but the cookies are all gone," he said and headed across the yard. This time he went through the gate and left it hanging open.

Sassy must have been in Jasper's house, because she didn't come running hell-bent for leather to get out of the yard. I went back into the kitchen, picked up the sandwiches and a new bag of peanut butter cookies, and headed outside. That's when I noticed Sassy lying beside Jasper. She had a god-awful ugly collar around her neck and a leash that looked like a rawhide chew toy.

"I thought my stomach had plumb growed shut to my backbone," Jasper teased when I set the sandwiches on the table.

"As thin as you are, that wouldn't take a whole lot," I shot back.

Jasper chuckled and poked Everett with his bony elbow. "How about you?"

"I was so hungry that your dog was beginning to look good. I figured a little barbecue sauce would make her taste like pork," Everett added.

Jasper shook a finger at him. "Don't you even let evil thoughts like that enter your mind. Good thing Sassy was asleep, or she would have bit a hunk out of your leg. I wouldn't punish her for doing it."

As if she understood every word, Sassy opened one eye into a slit and growled deep down in her throat.

"See there?" Jasper said. "She's warning you to not say such things."

"You two sound like Grandpa and Granny," Connor chuckled. "I loved to listen to them bicker when I was a little boy."

Everett picked up a bag of barbecue chips and opened it. "There was never a dull moment in our house when I was growing up, so I was used to that kind of lifestyle. Dad would accuse Mom of spreading gossip with whatever news she overheard on the party line. She would argue that what she was telling him was the gospel truth and that it came from a reliable source."

"Was she one of those *number, please* operators?" I asked.

"Nope," Everett answered. "But she loved to ease that receiver up off the base and listen in on other people's conversations. I tried it a couple of times when I was a kid, but I never could master the art of listening without the other two parties hearing the click."

"'Click'?" Connor asked.

"When someone who was on the party line picked up the receiver, there was a certain noise," Jasper told him. "You had to hold the button down and ease it up very gently. If you were lucky, someone would be laughing so hard on the other end that they didn't realize anyone was eavesdropping."

"And you always had to put your hand over the mouthpiece because if the two parties heard you breathing, it was all over," Everett added.

"When did the party lines end?" I asked.

"People around here stopped using them in the early sixties," Jasper said.

I poured myself a cup of tea and took a sip. "There are still some of Aunt Gracie's phones in the house. One in my bedroom and one in hers."

"Black phones with no dial," Everett remembered with a smile.

I chose a turkey-and-cheese sandwich from the stack. "Yep, and very heavy. People who own them should have to register them as weapons."

Connor chuckled. "Want me to go down to the police station with you?"

"Why would I do that?" I asked in between bites.

"If you have WMDs in your house, shouldn't you let the chief of police know?" he teased.

"I'd say what folks heard when they were eavesdropping was far more deadly than any weapons of mass destruction can be these days." Jasper's face was set in stone, and his eyes were haunted.

"Why would you say that?" He looked like he was about to have a stroke right there, with a sandwich in one hand and a red plastic cup of sweet tea in the other one.

After a second or two, he smiled and pointed toward Sassy, who was sitting at his side and begging for bites of his lunch. "How do you like Sassy's collar? I rigged it up by using an old belt that got too big for me. The leash is another belt that never did fit me."

"That is pitiful looking," I told him, deciding to live with his rapid subject change. "I'll order her a proper collar and leash this afternoon. It should be here in a couple of days."

He pursed his lips and said, "She's *my* dog, so you *will* bring me the receipt, and I will pay for it."

"Yes, sir." I saluted him.

"Not bad," Connor chuckled. "Were you in the service?"

"Nope. You better grab that last sandwich before . . ." My thoughts shifted so quickly that I forgot what I was about to say.

"Before what?" Connor asked.

"When you asked about the service, my mind went to Aunt Gracie, and Davis, and Jasper leaving for the military, and I wondered if she wanted to go with them," I admitted.

"Girls didn't go into the service back then," Jasper said.

"Did Aunt Gracie go to college?"

"No." Jasper shook his head. "When me and Davis went into the military, Gracie went to work in a dress shop in Poteet. A few years later, after I came home and Davis didn't, she bought the place and ran it until she retired. She hadn't been retired very long when she took your mama in and kept you so Sarah could work."

"What happened to the dress shop?" I made a mental note to ask Mama about that part of Gracie's life.

Jasper scratched his head and frowned. "Let's see now. She sold it, and the next owners didn't take care of business right, and so it closed up after a couple of years. There was a doughnut shop in the building for a while, but it folded up years ago, too."

"My mother loved to shop in Gracie's store," Everett said.

Party lines, dress shops, Jasper being careful not to tell me what he knew—how did it all fit together?

Connor covered my hand with his, and a spark sizzled between us. "Now, what are you thinking about so hard?" he whispered.

He removed his hand, but the chemistry was still there when I looked up into his eyes. "The past," I said, but my voice sounded a little deeper than normal in my own ears.

Jasper and Everett were talking about what stores were in Poteet back in their younger days, so Connor continued to whisper. "That's done and gone. The present is what we have. The hope is that we will even have a future."

"I thought you were a soldier, not a philosopher."

"I am many things, Miz Lila, and I'm sure you are, too. Maybe we can get to know each other a little better even after strawberry-picking season is over?"

"Maybe so." I nodded, but I'd have to think long and hard about that. "After all, we *are* friends."

"That's right, and I'll be at your house on Saturday morning with muffins." He grinned.

Chapter Seven

The last thing on Aunt Gracie's to-do list was to clean out her room, give anything usable to the women's shelter in San Antonio, and toss the rest of the stuff in the trash. I spaced out as I stood in the doorway and stared at the four-poster bed where she'd died. My feet didn't want to take a step inside the room, and yet my heart ached to find closure. I shifted my focus over to the vanity, with its big round mirror where she sat to put on her makeup. The very idea of going through her things seemed like an invasion of privacy.

"Don't come back and haunt me." I opened the door all the way, entered the room, and stepped back in time almost a hundred years. Over in one corner was a wooden cradle filled with dolls that had been Aunt Gracie's when she was a little girl. Their names were Dolly, Emma, and Maudie. I'd rocked each one of them to sleep when I was little, and then Aunt Gracie and I would tiptoe over to the cradle and lay them down for a nap. Those sweet babies were definitely not going into the trash can.

I picked up Emma and sat down in the wooden rocking chair. *"Shhh, hush, little baby. Lila loves you,"* I sang to the doll like Aunt Gracie had taught me to do before I could even pronounce the words.

As I rocked the doll, I scanned the rest of the room. Nothing had changed since the days when I played here, back when my feet didn't even touch the floor. The red satin bedspread looked like it belonged in a brothel instead of on a fancy white four-poster bed, and it sure didn't match the pink-rose wallpaper. Her makeup sat on a mirrored tray on the vanity, which had probably been bought at the same time as the bed.

A vision of Aunt Gracie sitting on the white velvet stool came to my mind. I must have been about six years old, and it had to have been on a Friday night because she was getting ready for her poker game.

"Someday, when you are old enough, I'll show you how to apply makeup," she had said. "The trick is to put it on in such a way that it looks like natural beauty. Don't plaster it on to try to cover your freckles. Own them and everything else that makes you who you are. Don't be ashamed of your height, your hair, or your body. God gave them to you."

I kissed Emma on the forehead and laid her back in the cradle with her two sisters, then crossed the room and stared at my reflection in the mirror—freckles and red hair—neither one had changed with age. I could not force myself to throw away the makeup or give away the tray.

Seemed like I'd been drawn to the vanity, so evidently that was the place to start. I opened the first drawer on the right. It was organized, with bobby pins, a hairbrush, a comb, and a tube of the stuff I remember her rubbing into her dark hair to make it shine—all in a sectioned tray that fit perfectly in the drawer. The second one held a dozen pair of red silk underpants. Had I somehow gotten in the wrong room? Surely Aunt Gracie had not worn those things. I tossed them all onto the bed and dug deeper, thinking that there would be white cotton granny panties in the drawer, the ones old ladies were supposed to wear—like what I basically had in a size larger than Aunt Gracie would have worn. All I found at the very bottom of the drawer was one of those antique-looking pink diaries that little girls used back then. Nowadays, they have a blog or a journal on their laptops.

I picked it up and held it in my hands for several seconds before using the little key taped to the back to unlock it. The first entry put a smile on my face: *Dear Diary, Mama gave you to me for my birthday. November 11, 1940. Davis and Jasper told me that I would throw you in a drawer and forget you, but I promise I won't. I may not write in you every day, but I promise to tell you all about my life at least once a week.*

On Valentine's Day she wrote that she'd asked for a red bedspread and panties that weren't white instead of a heart-shaped box of candy, but she had not gotten either. Her mother had told her that good little girls did not wear colored underwear and red was for grown women who weren't very nice. Gracie penned that someday she would have both, no matter what anyone thought.

"Her first act of rebellion," I whispered.

Every entry mentioned Davis and Jasper. They went to their freshman year of high school in Poteet, sat together on the bus, talked about their parents and what they would do when they left Ditto and were out into the world. I remembered having the same feelings, but I didn't have best friends like Davis or Jasper to share them with. Looking back, the people I had known were more like acquaintances than friends, and even most of them had left the area.

Things began to change toward the end of the summer between their freshman and sophomore years. Jasper wasn't mentioned as often as Davis. In the fall of that year, he held her hand on the bus ride home and brought her a bouquet of roses he'd picked from his mama's flower garden out behind their house.

Davis had kissed her after the big hot dog and marshmallow roast on her fifteenth birthday, and she'd liked it. Several hearts were drawn around the entry for that day. She wrote that someday she and Davis were going to get married. The next entry in the diary was entered the day after her birthday. *Can a person die from a broken heart? I will never trust a man again.*

My breath caught in my chest, and I could feel the pain and anguish behind that question. Something happened on that day more than eighty years before that had broken Aunt Gracie's heart. That's why she went to her room and refused to come out for a whole week.

Jasper's words came back to me: *If she wanted you to know, she would have told you.*

I flipped through the page in hopes of finding out why she had written those words, but the rest of the diary was blank. I laid it down on the red bedspread beside the pile of red silk underwear and headed downstairs.

"I'll probably never know, but whatever happened that next twenty-four hours is what shaped the rest of her life," I said as I began to make sandwiches for the strawberry crew.

Poor Aunt Gracie had had her heart broken when she was only fifteen years old. She had gone on to live for more than another eight decades, proving that the incident hadn't killed her like she was afraid it might that day when she wrote in her diary, but it destroyed something in her. I had a feeling it had something to do with Davis, the third friend in the trio, the one who had gone away to war and didn't come back. Yet she went on after that to be a businesswoman, and a surrogate grandmother to me. I hoped that I had half her strength and determination as I got older.

Chapter Eight

*Y*ou remembered!" I said when I slung open the front door on Saturday morning.

"Of course I did." Connor handed me a box from the bakery he'd mentioned. "I promised my new friend muffins for breakfast. My grandpa would take a switch to me if I didn't deliver what I promised, even if I am thirty-four years old. They're not from his kitchen; I drove up to San Antonio and got them special for you."

I stepped back and motioned for him to come inside. "Now, that's a real friend, for sure. Thank you so much for doing that. The coffee is ready. You will eat with me, won't you?"

"Unless you plan to eat a dozen muffins for breakfast," he answered. "I have to admit, I only bought six orange-cranberry. The other half dozen are blueberry."

"I like them, too." I led the way back to the kitchen. "Maybe we'll share some of each."

While I poured coffee, he opened the box and laid out a napkin at two places. He was dressed in camouflage pants and an army green T-shirt that stretched over his broad chest like it had been sprayed on with a can of paint.

"What did you do in the army?" I asked.

He wiggled his eyebrows. "I could tell you, but then I'd have to kill you. What I did was classified. How about you? What was your job?"

I picked up an orange-cranberry muffin, peeled the paper back, and took a bite. "Oh. My. Gosh. These are even better than the ones I got in Austin. To answer your question, I did taxes, payroll—all those things that big corporations need someone to do for them . . . but I quit."

"Really?" His voice couldn't hide the surprise.

"Really. But I'll go to work for my mama and Annie this next week."

"Are you going to be a cook?"

I shook my head. "No, but I will take care of the finances for them and organize the catering jobs so that they can do the cooking. Think you will be bored by the change from the military to selling strawberries and learning about the oil business?"

"So far, so good." He flashed a smile that lit up the room. "Grandpa keeps a calendar on his phone, and every day there's something for us to do. It amazes me how quickly he learned how to use a cell phone."

A faint whiff of his shaving lotion—something woodsy—drifted across the table. I caught myself before I took a deep breath to get an even better sniff of it. "Aunt Gracie never would have one. She said that her landline was good enough, and she wasn't going to carry the world around in her apron pocket."

"Smart woman," Connor said with a nod. "All this techno stuff is going to be the ruin of the world, for sure."

"That sounded like something Jasper would say." I reached for a blueberry muffin at the same time he did, and our hands got tangled up inside the box.

"Our hands have got to stop meeting like this," he flirted.

"But my hand enjoys it so much," I teased right back.

His eyes sparkled. "So does mine, but we are friends who have muffins together on Saturdays. Our hands will be disappointed, but we shouldn't ruin a good friendship."

"Oh, then this is not a one-time thing?" My hand was still tingling from the heat that had passed between us.

"Oh, no!" he declared with a shake of his head. "Now that the strawberry picking is done, we might both be so busy that we can't catch up except on muffin mornings. And since we are friends, maybe I could enlist your help in getting the strawberry pavilion folded up and put away until fall?"

"Sure," I agreed with half a giggle, "but only because we are friends." If he could pretend to ignore the sparks, then so could I.

"And you get muffins on Saturday?" He wiggled his dark eyebrows.

"Well, there is that." I peeled the paper off another muffin and bit off a chunk. I needed time for my mind to catch up with my heart, which was a mile ahead of it. Yes, Connor was handsome. The scar on his cheek jacked that up to downright sexy. Yes, his eyes mesmerized me. Yes, he had admitted to feeling chemistry between us.

But was that just one of his many pickup lines? Was he playing me to get me to fall in love with him so he could talk me out of my house and land and leave me with nothing but a broken heart? Those questions sobered me up—or maybe, I should say, they cooled me down. The last words in Aunt Gracie's diary came back to me, along with a question. If I fell in love with Connor, would I find out whether a broken heart could kill me?

"So, we have a muffin date every Saturday morning?" I asked.

He stood up, crossed the room, and brought back the coffeepot. He topped off my mug and then filled his. "A muffin friendship catchup on Saturday, then, and a friend that helps me tear down canopies."

"Sounds good to me," I said.

Does it really? Aunt Gracie's voice was back in my head. *Remember what I told you to do when opportunity knocks on the door?*

Invite it in and feed it chocolate cake. What makes you think Connor is an opportunity for anything other than a friend that's close to my age?

"Earth to Lila . . ." Connor's deep drawl took me away from my visit with Aunt Gracie.

Mama had told me to be careful of Connor because he wanted to buy my house. Apparently, Aunt Gracie did not agree with my mother.

I wondered if someone who had passed from this earth and into eternity could see into the future. If so, I wanted her to stick around in my head a while longer, and for a split second I was angry with Connor for interrupting our virtual conversation.

"I'm sorry," I said. "You have to remember that I'm used to being alone a lot, so I talk to myself and argue with the voices in my head. Sometimes I even forget that there is a real person in the room."

"Well, that's a first," he said with a sigh.

"'First' what?" I asked.

"Most women don't think of other things when I'm flirting with them." Even his whisper had a sexy drawl to it.

"To begin with, I'm not most women," I said, stifling a chuckle. "And flirting involves romance. We are friends who help each other out and have breakfast together on Saturdays." *Brain, take that reminder!*

"Yes, ma'am!" He gave me a smart salute.

"Connor Thurman, you are not in the army anymore!"

"Thanks for the reminder," he said with a quirky little grin, echoing my thoughts. "And, darlin', I'm glad I'm in Ditto, Texas. I've seen enough of the world for the rest of my life."

"You can tell me about it while we tear down the stand," I told him.

"I guess that's my cue to finish my coffee and last bite of this muffin," he said as he popped the remainder into his mouth.

"We're burnin' daylight," I told him.

Connor pushed back his chair and carried the paper wrappers to the trash can. "There you go. I did the dishes, and you stole that line from *The Cowboys*, which happens to be one of Grandpa's favorites."

I put the leftover muffins under a glass cake dome and put the two coffee mugs in the dishwasher. "It was one of Aunt Gracie's, too. Now, let's get movin'."

Connor leaned on the doorjamb. "Do you think I'll ever understand you, Lila?"

"Maybe when I see green tractors flying in the sky," I smarted off.

"You were right about not being like other women." He opened the door for me and stood to one side. "Hey, there's a package on the porch. Must've just gotten delivered, because it wasn't here when I arrived."

I bent to get it. "That should be Sassy's new collar and leash."

When I straightened up, Connor had a smile on his face that reminded me of an old saying I had heard from Aunt Gracie: *Grinnin' like a possum eatin' wild grapes through a barbed wire fence.*

"What's so . . ." I frowned. "You were checking me out, weren't you?"

"I'm not blind. I can admire a beautiful woman from all angles even if we are only friends."

I fought a blush creeping up from my neck but lost the battle. I turned my back so Connor wouldn't see my red cheeks, carried the box inside, and headed toward the back door.

"You don't have a comeback for that?" he asked as he followed me.

The stack of mail on the credenza had nothing to do with our banter, but I noticed that a couple of pieces had fallen onto the floor. I bent over and picked them up and added them to the ever-growing pile.

"Just being sure you got to see another angle," I threw over my shoulder. If he could flirt, so could I, even if I did feel like I was playing with fire. "But remember that what is good for the goose is good for the gander. I will pay you back."

"I will gladly pose for you anytime you want," he said.

I opened the back door and stepped outside. "Don't promise what you aren't willing to deliver."

"Never have and never will!" Connor waved at Jasper, who was out on his front porch.

I let him have the last word and held the box up for Jasper to see. "Sassy's collar and leash are here."

He started to stand up. "I'll get my wallet, and I won't have any sass from you about me paying for it."

"How 'bout you pay for lunch tomorrow at Annie's and we'll call it even?" I suggested.

He settled back down into his chair, and I could almost hear his bones squeaking like the hinges on the back door. "It's a deal, but you could be getting the short end of it."

"I doubt it because I'm going to order dessert, too," I teased as I carried the box across the yard. "You open the box, and I'll help put the new collar on her."

"Sassy!" Jasper called out, and the dog came running across the yard. "Your Christmas present has arrived early."

"It's March," Connor chuckled. "I think the present has come late."

"Shhh . . ." Jasper scolded. "Sassy don't know much about holidays just yet, so she'll believe whatever I tell her." He opened the box and grinned. "You done good. The collar matches her eyes, and the leash is one of them good ones that gives her room."

Sassy stopped at his feet and looked up at him with big blue eyes. Her tail thumped against the wood porch boards while he removed the old collar from around her neck.

"I can put the new one on," Jasper declared. "That way she'll know it's really from me."

"Okay, then," I said. "Connor and I are going out to take down the strawberry stand."

"I'm going to take it down, and Lila is going to keep me company," Connor said.

I propped my hands on my hips and glared at him. "I can and will help. That's what friends do."

"Y'all remind me of me and Gracie when we joked around," Jasper said as he finished buckling the collar around Sassy's neck.

"Did you ever flirt with her?" I gave Connor a dirty look and then focused on Jasper.

"Yep, I did," Jasper chuckled. "When I got home from the army, I tried my best lines on her. She let me know right quick that we were best friends and would never be anything more."

"Because she had feelings for Davis and he was gone?" I asked.

Jasper's bony finger shot up and moved so fast that it was nothing but a blur. "I'm old, Delilah Grace, but I'm not stupid. You are fishing, but today the fish ain't bitin'. Now, look at how pretty Sassy looks with her new collar. Thank you for getting these things for her."

"You are welcome."

Connor laid a hand on my shoulder and gave it a gentle squeeze. "Come on, woman, we're burnin' daylight. I have to be in San Antonio by five this evening."

I brushed his hand away and tried to give him another dose of evil eye, but I giggled. "Two things: don't steal my lines, and don't call me *woman*."

He started to salute, but I grabbed his arm. "And one more thing . . ."

"And that is?" he asked with a big grin.

"Don't salute me. You're not in that world anymore."

"Yes, ma'am!" he said with a nod and a bit of sarcasm.

Jasper slapped his thigh, threw back his head, and laughed. "Thank y'all for reminding me of Gracie today."

"Anything we can do to make your day," I said. "You want to go to Mama's house with me this afternoon? You haven't been off the place all week."

"We'll go to church tomorrow, get us a big old juicy burger from Annie's, and visit Davis and Gracie after that. That's enough getting out for this old man this week. Besides, Sassy would miss me real bad if I left right after she got her new collar," Jasper said. "But we will test out her leash and come out to watch y'all tear down the strawberry stand. I always hate to see the season end. I only see some of the folks once or twice a year if they don't go to my church."

He chuckled again when he bent forward and snapped the new leash to Sassy's new collar. "Davis and Gracie bantered more than me and her. Their eyes would sparkle when they were arguing. I miss that so much, even after all these years. The only ones who put fire in her eyes after he died was you and Sarah, but it was a different kind of twinkle."

"Tell me a story about something they argued over," I said.

Jasper smiled, but I saw the haunted look in his eyes.

"Another time, maybe, if I don't forget by then." His voice quivered and he cleared his throat. "Sassy wants to go for a walk right now."

The puppy yapped, and Jasper followed her through the space between the house and the garage—or carriage house, as it was called back when it was built.

"I don't know which one of you is taking the other for a walk," Connor called out.

"Don't matter, as long as we both get to go," Jasper yelled over his shoulder, then turned around and came back to where we were sitting.

"I guess Sassy got tired," I said.

The dog plopped down beside the chair where Jasper had been sitting, put her paws over her eyes, and went to sleep as if I'd commanded her.

"Never know what this critter wants. Most days she probably don't have any idea what she wants," Jasper said. "I was thinking about a story to tell y'all while we took that short walk."

"Is it a story about Gracie and Davis bantering?" I asked.

Jasper chuckled and then laughed so hard that his eyes disappeared into wrinkles. "It was the spring after strawberry season was finished." He pulled a red bandanna out of the pocket of his bibbed overalls and wiped his face. "There was still quite a few that could be harvested. Gracie, Davis, and I decided to pick enough to make us up a batch of strawberry wine."

"How did you know how to even start?" I asked.

"Gracie found a recipe for it in one of her grandmother's old cookbooks. She snuck it out of the house . . ." He paused and rubbed his chin. "I betcha that cookbook is still somewhere in the house. All the recipes in it are handwritten. Anyway, we had to hurry up and copy it down so she could put it back before her folks missed it—or worse yet, before Miz Rita or my grandmother missed it. Miz Betty wouldn't have ever looked at a cookbook. Davis's mama and Granny took care of all that. Gracie's handwriting was better than us boys' chicken scratch, so she took care of that job while me and Davis got us a pail and went to pickin' strawberries."

"Doesn't it take a long time to make wine?" Connor asked.

Jasper's grin got bigger. "Not if teenage kids are making it."

"Where did you . . ." I paused and looked out across the property.

Jasper pointed toward the oil pumpers out in the distance. "There used to be a barn out there. Mr. Clarence stored hay when he ran cattle. It was blown away by the same tornado that wiped out mine and Granny's old place. In those days, us two boys hauled hay for him in the spring and summers, but that's a story for another time. We were talking about the wine we made. Most of the stuff we needed, other than the strawberries, Gracie swiped from the kitchen." He dragged the red bandanna from the pocket again and wiped his brow. "A few years ago, Gracie and I watched an episode of *I Love Lucy* where she stomped grapes with her feet. If we'd have stomped them strawberries like Lucy did the grapes, we would have got ourselves caught for sure since we couldn't have washed all that red stain off our feet." He dissolved into laughter, wiping his face again.

Connor and I got tickled, more at his amusement than with the memory in his head. We had been listening to the story while we loaded up the two tables. Before we folded the chairs and put them into the bed of Connor's truck, we sat down to really listen.

Jasper stuffed his bandanna back into his pocket. "According to the recipe, we was supposed to let it age for a year, but that's a lifetime to kids. On the Fourth of July, Gracie's folks threw a big party . . ." He paused, and a frown took the place of his smile. "They said that Gracie was old enough to come to the big wingding, but she refused to go, since they wouldn't let me and Davis go unless we wanted to be part of the help. That girl was so mad, I thought for sure she'd either kick holes in the barn or else storm inside the house and ruin the whole party."

Connor leaned forward in his chair. "Is that the end of the story? What happened to the wine making?"

"I'm gettin' to it," Jasper declared. "I'm trying to remember just how it went. After the big argument with her folks over that party, they grounded her to her room, which was fine with her. She waited until the people were milling about the front yard where tables had been set up, and she walked right out the back door. Me and Davis were waitin' for her in the barn. We sat on the grass and listened to her fuss about the party. Then, after dark, we watched the fireworks. That's when Gracie got the bright idea of us opening our two bottles of wine that were aging."

Sassy stood up, yawned, and pulled on the leash. Jasper stopped talking and rubbed her head. "You got to learn to be patient, little girl. We'll try for a walk again when I finish my story."

"Where did you get the bottles to put the wine in?" I asked.

"Mr. Clarence and Miz Betty always had a glass of wine with their supper. Gracie just pilfered a couple of empties when they were thrown away. She even saved the corks. That night we passed the first bottle around until it was all gone and then opened the second one and did the same thing."

"Did you get drunk?" Connor asked.

"After all these years, I'm not sure if we were drunk or just thought we were, but we sure giggled a lot, and we all had a headache the next morning," Jasper said. "And now I've told you about my favorite memory from strawberry season, and it's time for Sassy to have her morning walk. Besides, you've got work to do, and I'm keeping you from it."

"But we want to hear more about the first time y'all got drunk," Connor said.

Jasper shook his head and stood up. "Not much more to tell there except to say that that night was the first time Gracie was really rebellious, but it wasn't the last. More stories later. Sassy and I are going for our walk so she can show off her new collar and leash." He and the pup slowly walked across the grass and around the house.

"Did Miz Gracie ever tell you that story?" Connor asked me when Jasper had disappeared down the lane.

"Nope." I stood up and folded the chair I'd been sitting in. "She once told me that the past was gone and should be forgiven. The future was just a glimmer of hope on the horizon; the present was what we had, and we should live it to the fullest."

"Good advice," Connor said. "But forgiveness is tough, and not planning for the future is even rougher, don't you agree?"

"Wholeheartedly," I told him and thought again of the last entry in Aunt Gracie's little pink diary about dying from a broken heart.

And that's the reason I'm ignoring the sparks between us. I don't know if I can trust you for anything more than what we are today.

Chapter Nine

How long are you going to ignore all that mail? Aunt Gracie's voice was loud and clear in my head that afternoon when I walked past the stacks of unopened envelopes and magazines piled up on the credenza. I had put off opening the mail for weeks. By just scanning through the messy piles, I could tell that a lot of it involved sympathy cards, and reading through them would make her passing so final. If I didn't read them, then I could pretend she was out visiting Jasper and would be coming through the back door at any time.

"Maybe tomorrow," I muttered as I shot the mail a dirty look and went on into the kitchen.

The leftover muffins from that morning were my lunch, along with a banana and a tall glass of sweet tea. Mama would fuss at me for not eating my vegetables, but one day a week with no green beans or broccoli wouldn't hurt me. When I had finished eating, I headed through the foyer and set my foot on the first step going upstairs. Refusing to even glance at the stacks of mail, I said, "Today, I'm going to clean some more in Aunt Gracie's room."

A piece of mail fluttered through the air and landed at my feet. "Okay, okay, I get the message," I declared with a long sigh. "I'll clean off the credenza before I go upstairs, but understand that I'm doing this against my will."

My bare feet made slapping sounds against the hardwood floors as I marched to the utility room, dumped the laundry basket full of towels that needed to be folded on top of the washing machine, and carried it back to the foyer. I brushed all the mail into the basket and sat down on the floor to go through it piece by piece.

"I will not . . ." The words were barely out of my mouth when I remembered having to write *I will not chew gum in Mrs. Hudson's class again* fifty times. "I will not toss the mail on the credenza and wait so long to go through it again," I said aloud. "If I do, I will have to write sentences."

Envelopes that were clearly junk mail were tossed across the foyer toward the door; I would bring a trash bag in later and gather them all up. Then I began to sort through those that looked like they held greeting cards; they went to my right. The others that had a business-return label went to the left. All kinds of companies packaged their promotional materials that way just to throw a person off, so I wasn't expecting much. I would give them a fighting chance, but most likely they would wind up in the pile to be trashed.

My hands trembled when I picked up that first card, but I was determined to bite the bullet, so to speak. I opened it to find a sympathy card with a field of Texas bluebonnets on the front. I glanced up at a small picture sitting on the credenza—Mama and me before I was even walking—in a field of blue flowers. Inside the card was a nice little greeting, but it was the note on the side that brought tears in my eyes.

I don't know who will be reading this, but I'm so sorry for y'all's loss. Miz Gracie saved me. I came from a big family, and my folks thought only the boys should have an education. Girls didn't matter so much, since all they would be doing was keeping house and rocking cradles. I was about to quit school after the eighth grade, but Miz Gracie gave me a part-time job in her store—taught me all about how to be a modern young lady. Then she gave me the money to go to college. I am now a retired schoolteacher,

*and I owe it all to Grace Evans. I just wanted whoever is
reading this to know how much good she did.*

By the time I reached the sixth card, the dam holding back tears let loose. By the tenth one, I was really sobbing. Aunt Gracie had touched so many people's lives, yet she'd never bragged about her generosity. She used to tell me that crying was good for the soul. If that was the truth, then my heart shouldn't even have a speck of dust on it.

I didn't want to read anymore, but staring at the stack of unopened ones was like passing a car wreck on the side of the road. I couldn't look away from the accident any more than I could throw all the rest of the cards into the trash can without opening them.

"Lila, where are you?" Mama's voice sounded like it was a mile away.

I rubbed my face on a corner of my shirt, but another batch of tears started up as soon as I did.

"Delilah Grace, are you home?" Her tone was somewhere between angry and worried. "I've called you a dozen times, and it's going straight to voicemail."

I reached for my phone, but it wasn't in my hip pocket.

"In the foyer," I called out between sobs.

Something rattled on the cabinet, and then I heard Mama running across the kitchen and into the foyer. She sat down beside me and wrapped me up in her arms, patting my back the whole time. "What's the matter?"

I pointed at the sympathy cards strewn all around me. "Those happened."

Mama dried my tears on a tissue she pulled from her purse. "I should have been here with you when you tackled this job."

"Almost every one of them has a story to tell about how Aunt Gracie helped them," I said between hiccups. "And there's at least fifty more of them that need to be opened."

"She believed in women empowering women," Mama said, her voice cracking. She took a deep breath and went on. "Long before the concept was even a popular thing. I'll help you go through the rest. You should have called me before you even started. What do you think we should do with them?"

"I'll put them in a box with other things like her diary and store it up in the attic. Maybe someday I'll get rid of them, but not for a while." I opened another one, and the greeting alone brought on a fresh river of tears, and the little note—from someone named Martha—was so sweet that I wished Aunt Gracie could read it for herself.

Then, in a split second, anger replaced the tears. "Why do people wait until someone is gone to tell the survivors how much that person meant to them?" I asked through clenched teeth. "These people should have written letters to Aunt Gracie while she was alive, not to us after she is gone."

"Maybe that should be a lesson to us," Mama said. "I'm pretty sure they *would* have written thank-you notes to her through the years. You might even find some tucked away in the attic. She never was one to throw anything out."

I put the card back in the envelope and gently laid it with the others. "Someday, when and if I ever have children, they can learn just how great Aunt Gracie was by reading all these notes. Why didn't she ever get married and have children?"

Mama took another tissue from her purse and handed me a fresh one. "I asked her that many years ago. She said even though we had only a slight connection through her mother, birth and blood didn't always make a family. She also told me that Jasper was as much her brother as real kinship could have ever made him, and that she had me for a daughter and you for a granddaughter. Do you know what she would tell us right now?"

I dried my eyes and took a deep breath. "To pull ourselves up by the bootstraps?"

"Something like that," Mama answered. "She would say that she raised us both to be strong, and that we need to stop weeping and wailing and get on with life."

"'Life is short, at best,'" I said, quoting something she'd said many times, "'so don't waste a single second of it.'"

"You sound just like her." Mama stood up and headed back to the kitchen. "Have you eaten lunch?"

My bones creaked when I got up and followed her. "I had a leftover muffin and then started sorting through the mail. I could make sandwiches and open up a can of soup."

"Let's go to Annie's. Her Saturday special is pinto beans and corn bread."

"And greens with hot sauce?" I asked.

"Yep, and fried potatoes on the side." Half a smile broke through the sad expression on Mama's face.

"That was Aunt Gracie's favorite meal. Seems only fitting, after this morning," I said. "I'll get my purse and meet you out front."

"Let's take Aunt Gracie's car today," Mama said. "It hasn't been driven since the week before she passed away."

"I'm not sure I can drive it without crying."

"Yes, you can, and you will," Mama declared. "She intended for you to have it, along with everything else. It needs to be driven often so that it doesn't just sit in the garage and rust. I'll be waiting on the front porch."

I went through the foyer, picked my purse up off a ladder-back chair, and walked out the front door. The garage had been added onto the house long after it was built and was set just a little ways off to the right. Aunt Gracie had an automatic door installed after I was away to college, and as luck would have it, I forgot to get the thing out of the bowl on the credenza.

"Got to go back inside and get the opener thing," I told Mama.

"You should keep it in your purse," she suggested.

"You are right," I agreed.

I stepped over the mess of junk mail I'd left on the floor, got the opener, and hurried back outside. An old song popped into my head that said something about always being seventeen in your hometown. I was realizing that it was the absolute truth. I had been out on my own for more than a decade, and here I was, obeying Jasper and my mother even better than when I was living at home. Maybe it was because I had just had a meltdown over dozens of sympathy cards.

The garage door felt like curtains opening before the first act of a play—slowly, as if it was teasing me and Mama. The garage used to be so clean that a person could have eaten off the floor. The tools were still put away neatly, and the 1957 Ford Fairlane—red, with a swoosh above the front doors—sat in the middle of the floor like a king on a throne. But there was a layer of dust everywhere.

"Those last months of Gracie's life must have been tougher than I realized. The yard needs desperate help, and there's dust on everything in the house. Look at her precious Ford, Mama. It used to shine," I said as I slid behind the wheel.

Mama got into the car. "I used to say that Grace Evans never met a speck of dust she couldn't conquer. She never let on that she didn't feel good, so I didn't know."

Brave and selfless, I thought as I started the engine and backed out of the garage.

"She told me that she bought this to celebrate her thirtieth birthday," Mama said.

"Jasper said that her mother drove a Caddy."

"That's right. Her father got a brand-new Chevy truck every year," Mama said. "When I asked her why she bought a Ford, she said that Davis always liked Ford vehicles. He must've been a very good friend for her to keep him in her heart so long."

I thought of the red bedspread and red underwear, and of that entry in her diary about what her mother told her. The red car was probably part of that same rebellion, but I wasn't ready to share what I'd read—not even with my mama.

I put the car in Drive and slowly made my way down the lane. "I feel like I'm driving a boat instead of a car."

"But aren't these wide seats nice?" Mama said. "Your father had an older car with wide seats . . ." She blushed scarlet.

"Was I conceived in a big back seat?" I asked.

Her cheeks turned a deeper shade of scarlet. "Most likely you were. God, but I loved that boy, and God only knows why, because I knew in my heart he wouldn't settle down. Still, I couldn't refuse him anything he wanted. I knew my folks would disown me if they found out about him, but at the time, I didn't care. I just wanted to be with him."

I wasn't sure how to respond to that. "You have loved him forever, and he loved you for a season."

Mama nodded. "Well put. And together we made you, and that way I got to keep a little piece of him forever."

"Weren't you mad at him for leaving you when you told him you were pregnant?" I asked.

"I should have been, but a part of me knew that he didn't love me like I did him," Mama answered. "I was angrier at him for not ever getting in touch with me in the next years. He should have cared about his child. The only one that showed me any love was Aunt Gracie. Mama and Daddy had different rules for me and my brothers. They kept a tight leash on me, but the boys could get away with anything. Thank goodness for Aunt Gracie." She dabbed at her eyes with another tissue that she'd pulled out of her purse. "You'd think I would be done grieving by now."

"I'm not sure we'll ever be over it totally, not even after we reach that final step of acceptance," I said around the lump in my throat.

Silence filled the car for a few seconds before she went on. "She came to the house when she found that my folks were throwing me out because I was pregnant. According to them, I had disgraced the Matthews name. While Mama was cramming my things into garbage bags, I called Aunt Gracie. I'd only just gotten out to the front lawn with everything I owned in two black plastic bags when Aunt Gracie drove up in this very car, in her best red pantsuit, and stormed into the house without even knocking. She lit into my folks like a mama bear and told them what she thought of them for what they were doing, in a voice so loud that folks all the way to Poteet probably heard her. There was a lot of screaming and Bible verses quoted, but she finally came outside and told me to put all those bags in the back seat of this Ford."

"What did she say to you?" I asked.

"She said that I was not to look back but to keep my eyes forward."

"Did you?"

"Of course I did."

I turned toward Poteet and tried to imagine Aunt Gracie raising her voice but couldn't. "Was she talking about right then or the future?"

"Both," Mama said. "She wanted me to go to college that fall, but by the time I graduated, I was sick of school. Sometimes I wonder if our lives would have been different if I had taken her up on her offer to pay for me to go."

"Hindsight is twenty-twenty," I reminded her. "We have always had plenty, Mama. I never knew that we weren't as rich as all the fancy kids I went to school with."

She laid a hand on my shoulder. "I'm glad."

"Do you think your folks are still alive?" I asked.

"Have no idea," Mama answered. "I've never heard from them, but Jasper told me they had moved to Wyoming."

"Want me to get in touch for you?" I asked.

"They know where I am," she said with a serious expression on her face. "Let's talk about . . . Oh my goodness!"

"What?" I almost stomped on the brake.

"Beans and corn bread is one of Jasper's favorite meals, too. We should have asked him to come with us," she said.

"We'll order a take-out box for him."

I snagged a parking place close to the front entrance of the small café. "He'll like that. It's hard to think that Annie won't be running this joint in just a couple of weeks. Both this place and Madge's Diner have been around longer than I've been alive."

"Honey, they've been in business since before I was born. Madge told me once that Gracie bailed her out during the tough times when the pandemic shut down so many places." Mama got out of the car and ducked when a loud clap of thunder right above our heads sounded like it was raining potatoes down from the sky. "Good Lord! Where did that come from?"

I pointed to the southwest. "Looks like we're in for some bad weather. Must have something to do with Annie's Café. It rained when Jasper and I came for Sunday dinner last week."

She laughed at my remark as dark clouds obliterated the sun and lightning shot through the sky. Thunder followed and several folks came running out of the café.

"Want to go in or head back home for a sandwich?" I asked.

"I've got my heart set on a bowl of beans. We can wait out the storm inside. Even if we get wet, I don't expect a little rainwater will melt either one of us."

A memory popped into my head of a day when I must have been four or five years old. A spring shower came up, and since there was no lightning, Aunt Gracie and I had gone outside and played in the rain. We had held hands and played ring-around-the-rosy and giggled for the better part of an hour. Then we had run inside, gotten into dry clothing, and had hot chocolate and cookies. I remembered asking her if she had done that when she was a little girl, and she shook her head.

"Mother said I had to be a lady and live up to the Evans name." Her voice became harsh and she shook her finger. "'Ladies do not dance around like heathens in the rain. What would people think?'" Then her tone softened, and she smiled at me. "Don't ever let anyone tell you that you can't dance in the rain."

We barely made it into the café before raindrops the size of lemons began to fall. The place had emptied out except for Annie and a couple of waitresses, who were having a glass of tea in a back booth.

Annie waved from the back of the dining area. "Did the storm blow y'all in here?"

"Almost," Mama said. "There's only one place in Poteet to get pinto beans and corn bread."

"You're in luck," Annie said. "There's probably enough left for a couple of plates."

"Think you could make that three?" I asked. "We'd like to take some to Jasper."

"I'm sure I can," Annie said and motioned for one of the waitresses. "Gina Lou, fix these people up and bring me a glass of sweet tea to have with them while they eat. Allie, you can flip the sign to Closed."

The blonde waitress headed for the door just as it opened, and a tall fellow stepped inside. He hung his yellow slicker on the back of a chair and sat down at a table across the room.

"Hi, ladies. The storm hit the ranch half an hour ago. It's moving slow, and the weatherman said it could settle right over Poteet until midnight or later," he said before he blinked a couple of times and then smiled. "Lila Matthews, is that you?"

His voice sounded slightly familiar, but I couldn't put a name to it or to his round face. His spurs jingled when he crossed his legs at the ankles, and his black cowboy hat looked weather beaten. "You don't know me, do you?"

"I'm sorry," I said. "Your voice sounds—"

"Derrick Marston," he said as he removed his hat. "I sat in front of you in homeroom all through high school. Had a big crush on you but was too shy to say anything."

"I remember you now." He had been a foot shorter than me and his red hair was longer these days. "So, are you still living around these parts?"

"Oh, yeah," Derrick said. "I'm running the Double M down south of town for my dad. I heard you had come home—and, honey, I'm not shy anymore. So, can I take you to dinner some evening, and maybe a movie?"

"Of course you can, but it might be best to call her and not spring that on her right here in public," Mama jumped in. "Gracie left her place to Lila, and she's living in Ditto. If there's a phone book lying around your ranch, you'll find the number for Grace Evans in it."

"Fair enough," Derrick said. "Annie, darlin', will you bring me a burger and double order of fries?"

Gina Lou looked like she could chew up nails and spit out staples, but she forced a smile.

"I'll take care of that for you, Derrick," Gina Lou said through that rigid smile. There was something painful in her gaze, yet she'd been so quick to wait on him. She tucked a strand of blonde hair back into her ponytail and smoothed her apron. Her T-shirt, which had ANNIE'S CAFÉ written across the chest, was tucked into her jeans to show off a tiny waist. If she could sing, she could have run Dolly Parton some serious competition in Nashville.

"Thanks, Gina," Derrick said and pulled his buzzing cell phone from his pocket. He stood up and went to the far corner of the room, talked in a low tone for a minute, and then called out, "Cancel that order. Looks like my prize bull has broken through the fence. Nothing like trying to corral a bull in a vicious thunderstorm. I'll call you later, Lila."

I waved and waited for him to put his slicker on and disappear outside before I raised an eyebrow at my mother. "I'm perfectly capable of taking care of my own love life. I wasn't attracted to Derrick in high school, and even though he's now six feet tall and let his hair grow out, I'm still not. I don't want to go out with him, and when he calls—"

"Thank God!" Gina Lou burst out.

"Why would you say that?" Annie asked as she set platters of food in front of me and Mama.

"I dated him for several months and flat out fell in love with him."

"What happened?" Mama asked.

Annie pulled out a chair and sat down at the table with us. "Same old love story as you had all those years ago, Sarah. She thought she was pregnant, but it was a false alarm. He wasn't willing to step up and face the responsibilities."

"Hard lesson learned," Gina Lou said as the corners of her lips trembled.

Mama took a drink of her tea. "Been there, done that. Honey, you are better off without a man like that."

"Don't I know it," she said. "But I'm still working on getting my heart caught up to my common sense."

"You still want me to go out with him, Mama?" I had no intentions of going anywhere with Derrick, but I had to ask anyway.

"Not if he's that kind." Mama took another long drink of her sweet tea. "He was so polite and sweet when he came into Madge's Diner, and always left a good tip."

"He was sweet to me," Gina Lou said with a long sigh. "Until he wasn't."

"He's a charmer, all right," Annie said, "and I bet he was happy to run into you. He's been bragging around town that he's going to own Gracie's place by Christmas, even if he has to buy the cow to get the property. He wants to tear it down and plow up the strawberries."

"Why would he do that?" I asked.

"As soon as marijuana is legal in Texas, he's going to be a big weed king," Gina Lou answered. "That place is only the beginning of his big dream to make millions growing pot."

I wondered if Connor had the same thing in mind. After all, his relatives had started with cattle, moved to oil, and toyed with strawberries. Were they getting ready to cash it all in for a marijuana farm? Then a picture of a big black-and-white cow passed through my mind. "We have a dog on the property, but not a cow."

"*You* are the cow," Gina Lou giggled. "He used to talk about how he would buy up the whole town of Ditto for his new enterprise."

"Well, this cow isn't for sale," I huffed. "So Derrick can go find some other cows to build his empire on."

Chapter Ten

I mumbled all the way down the stairs that Sunday morning, shot a dirty look toward the kitchen clock hanging on the wall, and poured myself a bowl of junk cereal for breakfast. Even as a child I hated daylight saving time. Changing the clocks in the spring and then switching back in the fall always seemed stupid to me—but then, Aunt Gracie might have instigated that in me since she complained every time we had to make an adjustment.

She always said that someday she was moving to Arizona, where they stayed on God's time. For at least two weeks, my whole world was always turned upside down. The clock would say that it was noon, but my stomach would declare that it wouldn't be hungry for another hour. My eyes would pop wide open an hour before the alarm went off, and no amount of beating my pillow would help me fall back to sleep. That first day always dragged like a snail making its way through molasses in zero-degree weather. Just when I would get adjusted to the new norm, winter would come along and we would get that hour back—of course, I didn't want it by then, but who asked me?

I could almost hear Aunt Gracie fussing at me. *I give you a house and enough money to choke a horse, and what do you do? Complain over one little hour. Pull up your big-girl under britches and suck it up.*

"Hey, I got this attitude from you," I protested.

But Aunt Gracie was right: one little hour shouldn't spoil my Sunday morning. I had just taken the last bite of my chocolate-flavored cereal when the phone rang. I hurried up and swallowed before I grabbed the receiver. "Hello?"

"Mornin', Lila," Jasper said. "I won't be going to church this morning."

"Are you feeling all right?" I asked. "You aren't feeling sick, are you? I've never known you to miss church."

"This time change turns everything upside down for me. Always has, and me and Gracie decided a few years ago—after you left to go to college—that we wouldn't go to church the morning after we fiddle with the clocks. So twice a year . . ." He paused and coughed. "That was just springtime allergies. Don't go thinkin' I'm about to kick the bucket."

"Can I bring you anything?" I asked. "Do you have medicine?"

"I don't need pills. Never have been much for all the medicine doctors dole out. The side effects seem worse than what they're tryin' to cure, if you ask me. My granny brewed up lemon tea with honey for me during this time of year. I've had a cup this morning, and I've got the beans and corn bread you brought me last night, so I'm well fixed for the day. Me and Sassy are just going to stay inside and rest up. We'll be fine when we get used to this time change. Always took me and Gracie at least a week to get adjusted."

"If you get to feeling worse, will you call me?" I asked.

"You know I will." Jasper's chuckle was followed by another raspy cough. "You said I had to live until fall so we can celebrate my birthday."

"That's right," I agreed. "Want me to bring you a bottle of Aunt Gracie's whiskey?"

"No, darlin', I've got my own brand. I'll put a shot in my hot lemon tea this morning. The whiskey will knock out this little old cough real soon," Jasper said. "See you later this evening or tomorrow. Bye, now."

The click as he hung up told me he had called from his landline. I shook my fist at the ceiling. "And there you were, telling me not to grumble about the time change when you missed church because of it. Just for that, I'm going to clean out your closet this morning."

I was marching up the steps like a woman on a mission when the ringtone on my cell told me my mother was calling. I stopped midway, sat down, and stretched my long legs out four steps below me. "Hello, Mama."

"Who are you mad at?" she asked.

"What makes you think I'm mad at anyone?"

"I can always tell by your tone if you are angry, happy, or bored. Today, you are angry."

"I hate the time change," I declared.

Mama giggled. "Me too. But we'll get over it in a week or two. It's not fatal. What are you doing this morning since Jasper isn't going to church?"

"So you know about the time change rule?"

"Of course I do," Mama said. "Gracie said that the good Lord would understand because He wasn't the one that sanctioned moving the clocks back and forth like that."

"I agree with both of them," I said. "How about you? Are you going to church this morning?"

"No, I'm not," she said. "And I agree with them, too. By next weekend I'll be in tune with the change, and I'll be able to think about the sermon. Today, I might fall asleep and snore at the wrong time. I'm not even putting on shoes today. So, like I asked, what are you doing this morning?"

I looked down at my own bare feet and felt a bit liberated to not have to wear shoes, either. "Today, I'm cleaning out Aunt Gracie's closet. Want to come help me?" I could almost feel her shiver at the idea.

"Thanks, but no thanks," she said. "Annie is coming over this afternoon to talk about our new project."

I stood up. "Do I need to be there?"

"Not really, but you are welcome if you get bored or weary from cleaning Gracie's closet. We're going to organize recipes into folders."

I went on up the stairs to the landing, slightly amused that Mama said what she did to keep me moving toward the job at hand. She and I both knew I was procrastinating so I wouldn't have to admit that Aunt Gracie was really gone. "I'll keep that in mind. Have fun."

"You, too," she said and ended the call.

When I looked into Aunt Gracie's bedroom and saw the stack of red underpants on the same color bedspread, I almost closed the door. What was in her room had been private for almost a century. What right did I have to go through any of her things?

I gave you that right in my will. Her voice in my head sent chills down my backbone. Evidently, she intended for me to dive into her past.

"I've got to do it, and I've got all day with nothing else to do," I said out loud and looked up at the ceiling. "If you've got anything else to say to me, just spit it out."

Her voice didn't pop into my head, so apparently she had finished fussing at me. That told me there wouldn't be a single piece of paper or another journal hidden anywhere that would have a clue to the big secret. Aunt Gracie had put everything to rights before she passed away, and she didn't care if I found the diary or riffled through her closet and drawers.

I crossed the room, opened the closet doors, and took the first dress off the hanger. I laid it out on the bed to take to a women's shelter and stared at it for a full two minutes. Today's women lived in jeans and T-shirts. No one would want a 1940s dress with a tiny waistline, buttons all the way up the front, shoulder pads, and a pristine white collar. One that fit a woman who was only a couple of inches over five feet, or maybe a little taller if she wore heels.

I had never seen Aunt Gracie in that dress—but then, she would have worn it years and years before I was born. A memory played at the corners of my mind, but I couldn't place the picture. Maybe I'd seen something similar in a magazine. Then boom! The memory took form, and there it was. A lady in a play at the university materialized.

"That's it!" I snapped my fingers.

The Drama Department had put on a play my senior year. I couldn't remember the title, but it had been based on a book, and the main character wore a dress exactly like the one lying on the bed. I was sure the school would love to have all these old dresses for their costume collection and made a mental note to ask them for a mailing address that week.

Still thinking about that, I went back to the closet and noticed I had missed a note pinned to the bottom of the hanger. *This is the dress I wore to my high school graduation. Davis and Jasper both told me I was beautiful that evening. I'll never be as pretty as my mama, but they made me feel like I might be someday. Daddy was too busy to attend, and Mama didn't come back for the event, but I had my two best friends, and that was all I wanted.*

The next outfit was a straight pink skirt and matching jacket. This time a note was pinned to the jacket lapel. Gracie had done a lot of preparation before she died. *I wore this on my first day at the dress shop. I was so nervous, but Phyllis said that I had a natural knack for selling clothing. Davis and Jasper have gone off to basic training. I promised that I would write them every day, and as soon as they sent me an address, I would send all the letters I had written up to that time. I will miss them horribly. Maybe working at the shop will help pass the days. Daddy and I seldom speak to each other anymore—his fault, not mine. Mama remarried last month and moved to Boston. I hope she's happy in her new world, but I'm glad she is gone.*

I arranged the notes on the bed and wept when I reached a black dress with a matching coat. *I wore this to Davis's memorial service. Jasper is still off somewhere fighting in the war, so I stood by myself by the flag-draped casket and cried for what might have been if circumstances had been different. His mother and I didn't speak to each other, but we did exchange a look through all the tears we shed that morning. We both loved him so much. My precious Davis won't be coming back to me. My heart was broken before. Now it's shattered and can never be put back together.*

The next outfit was that bright red pantsuit. The note pinned to the lapel of the jacket made me giggle. *This was the last thing I brought home from the shop before I sold it. Red has always stood for independence to me. I'm not sure that Sarah's mother ever knew anything but submission to her husband, and she would have never been brazen enough to wear red—or pants, either, for that matter. She was furious with me for taking Sarah in, but then, I was just as angry with her for not supporting her only daughter.*

I was surprised to find a pink dress in her closet, even if it was the hottest shade I had ever seen. A couple of sizes larger than the ones I'd found before, it had tiny white polka dots and a pleated skirt. I carefully removed it from the hanger and unpinned the note from the lace collar. *This is what I wore on the day Sarah went into labor. I wanted the baby to be a girl, and I got my wish. I wanted Sarah to go to college the semester after the baby came, but she wouldn't. She told me she hated school and was happy being a mother. Each woman should have the opportunity to choose her destiny. I chose mine, so I didn't argue.*

There was what she had worn when I graduated from kindergarten and right next to it was the one she had worn when I finished high school. The next one I remembered well because I had a picture of her standing beside me when I graduated from college. I flipped through the rest of the clothing, looking for notes, but there were no more.

"I should have known you'd leave notes for me—but why pinned to just part of your clothing?" I whispered.

To help you remember, was all I got from the voice that often popped into my head.

Who would have thought I would find Gracie's life story in her closet? I carefully arranged all the notes into chronological order and carried them to my office. Mama had given me a small picture album with a beach scene on the front for Christmas and said that someday she was going to go there. When I asked her if she was going to swim in the ocean, she shook her head and said, "I want to smell the salt air, let the warm sand drift through my hands, and listen to the waves splash against the shore."

I found the album in my desk drawer and carefully slid each note into a protective sleeve.

Mama used to say that my mind reminded her of a hamster on a wheel. One minute, I was talking about one thing, and before I could finish a sentence, I would jump course and ask a question about something totally different from what we'd been discussing. My gaze went from the album and then over to the closet shelf where I stored my office supplies.

"Good Lord!" I gasped. "I've already forgotten what those outfits look like, and I haven't even started going through the other boxes."

I laid the album on my desk and hurried back to Gracie's bedroom. There might be something on the shelf in her closet that would continue the story of who Aunt Gracie was before I knew her. I stopped in my tracks when I looked at the clothing piled up on the bed and forgot all about taking down the boxes on the closet shelf or going through the stuff on the closet floor.

I slid my phone from the hip pocket of my jeans and snapped a photograph of each outfit that had had a note attached to it. Then I went back to my office and printed them all in the right size to go behind the notes in the album. It took the better part of an hour to get them arranged, and I ripped a tiny tear in the note about the red pantsuit. Tears rolled down my cheeks as I carefully taped it back together. These little pieces of paper were like an autobiography, and not one of them should be destroyed.

I could not give all her things away to be used as costumes. No, ma'am! I had to keep these milestone markers. Someday, when I had children, the stories I would tell them about the wonderful woman who helped raise me would keep her memory alive. I went back to my room, tossed my winter coats and jackets out of a plastic storage container and onto the bed. I didn't take time to hang them up but carried the empty box over to Gracie's room, picked up the first dress, folded it neatly, and laid it in the container.

Just when I'd finished with the last item, the phone rang with a generic ringtone—it couldn't be my mother or Jasper. I answered cautiously on the fourth ring. "Hello?"

"Is this Delilah Matthews?"

"Who's asking?" Saying yes could mean the beginning of identity theft.

"It's Derrick," he chuckled. "Don't you recognize my sexy voice?"

I rolled my eyes toward the ceiling. "No, I didn't. I'm sorry." Of all the people breathing the air on this earth, he was the last person I wanted to talk to. I was furious with him for jerking me out of Aunt Gracie's past and into the present.

"That's all right, darlin'. We can remedy that, starting with dinner tonight. I'll pick you up at seven, and we'll come back here to the ranch for grilled steaks. How do you like yours cooked?"

"I have already made other plans for tonight, Derrick," I said through clenched teeth. I was starting to get why Gina had reacted the way she did.

"So, you are seeing someone else?" he asked.

"That is none of your business. Just know that I don't want to spend time with you."

Mama said that a person could catch more flies with honey than vinegar, but I wasn't interested in catching bugs of any kind.

He laughed softly. "Your loss, darlin', but I intend to change your mind."

"Don't waste your time," I snapped.

"I like a woman with a little spirit," he said.

"And for the last time, my property is not for sale," I told him.

"Well, if it ever is, I've got first dibs on it," he said. "I'll top any other offer you might get."

"Goodbye, Derrick," I said as I ended the call.

I fumed as I picked up the last outfit—the red pantsuit—and folded it. *Red for independence* is what Aunt Gracie had written. I'd always heard that red-haired women should wear greens or the jewel tones of autumn, but I was buying something red the next time I went shopping.

I left the bedroom with the container and padded barefoot down the hall toward the door with the steps leading up to the attic—the place where spiders and other bugs lived. Aunt Gracie had an exterminator come every few months and take care of all things creepy and crawly. He always started up there in that dark place and worked his way down to the basement.

Please let him have been here recently, I prayed silently as I climbed up. But if there was an eight-legged critter, it must have been hiding in a far corner, because I didn't even see a web anywhere. The whole area was covered with dust, but there weren't any little mouse tracks on the top of the old steamer trunks or the little rocking horse in the corner. Evidently, the exterminator was still doing a good job.

"I should have at least put on a pair of flip-flops or socks," I muttered. "I'm going to have to wash my feet when I leave here, or I'll track dust everywhere I go."

I had always been more than a little bit terrified of the place, and I'd only gone up there one time during my great Ditto ghost-hunting days. That morning, I'd found a spider the size of a saucer—if I'm lyin', I'm flyin', and my feet ain't left the ground—sitting on the little wooden horse. I took it as an omen that the evil thing was protecting the ghosts that lived in the attic, or else it was scaring them away. Either way, it could have the whole place to itself—at least until the man came with the spray gun that would send him to wherever dead bugs go when they are poisoned, stomped, or hit with a flyswatter or shoe.

I set the container beside the dollhouse that Aunt Gracie would bring to the dining room and let me play with when I was a little girl. It was a replica of this house, right down to the wallpaper and the tiny furniture—all but the attic, which was totally empty.

"My mama had that made for my birthday when I was six," Aunt Gracie had told me with a smile. "I loved the times when she would sit on the floor and play with me."

"Why don't she live here anymore?" I remembered asking.

"That's a long story for another day," she had said. Then she'd sat down beside me, and we played for at least an hour.

I picked up the little sofa, which must have looked like the one that had been in the house in the thirties. Had Gracie giggled when she'd looked at the furniture in the living room during those days and then back at her own little house? Or did she want to rip off the blue velvet upholstery and replace it with red? I had put the tiny piece back in its place and turned to walk away when I stubbed my toe on the edge of an old steamer trunk. I sat down with such force that dust boiled up all around me. I sneezed three times in a row and pulled an old tissue from my pocket. I'd already used it a couple of times to wipe tears from my eyes, but it came in handy once more.

"What is the matter with me?" I groaned. "Weeping at notes, stumbling around like I'm tipsy on tequila shots . . . Are the ghosts in this house turning me into a blubbering fool?"

I slapped the trunk with an open hand, and more dust flew around me. When I stopped coughing, I noticed a small handwritten sign taped to the top of the trunk: Keep out! This belongs to Mary Grace Evans.

The handwriting was in block letters and was definitely that of a child. The hinges creaked when I opened the chest. The guilt for prying into something that definitely said to keep out didn't keep me from peeking inside. As I picked up a yellowed piece of paper and then another, I wondered if Gracie's mama had stuck things to the fridge with magnets. Maybe that was too low class for them to have even considered. From what Jasper had told me and what I'd pieced together from things I'd learned, her parents were bougie.

But then, on the other hand, her mother had taken the time to play with her when she was a little girl. Maybe when Aunt Gracie had gotten too old to have her work put on the refrigerator, her mama stored all those things in the small trunk and put it in the attic. I could picture a little girl with dark brown braids finding it in the attic and writing that little note—maybe for the exterminator, so he wouldn't open it up and ruin everything with the spray.

From her report cards, it was apparent that she was a brilliant student—all As on every one, not a single B. She could have easily gone to college with those grades. I made a mental note to ask Jasper why she hadn't furthered her education. Had she wanted to be a teacher or maybe even a doctor? Why hadn't I ever asked her to tell me more about her life while she was still with us?

My phone rang and startled me so badly that I dropped one of her report cards on the floor. I slipped the phone out of my back pocket and said, "Hello, Mama."

"Do you think you could come over here . . . like right now?" she asked.

I picked up the card, blew the dust off, and gently laid it back in the trunk. "Sure, but what's the hurry?"

Her voice caught. "We just need to talk."

"Then I'll be over in half an hour. I'm up here in the dusty attic right now, and I need to take a quick shower." Worry replaced any guilt that had washed over me when I'd opened the small trunk.

"That will be fine," Mama said, and the screen went dark.

Chapter Eleven

Mama was probably the second-strongest woman I knew, coming in just behind Aunt Gracie. She had always been one to grab the bull by the horns, spit in his eye, and dare him to charge her. So I wondered what on the great green earth could have happened that had upset her. I didn't take time to blow-dry my hair or even slap on a little makeup to cover up my freckles. I just jerked on a pair of jeans and a T-shirt and hopped in my vehicle. It seemed like the five-minute drive from my house to hers took every second of an hour. All kinds of scenarios went through my mind. Maybe she had found out she had a disease—something wrong with her heart. Aunt Gracie had died peacefully in her sleep from a heart attack, so the gene could be in the family. My hamster mind jumped from that to wondering what it would be like to simply go to sleep and not wake up in the morning. Did God have a pair of wings ready, or was He going to have to keep those Pearly Gates closed just a little while longer?

I braked hard at the end of her driveway and slung gravel halfway to Poteet. I parked beside Annie's vehicle, got out of my SUV, and jogged across the yard to where Annie and Mama were sitting on the porch. Neither of them looked deathly sick, but their expressions said they were worried.

"Are y'all okay?" I asked after a couple of short bursts of breath.

"We're fine," Annie called out from the porch swing.

"Then what's this news that I needed to get over here for?" I waved at the gray gravel haze blowing across the porch. "After the day I've had, I feel like I'm spittin' dust."

"Oh. My. Goodness!" Annie giggled—a bit nervously, which concerned me. "You sound just like Gracie sometimes."

Mama nodded and headed into the house. I had barely sat down on the top porch step when she returned with a longneck bottle and handed it to me. "This should settle anything you've breathed in. Annie and I have been talking, and . . ." She took a deep breath and rubbed her forehead. "I'm so sorry, Lila."

"For what?" I was getting pretty worried; not even a couple of drinks of icy-cold beer settled my nerves.

"We were taken up in the heat of the moment, and . . ." Annie said, and then there was another pregnant moment of silence.

"Somebody tell me what's going on before *I* have a heart attack," I whispered.

"We don't want to open a catering business," Mama blurted out. "And I feel horrible that you quit your job."

Had I heard her right? Was she teasing me? I was completely tongue-tied, and my chest tightened.

Everything happens for a reason.

Aunt Gracie had said that too many times to begin to count. I'd even said the same thing when she'd left me her property and I made the decision to move to Ditto.

I repeated the words in a whisper: "Everything happens for a reason."

"What was that?" Annie asked.

"She said, 'Everything happens for a reason,'" Mama told her. "Gracie said that all the time, and I believe it—but, Lila, what brought it to your mind at this moment?"

I took another long drink of the beer. "On the way over here that evening when y'all told me about the decision to start a catering business, I was having a little hissy fit about needing some excitement in my life. That gave me a reason to quit my job that had become so boring since everything shut down a few years ago. Now I will have time to find my true passion in life. I don't know what it is, but I believe with my whole heart that it's out there somewhere, just waiting for me to open my eyes."

"Or stumble over it?" Annie asked.

I thought of the notes on the outfits in Gracie's closet and of stubbing my toe on the small chest—both in the last few hours—and had to smile. "Most likely, that's exactly what will happen."

"You're taking this better than I ever thought you would—and again, I'm so sorry to disrupt your life twice in only a few days," Mama said.

"Aunt Gracie was right when she said that about things happening for a reason. We might not know what they are today, but it'll all come out in the light." I was amazed at myself for not being disappointed or even upset.

"Whew!" Annie wiped her forehead in a dramatic gesture. "We were both sitting here going over every which way about how we could tell you."

I took a couple more sips of my beer. "What made you change your minds about catering?"

Mama's eyes were filled with excitement. "We want some time to do what you just said. Find our passion, and it's not really in the food business. When I slowed down, I realized I was diving into something out of desperation."

"And a need for security," Annie added with a nod. "Not financial but mental. Like your mother, I've worked since I was just a kid. I thought I had to be busy, or I would be . . ." She struggled to find the word.

"Bored?" I finished for her.

Annie smiled and nodded. "That's the word. Every minute has been accounted for most of my life, so the idea of having whole days in a row with nothing to do scared me."

My chest tightened, and fear washed over me when I thought of the same thing. When Mama and Annie had suggested a new path for their lives, I had jumped right in without mulling it over for a while. But I'd had a new job and an exciting new adventure ahead. Now there was a void—no calling the lawyers to help me set up a corporation, no talking about a warehouse with a kitchen in it. I would have to find my own path, and that would be new territory for me. I closed my eyes, and the first thing that came to mind was snow cones. It was kind of silly, but maybe even that was a reason to set something else in motion.

"Let's go get snow cones. My treat, and y'all can ride with me."

"Where did that come from?" Mama asked.

"I don't know." I shrugged. "But it sounds like a good idea."

Annie stood up. "I agree."

Mama pushed up out of her chair and started across the porch. "I'll get my purse."

I finished off the last of my beer and set the empty bottle on the porch. "You don't need it. I'm paying today."

Mama cocked her head to one side and almost grinned. "What if something happened and I needed to drive home? I don't go anywhere with anyone without my driver's license."

"Suit yourself," I said. "We're going to San Antonio. There's a little place up there that serves the best shaved-ice snow cones you'll ever eat. Aunt Gracie took me there once when I was bawling and squalling about a boy calling me a beanpole."

Mama went inside the house. "All the more reason for me to take my purse."

"Mine is in the car," Annie said. "We might even have time to check out a store or two if we are close to a mall."

Three pickup trucks and one car passed us on the twenty-mile trip from Ditto to the southside of San Antonio, where the Lone Star Water Ice stand was located. Mama and Annie were so busy talking about the few times they'd actually carved out half a day to go to "the city" that they didn't even notice what served as heavy traffic in our small town.

The little building sat on the back corner of a small shopping mall, so parking wasn't a problem. I pulled into a spot, turned off the engine, and unfastened my seat belt.

"We aren't going to get them at the drive-up window and eat them on the way home?" Annie asked.

"Nope," I told her. "There are two windows: one for drive-up service, another around back. There are some picnic tables back there, so we can visit while we eat."

"That building looks like an old hippie wagon from the sixties," Mama giggled.

"How would you know anything about those?" I led the way around the building, which had not changed one bit since Aunt Gracie had brought me here all those years ago. Bright flowers the size of the hood of a car were painted all over it. Some of them overlapped others, but the Texas flag was somewhere in each one.

"I didn't, but Aunt Gracie talked about buying one when you were a baby. She said that she dreamed about her and Jasper traveling around in it," Mama answered.

"Well, would you look at this?" Annie said when we rounded the side of the place and she saw the wooden picnic benches scattered about under the massive oak trees. "This is lovely, and there's a nice little breeze blowing."

"Y'all don't have plans for anything else today, do you?" I asked.

"Not a single one."

"Good, because I thought after we get done here, we might go to the mall and walk off the calories we're about to eat."

"This is Sunday," Annie reminded me.

"Yep, and the mall closes early, but we'll have a couple of hours to shop, and we've got that extra hour of daylight, so we'll be home by dark."

"And not a one of us have a curfew, so if we aren't home by midnight, we won't get into trouble," Annie declared.

"Aunt Gracie would want us home by dark," I said and swallowed the lump in my throat that formed at the memory.

"Yes, she would," Mama agreed. "She worried about us both."

The wooden benches showed their age and had several initials carved into the seats. Annie pointed to the one closest to the window where we would order. "I thought I could read the sign if I was this close, but no such thing. I didn't bring my reading glasses, so one of you will have to tell me what's on that menu up there."

"I didn't bring mine, either," Mama said, "but I usually get a rainbow with cherry, grape, and banana when we're at the one in Poteet."

"Okay, listen closely." I slowly read off each flavor and then said, "I'm getting a piña colada."

Annie squinted and frowned. "I can't make up my mind between a pineapple or a coconut crème."

"I want a piña colada, too," Mama said. "Never had one of those, but I'm game for something new."

I thought of what Jasper had told me about Aunt Gracie having regrets over never going anywhere. Had she, in that final breath she took, wished she would have sold the last twenty acres and her house and traveled the world? Her red pantsuit wasn't her only act of rebellion, according to Jasper's hints. He had said when she'd come out of her bedroom after whatever had happened when they were teenagers—maybe no more than fourteen—that she never again let anyone tell her what to do. And yet she had stayed right there in that house in Ditto and took care of things, even when her father had passed away.

"Make mine the same," Annie decided. "That way I get coconut and pineapple flavors both."

That antsy sensation when someone was either staring at me or was nearby swept over me. A prickling feeling that raised the hair on my neck was a dead giveaway that someone or something was near. I glanced over my shoulder to see a coyote peeking out from around a tree. When we made eye contact, the animal turned tail and ran, but the strange feeling didn't disappear.

"Hey, Lila," a very familiar deep voice floated through the air as Connor came around the building. "Fancy meeting you here."

"Hey. I could say the same thing to you." I could hear a bit of breathlessness in my own voice. "I didn't expect to see you at a snow cone stand."

"Grandpa brought me here when I was a little boy and . . ." Connor stopped talking when the lady in the window asked us for our order.

"What are you ladies having?" she asked.

"Three piña coladas," I answered.

"Make that four," Connor said and handed her a bill. "I'll treat today if I can sit with y'all while we eat them."

"Thank you, and of course we will share our table with you."

The lady took the money and made change. "Be right back."

"Who introduced you to this place?" Connor asked.

There had to be at least a foot between us, but I had the same feeling I'd had when I took sandwiches out for lunch during strawberry-picking season. There was definitely chemistry between us, but that didn't mean I had to give in to it.

"Aunt Gracie brought me here."

"When you were a little girl?"

"No, when I was a teenager." I remembered the day well. We had had snow cones before we went to the mall, and she bought me a new outfit for church on Easter Sunday.

"Was there an occasion?" he asked.

"Easter." No way would I tell him that a boy had hurt my feelings and made me angry at the same time. "We went shopping after we sat at that bench where Mama and Annie are now."

The lady came back with four disposable cups full of shaved ice and flavorings, along with spoons and napkins. "Enjoy," she said.

"I'm sure we will," Connor said.

We each carried two of the cups to the table, set them down, and then took a seat on the other side from Mama and Annie. Not even the freezing ice toned down the heat rushing through my body when his shoulder touched mine.

"Hello, ladies," Connor said. "Lila gave me permission to sit with y'all. How's the catering business coming along?"

"We put a pin in it for a while," Annie said. "We aren't sure that's what we want to do for the next twenty years."

"We've worked all our lives and never been anywhere or done anything else," Mama added.

"You could do some traveling," Connor suggested. "Try a road trip or a cruise."

"I'll drive you or go with you since I don't have a job," I offered.

Mama reached across the table and laid her hand on mine. "Darlin' girl, I'm not even fifty. I believe I can drive myself. You are welcome to come with us on any of our adventures, but it won't be to babysit us. And besides, who would take care of Jasper if you went with us?"

"Amen," Annie agreed. "Connor has a good idea, Sarah. Let's plan a road trip and leave the week after we are free from working. Maybe just a short one here at first. We'll each make a bucket list when we get back to your house."

"That would keep y'all from getting bored from not having a set schedule," Connor said between bites. "Coming to Ditto was an adjustment for me after being on edge all the time. I'm still not completely in tune with my new norm."

I'd wondered if he might not stick around once he got bored with growing strawberries and sitting in meetings. Losing him as a friend would be tough, but if we were to take it to the next level . . . well, that would be a heartache waiting to happen.

Mama nodded. "A vacation sounds good. Got any suggestions, Connor?"

"Lots of them," he answered. "How long do you want to be gone?"

"A week, maybe two to start with," Annie replied.

"Are you country music fans?" he asked.

"Yes," they said in unison.

"Well, then, you might try going to Nashville," he suggested. "You could go to the Grand Ole Opry and the Ryman, and take in all the other sites like the Country Music Hall of Fame. And if you plan your route to include Montgomery, Alabama, you could visit the Hank Williams Museum."

"Who knows, you might even get to see George Strait or Chris Stapleton while you are there," I added.

"I like that idea," Mama said.

Annie's eyes widened. "Me too. Let's do that, Sarah. Are you going, Lila?"

I shook my head. "Not this trip. Like Mama said, Jasper needs me to take him to church and be there if he gets sick. Aunt Gracie would haunt me the whole trip if I left him alone. He had a cough this morning that worries me."

Mama chuckled. "What if we decide to stay in Nashville?"

"Then I'll come visit you real often," I replied and then added, "And I'll miss you something awful."

"You know a lot about that area, so evidently you've been, right, Connor?" Annie asked.

"Yes, ma'am."

"Got any advice for us?" Mama asked.

"Stay in the hotel right on the strip and park your vehicle across the street instead of doing valet parking. You'll save some money that way, and you'll be within a block of the Ryman. You could easily spend several days going from one bar to the other, just listening to the music."

"How far is the Grand Ole Opry from there?" Annie asked.

"Across town, and for that you might want to splurge on a taxi or Uber. Traffic can get messy at night in that area. You could also check out Blake Shelton's venue," Connor suggested as he stood up. "If you need any more ideas, just holler. I'll be up here in San Antonio until the end of next week, but . . ." He pulled a card from his pocket, wrote on the back, and handed it to me. "Here's my cell phone number."

"I guess you learned the strawberry business really good for Everett to already have business cards made up for you."

"Yep, I guess so. All right if I call you later? I need to be getting back to the hotel."

"I'll be home thirty minutes after the mall closes," I told him.

When he had cleared the area, I narrowed my eyes at my mother. "Have you changed your mind about him?"

"Not where you are concerned," she declared in a no-nonsense tone.

Chapter Twelve

"Looks like we've got company," Jasper said.

I sat down in the spare chair on his porch. "Sounds like someone is coming—but maybe they're coming to see you, not me."

"Ain't dang likely." He grinned. "Most of the folks that might drop by here are in the cemetery. I've outlived all my friends."

"Hey, now!" I protested. "I'm still kicking."

"You are family," he declared and threw the tennis ball for Sassy to go fetch. For a man who was over ninety years old, he had a pretty good arm. Sassy took off after it and caught it midair just before it hit the fence.

"If I was still able to go duck huntin', she'd be a good one to fetch." His voice held a bit of wistfulness. "Me and Davis used to go out huntin' ever chance we got. Granny could fix up a duck or some venison real good."

"Did Gracie ever go with you?" I asked.

"She didn't like the idea of killin' anything." Jasper took the ball from Sassy's mouth and hurled it out through the air again. "But she would come out here and eat with us when Granny cooked, and she did like to go fishin'. Granny taught her how to mix cayenne pepper in the cornmeal to give the bass a little extra spice. She and I went out to the pond last spring and caught us a five-pounder. I cleaned it and she fried it up with hush puppies."

I thought I heard a noise but couldn't be sure if it was the doorbell or the wind chimes hanging on the front porch. "Did you hear that?"

"I'd say it was the doorbell. You going to answer it?"

Sassy brought the ball back to Jasper, laid it at his feet, and growled.

"Don't worry, sweetie," I assured her. "Very few folks use the front door or ring the bell. It's most likely a delivery person. If it's anyone who knows us, they'll come around to this side."

"You been shopping online again?" Jasper asked.

"It's called retail therapy. I'm trying to figure out what I want to do with my life, and poring through online sales helps me escape."

Jasper picked up the ball and threw it again. "You could go to town and buy what you need. That way you would see people. Kids today are losin' the ability to have decent conversations."

"Yep, they are, but that would require that I put on shoes. I already did that with Mama, and that's enough shopping for a while." I held my foot up and wiggled my toes. "I bought a new trash can for the kitchen and a new nonstick skillet. I don't reckon there would be many conversations around that, now would there?"

"Gracie has good cast-iron cookware. That's all you need, Lila." His tone was only a notch above scolding.

"Hey, is anybody home?" a feminine voice yelled. "Lila, are you back here?"

"What's Gina Lou coming around here for?" Jasper asked.

"Who?" I asked.

"Gina Lou, the waitress at Annie's," Jasper said. "I'd recognize that nasal twang of hers anywhere."

"Don't know." I shrugged and then called back, raising my voice, "Come on around to the backyard."

She had barely made it to the gate when the headlights of more vehicles lit up the space between the house and the garage.

"Looks like we're going to have a party," Jasper chuckled. "You got plenty of beer, or do I need to borrow Gracie's car and make a run into Poteet?"

"You aren't driving anywhere!" I fussed at him.

"Afraid I might find me another dog?" he teased.

"Afraid that you might wreck the car," I shot right back.

Sassy started for the gate when she heard the hinges squeak. I grabbed her collar just as she was about to run past me and held her back. "Hey, Gina Lou. Be sure the latch is tight when you shut the gate. What brings you out this evening?" I wondered if she'd brought friends. At least two more cars had pulled in.

"I didn't know if you'd recognize me away from the café." Her blonde hair flowed down around her shoulders, and that evening she was wearing a cute little sundress with strawberries printed on it. "I was in the neighborhood . . ." She rattled the gate to be sure it was firmly closed. "No, that's not right. I wanted to talk to you about Derrick and ask—"

"Did I hear my name?" Derrick put a hand on the fence and hopped over it without dropping a huge bouquet of lilies. When he realized Gina Lou was standing on Jasper's front porch, he stopped in his tracks and glared at her. "What the hell are you doing here?"

She popped her hands on that tiny waist and locked eyes with him. "Warning Lila about scumbags like you."

"Leave, right now!" he demanded, raising his voice.

"Hey, this is *my* property. You have no right to tell anyone to leave," I said.

He turned his glare toward me. "Don't believe a word this piece of—"

"What's going on back here?" Richie Brewer asked as he opened the gate and came into the yard. Maybe everyone in town was coming to buy the farm. But I was a little glad to see that Connor wasn't one of them.

"None of your business—and if you're here to try to talk Lila into selling the place to you, it's too late. I'm first in line," Derrick growled.

"What for?" Richie asked. "All you'll do is plow under the strawberries and plant marijuana as soon as Texas makes it legal."

"Party has turned into a brawl," Jasper muttered. "Want to take bets on who wins when the fightin' starts?"

"I'll put my money on Gina Lou." I crossed my arms over my chest. "You can both go home and forget that this property even exists. I'm not selling it to anyone."

Derrick's expression changed from angry to sweet in a split second. "These flowers are for you, darlin'. No strings attached. I didn't send anything when Miz Gracie passed away, so I brought them tonight. They are almost as beautiful as you are."

"You've used that line so many times that it's worn out," Gina Lou snapped.

"You"—he pointed his finger at her—"stay out of this, and go on back to whatever rock you live under."

"Hey, now," Richie barked, "that's no way to talk to a lady."

Derrick whipped around to face Richie. "She's not a lady, and you can stay out of this, old man."

"Derrick, you can take your flowers and go home. And don't you dare talk about Gina Lou that way. Richie, I don't need you to fight my battles!" I yelled over all of them.

"Lila, are you all right?" Connor asked from outside the fence.

"I'm fine!" I shouted. Now there were three guys in my yard, all bowed up like a bunch of fighting banty roosters.

"I brought pizza and beer," he said. "I had no idea you had company. What's going on?"

"None of your concern," Derrick said.

"These two are having an argument." Richie's tone said that he was aggravated. "Lila has asked them to leave, but they won't. I just dropped by to see if Lila had changed her mind about selling her property. I know that Everett's lease runs out the first of the year, and I wanted her to know I'm still interested."

Derrick shook the flowers at him. "And I told him that—"

"Don't believe a word he says," Gina Lou growled.

"I think the whole bunch of you better go," Connor said as he came through the gate and set the pizza and beer on my back porch. "She's asked you to leave . . ."

My hands clenched into fists. Men and their chivalry. "I don't need you or anyone else to fight my battles."

"Hey . . ." Connor held up his palms. "Let's all take a deep breath and give Lila some space."

Jasper went into his house with Sassy right behind him.

"Just because you are sleeping with her doesn't give you the right to boss us around," Richie said.

That put extra heat in my already scalding-hot temper. I pointed at him, then swung my finger around to include all three of them. But Connor snapped before I could speak.

"Hey, now! That was uncalled for, Richie."

Jasper opened the door, gently closed it and the wooden screen door behind him, and stepped out to the edge of the porch. He licked his finger, stuck it up in the air, and said, "Gina Lou, you come on over here and stand behind me."

She didn't argue, simply obeyed.

Then he raised what looked like a small can of hair spray up in the air. "This here is pepper spray. The wind is coming y'all's way, and I'm going to give you to the count of five to get the hell out of my yard."

"You wouldn't dare," Richie said.

"One . . . ," Jasper said.

"Old man, I could tackle you and take that away from you before you can count to five," Derrick declared.

"Two. Try it and we'll see how you look with eyeballs that match your red hair," Jasper growled.

"I'm leaving." Connor cleared the yard and jumped the fence in only a few seconds.

"Three . . . four . . . ," Jasper said.

Richie started across the yard at a slow pace. Derrick threw the flowers on the ground.

"Five," Jasper said and sprayed.

I could hear Richie coughing and sputtering as he picked up speed and jogged away between the garage and house. The sound that came out of Derrick's mouth sounded like something between a piglet caught in a barbed wire fence and an ambulance siren. He held his nose with one hand and ran toward the fence. He burst out of the gate and left it hanging open as he made his way to his truck.

"Now"—Jasper sat back down—"we'll let that stuff blow on out of the yard while Lila brings out a kitchen chair for Gina Lou to sit in. Don't let Sassy out. She'll be real mad at me if she gets into what's still floatin' around in the air. In a few minutes, the wind will carry what's left of the pepper spray away from us, and we'll all enjoy that pizza and beer over there on Lila's porch."

"I meant it when I said I could fight my own battles," I told Jasper.

"You didn't have any pepper spray in your pocket, did you?" he snapped as he sat down in his chair.

"No, but—"

"Don't fuss at me," he interrupted. His eyes twinkled, and the corners of his mouth turned up in a smile. "That was more fun than I've had since Gracie left me."

I went inside his small house and wasn't surprised to see that the place hadn't changed much at all since the last time I was in it. The same wooden table with three mismatched chairs around it filled up one end of the room. The sofa was different but well worn, as was the recliner at the end of it. I picked up a chair and carried it out to the porch. "Didn't see Sassy. She must be hiding in one of the bedrooms."

"Most likely." Jasper motioned toward the chair. "She's smart, and I told her to stay put or else she would be sorry."

Gina Lou sat down. "Why did you let me stay?"

"You didn't come here to hoodwink Lila out of her property, did you?" Jasper asked.

"No, sir!" Gina Lou declared.

"That's your answer."

I eased down into the rocking chair. "Why didn't you let Connor stay? Do you think he's out to sweet-talk me out of my house?"

"Don't know," Jasper said, "but until I do, he can get his butt off my yard with the rest of 'em. Me and his grandpa have been friends for years, but I ain't got a good solid read on Connor just yet."

"From what I've heard, he's a good person," Gina Lou said.

"Did you think Derrick was a good person at one time?" Jasper asked.

"Good point," Gina Lou said with a nod. "I guess now that the drama is over, I should tell you why I'm really here. Annie's is closing on Friday night of this next week and reopening on Monday under the new management, but . . ." She paused.

"The new owner isn't keeping the staff?" I asked.

Gina Lou shook her head. "She's bringing in her own people. I came to ask you if you might have some work for me. I used to clean houses and do odd jobs like yard work before Annie hired me when I was sixteen. She overheard you telling Sarah that you might need help cleaning that big house."

"Didn't college interest you?" I asked.

Gina Lou blushed. "Yes, but kids that come from my background don't have the money for that. There are seven of us, and I'm the oldest. I moved out so my folks would have one less mouth to feed, and pretty often I help them out with my tip money."

"What did you want to be?" Jasper asked.

"A teacher, maybe kindergarten or first grade," she said. "I taught all my little brothers and sisters to read and do a little math before they even started to school. But that's just a pipe dream."

"Yes, I can use some help with the housework and the yard." I hoped that I wasn't being impulsive again. But it felt like something Gracie might have done. "I'll pay you minimum wage, which is what you are getting at the café, right? And you can live here—free room and board should make up for the tips," I said. "It's a big house with four bedrooms, and I'm rattling around in it all day by myself. You won't have rent or a food bill."

"Are you serious?" Gina Lou asked.

"Yes, I am," I replied. "When can you start?"

"I can move in and start work on Saturday. My rent comes due the fifteenth, so that will work out great," she said. "I won't have a lot to move. The travel trailer that I've been renting is furnished."

"If you've got more than what will fit in your bedroom, there's room in the garage to store the rest of your things," I said. "Jasper, do you reckon the pepper spray has settled enough that we can go get that pizza and beer?"

"Yep, and I'm hungry. I hope it's meat lovers," Jasper said.

"A heart attack in a flat box, if it is," I teased.

"Bring it on," Jasper declared. "Sooner I get the business of dying over with, the sooner I get to see Davis and Gracie."

"You might have to ask forgiveness for spraying those guys tonight," I threw over my shoulder as I stood up and jogged across the yard.

"God told me it wasn't a sin," Jasper argued. "I asked Him if I should bring the pepper spray or the shotgun out to get rid of those varmints. He said the shotgun wasn't loaded, but the spray was ready to go."

At his age he might possibly have a hotline to heaven, so I didn't argue. I picked up the large pizza and six-pack of beer and carried them over to his porch. I wiped the dust off the stump that was our table and set the pizza on it, passed out a bottle of beer to each of us, and then took my seat.

"Since you have a one-on-one working relationship with God, maybe you better say grace," I joked.

He bowed his head, closed his eyes, and said, "For this food, we are thankful, Father. Bless it as you see fit. Amen."

"That was short and sweet," I said.

"God don't expect us to give thanks for the green grass, the blue sky, and the crickets," Jasper huffed as he picked up a slice of pizza. "He just wants us to remember to be grateful. It ain't meat lovers, but I like sausage and bacon almost as good."

"I'm so happy that . . ." Gina Lou's eyes filled with tears. "There are no words. Thank you, thank you so much."

"Gracie should've hired a housekeeper years ago, but she . . ." Jasper stopped midsentence and bit into his pizza.

"She what?" I asked.

"She was too independent for her own good."

He almost gave away a secret. Maybe not the big one, but there was a reason Gracie wouldn't hire someone to help her. It had to be connected to that time she had been told she could attend a party, but Davis and Jasper could only show up if they agreed to be the help. If I was right, she probably didn't want to make anyone feel like her friends did that evening. I still wanted to help Gina Lou—maybe it was easier for me because I hadn't lived here for a long time.

"*Thank you* seems like so little, but it's all I've got," Gina Lou said. "I liked Miz Gracie. She was always nice to me when she came in to pick up takeout on Sundays after church."

"We didn't do that very often because Gracie liked to give Madge our business since Sarah worked there," Jasper said.

My mind drifted back to the first sympathy card I had opened—the one that the retired teacher had written, about being so grateful to Aunt Gracie for helping her get through college.

The breeze picked up, and the new mint green leaves on the trees seemed to dance around like graceful ballerinas. If I had been superstitious like my mother, I would have been absolutely sure that Aunt Gracie's voice was a sign.

Pay it forward.

Fall classes didn't start until the end of August or first of September. By then I should know Gina Lou well enough to figure out if she was serious about becoming a teacher. If so, I could easily pay for her education, and depending on what path the rest of her siblings wanted to take, that might be something to think about, too.

"So, of the six kids still at home," I asked, "how many are brothers?"

"The baby, Jesse, is eleven. I have five sisters scattered out over twelve years. The next one below me is eighteen and graduates in May. Then Mama had four more in the next seven years before she got her boy. They're all real smart." Gina Lou finished her slice of pizza and polished off her beer. "I should be going. I want to go by Annie's and tell her not to worry about me, that I've found a job."

"See you on Saturday, then?" I asked.

"What time should I be here?"

"No set time. You can use that day to get moved in and settled, and actually begin work on Monday."

"Thank you, again," Gina Lou said as she walked out across the yard and disappeared into the dark.

I picked up the last of the beers in the carton and took a step toward the house. "Good night, Jasper. Thank you for saving the evening."

"Don't thank me," he said. "You are able to take care of yourself. I was just the one with the fire power. What are you going to do now?"

"Call Connor and tell him thanks for supper."

"Why would you do that?" Jasper scolded. "He was right in amongst all the trouble that got stirred up tonight. He's a good man but seems to me like all the local folks are way too interested in this property."

"Maybe you are right," I agreed and decided to wait until the next day to call him.

Chapter Thirteen

How can sadness and happiness fill my heart at the same time? I wondered as I tossed my purse on the floorboard of Mama's truck and slid into the passenger's seat. Was this the way Aunt Gracie had felt when she yearned to go see the world yet was anchored to the house and land?

"You look conflicted," Mama said. "What's wrong? Is it Connor? Are you having regrets about hiring Gina Lou?"

"How do you do that?" I asked.

"What?"

"Know when something is bothering me?"

She started up the engine and backed out of the driveway. "It's built into a mama's DNA. So fess up, kiddo. What is it?"

"I'm glad you are finally going on a vacation," I said, "but you've always been at home. I want you to go, and at the same time I don't want you to be gone."

She reached across the console and laid a hand on my shoulder. "I read a story one time that was about a person who had regrets on her deathbed. Her husband of more than fifty years told her that half of his heart was going with her but that half of her heart stayed with him. He made a promise that he would go see the mountains in the wintertime when the snow was knee deep. He would wade through it so that she could see it through his eyes and the half of a heart that was still hers that beat in his chest."

"What has that got to do with you being gone?" I asked.

"There was a bond between me and you and Gracie. It's not like a married couple, but it's there. What either of us do for the rest of our lives gives her the ability to see—"

"—the beach and hear the ocean waves," I butted in before she could finish.

"When did she tell you about that being something she wanted to do?" Mama asked.

"It was in one of her notes that she left behind." I went on to tell her about what I'd found in Gracie's closet.

"Maybe someday we'll go to the beach and let her see it." Mama choked up. "Until then, I'm only a phone call away anytime you want to talk . . . but I can call this whole thing off if—"

"No!" I said before she could even finish. "You and Annie both deserve this and need it. I would feel guilty if you stayed home because I was being selfish. Just remember that Aunt Gracie really liked Hank Williams—take time to really look at everything if you go to the museum."

"Family first," Mama said. "Aunt Gracie taught me that by example."

"She was so right—and what kind of daughter would I be if I told you to stay home? I want you to go. Gina Lou will be helping me take care of things. Lord knows, the dust bunnies in the garage have grandchildren. Aunt Gracie and Jasper haven't been able to take care of it in years."

Mamas weren't the only ones to understand facial expressions. I could see hers shift into worry mode in an instant.

"And Connor?" she asked.

"I don't know about Connor, but I'm not rushing anything. I promise I will be careful. Right now we are friends . . ." Just saying his name caused my pulse to kick up a notch or two.

"Do I hear a *but*?" she asked.

"Yes," I replied with a slight nod. "I haven't dated in a long time, so maybe that's why I feel sparks every time he's around. But there's no denying that there is chemistry between us. There's another *but*, Mama. If you will remember, I've been burned a couple of times in the past. I have learned the signs to look for when the relationship is just a flash in the pan, so you don't have to worry about me."

"I trust you," Mama said.

"Good. Now, let's talk about something that doesn't put a lump in my throat."

"Okay. What do I need for this vacation? I've lived in jeans and T-shirts from the café most of my life. What do you think?"

"I'd say new jeans, for sure. Yours are getting pretty worn. You and Annie will buy T-shirts at every stop you make, so don't buy too many to take with you," I told her. "A couple of pretty outfits, maybe capris and nicer shirts, for going out to eat or fancier places. And absolutely two new suitcases. Come to think of it, I've never seen a suitcase in your house, Mama."

She pulled into a parking space on the west side of the mall. "I've never traveled overnight, so I didn't need anything like that."

I unfastened my seat belt and threw open the truck door. "That is the saddest thing I've heard in years. I'm buying you a set of luggage today."

She started to argue, but I held up a palm. "Call it an early Mother's Day present."

She got out of the truck at the same time I did. "Can I have a red set?"

I slowed my stride to match hers. "Of course you can. Aunt Gracie would be so proud to see you roll a bright red suitcase into the hotel."

"Should we make reservations?" she asked.

"Only one day at a time," I suggested. "You might change your minds about the route as you travel. When the company sent my department for workshops, they usually put the bunch of us up in Holiday Inn Express hotels. They are reasonably priced and have free breakfast."

She opened the door into the mall entrance and held it for me. "Good to know. If you've got any more tips, text them to both of us."

"Will do—and would you look at that?" I pointed toward a display in front of a store. "There's a sale on luggage."

"And they've got a red set," she almost squealed. "We are two lucky women today."

I didn't feel lucky at all. I was about to have a housekeeper-slash-roommate whom I barely knew. I had feelings for a man I'd only known a short while, who could be trying to get into my pants *and* my land. And my mama—who, along with Aunt Gracie, had been my rock my whole life—was going away for God knew how long.

I could hear Aunt Gracie telling me to put on my big-girl panties; that I was not to treat Gina Lou like the help, the way Davis and Jasper had been treated; and that I could kick Connor out of my life if things didn't work out. She would also remind me that my mama deserved a nice long trip. If she could really see what was going on right now in Mama's life, as well as mine, she would be proud as a peacock.

Way back before I started working from home in my pajamas, it wasn't unusual for me to spend a whole afternoon and evening in a shopping mall. But I had forgotten how hard that had been on my feet and back until that evening. When I got home, I kicked off my shoes inside the front door and padded barefoot to the living room, where I eased down onto the sofa and propped my feet on the coffee table.

"My poor mama stood on concrete floors for eight to ten hours every day," I whispered. "I should have appreciated her efforts more."

Someone rapped on the front door. Thinking it was Mama, who might have gotten one of my bags mixed up with hers, I yelled, "Come on in, but you don't have to knock!"

"Hey, Lila," Connor's voice floated down the hallway. In a moment, his tall frame appeared in the archway. "Why is it that I don't have to knock? Is that part of the friendship-muffin pact?"

"I thought you were Mama. We just got home from the mall in San Antonio," I explained. "Have a seat."

He set a basket on the coffee table. "I brought cheesecake and strawberry wine from a little winery on the way down here."

"Mama and I had tacos in the food court, but we didn't take time for dessert, so that sounds great. How did you know that I like strawberry wine?"

"I didn't." Connor shrugged. "It goes well with cheesecake—and it's one of my favorites, anyway."

He sat down beside me and opened the basket, set out two large pieces of cheesecake, and unwrapped them. Then he brought out two stemless wineglasses.

I watched him pour the wine. "I figured you for a beer or whiskey man."

"I like those, but if I'm drinking wine, I like this kind—especially with cheesecake. It reminds me of strawberries and champagne." He handed me a glass and then picked up a fork and fed me a bite. "Now, chase that with the wine. I think you're going to like it."

Not a one of my previous boyfriends had ever fed me, and I liked the heat that flowed through my body.

"I've never had strawberries and champagne, but I can't imagine that it's any better than this." My voice sounded a little deeper than usual, but dang it, the sparks were flitting around like it was the Fourth of July.

"We'll have to remedy that sometime," he said with a grin. "I was surprised when you called me after the pepper spray incident. Jasper kind of looped me in with those other two guys. I figured that you were done with the lot of us."

"You were smart enough to run when he started counting—and you *did* come around with pizza and beer, so I gave you another chance.

Of course, you might just have been trying to sweet-talk me into selling this place to you."

"Let's get something straight." His tone and expression turned serious. "I would buy this property in a heartbeat, but our friendship means more to me than a few acres and an old house."

"Why?" I took another bite of the cheesecake and then a sip of the wine. If strawberries and champagne *were* better than this, I would have to splurge and try them together sometime.

"I've had a couple of fairly serious relationships, but there's something between us that I can't explain," he said. "I wouldn't jeopardize it by—what was it you said?—*sweet-talking* you into selling me this place. I noticed that one of the guys brought you flowers. Are you interested in him?"

I shook my head. "Nope. His name is Derrick—a classmate of mine from high school. Sounds like he's wanting to buy up Ditto to put in marijuana fields if Texas legalizes pot in the near future. Even if I wanted to sell, he wouldn't get a chance at it. I couldn't bear the idea of anyone plowing under the strawberries. They are part of the legacy of this place. The older guy is Richie, and he wants to buy the place as a hobby farm. He knows your grandpa's lease is up in January. I never thought about people coming out of the woodwork, wanting to purchase a couple of acres and an old house in Ditto, Texas."

"Or quitting your job to work with your mother and Annie?" he asked.

"Aunt Gracie often said that everything happens for a reason," I said, "but sometimes it's tough to ferret out the purpose of *what* and *how* at the time." I stopped long enough to take another bite of cheesecake. "Today, I went shopping with Mama for her trip. I bought luggage for her early Mother's Day present. She's worked all these years and supported me, but she's never even owned a suitcase." My voice quivered, and I had trouble swallowing the lump in my throat. "I feel guilty for taking her and Aunt Gracie for granted."

Connor laid a hand on my arm. "Sometimes I feel the same about going off to another country when I could have come here and spent time with my grandparents. I was too busy with my own life to visit them like I should have done."

"Where are your parents?" I asked, enjoying the little zing of sparks at the touch of his hand.

"Dad is retired from the military, and they live in the Bahamas these days."

"Do they ever come back for visits?"

He shrugged. "They try to come for a couple of days at Christmas. Growing up an army brat had its pros and cons. Dad said he wanted nothing to do with settling down permanently, especially not in Ditto, Texas. Mother loved the life of traveling from base to base. Grandpa and Granny were my stability, but the way I was shifted around with my parents kept me from ever realizing the importance of roots."

Even though we were talking about serious things, the chemistry was still there. Had the sparks been in living color, they would have looked like one of those fireworks that light up the sky with bright blue, purple, green, and red.

"Hindsight, and all that," I said.

"Yep," he agreed. "What else is new in your life? Have you found another job?"

"No, but I hired a housekeeper. Gina Lou from down at Annie's Café is moving in with me on Saturday. She'll be helping out with whatever needs to be done, and she'll be busy for months."

"If she gets caught up and needs some extra work, Grandpa could probably use her services. He's been pretty stubborn about hiring help since Granny died. I do what I can in between all the other things he has me trying to learn," Connor said with a shrug. "But the dust gets pretty deep before either of us has time to clean house, and Granny's roses are downright pitiful looking."

"Her dream is to be a teacher, but she doesn't have the finances." I told him about the sympathy cards. "I figure four or five months' work will get this place in order, and I can always find someone to come in a day or two a week. I'm thinking about paying her tuition and room and board at the college in the fall. Kind of paying it forward."

"That sounds like a wonderful idea," Connor said. "I'd be glad to help any way I can. Just let me know."

"Thank you, and I will." I took a long drink of the wine.

He leaned over and tucked a strand of hair behind my ear. "You are beautiful."

A blush crawled up from my neck and made my face feel like it was on fire.

"Is that a blush?" he asked.

"Busted!" I set the empty glass on the coffee table. "I'm not used to compliments."

"I wasn't blowing smoke up your skirt," Connor said. "I'm impressed by you more and more as I get to know you, and I was serious about helping pay for Gina Lou's education."

"Then thank you again, but I can cover it. I was about to watch a movie. Got time to stick around?" I asked.

"Love to," he answered. "I get so bored in the hotel room at night. I don't know why Grandpa doesn't just drive back and forth when he has to have all these meetings once every quarter. DVDs in the cabinet under the television?"

"No such thing. Aunt Gracie was adamant about keeping things as they are, but she and Jasper loved their movies, so she subscribed to nearly all of the streaming services." I picked up the remote and started pushing buttons. "Western, drama, comedy? Name your poison."

"What did Miz Gracie like?"

"Comedy or Westerns, for the most part, and so do I," I replied. "She said that watching funny shows made her forget the sad times, and Westerns took her back in time."

Connor nodded. "Then let's watch whatever y'all liked."

"How about *McLintock!*?" I said as I flipped through movies and sitcoms.

"I've never seen that one. Grandpa introduced me to every old Western that was out there, so I don't know how he missed that one," Connor said.

I pulled my feet up on the sofa and got comfortable. "You might as well take off your shoes."

"Are we good enough friends for me to do that?" he teased.

"You brought cheesecake and wine, so I would say that we are."

"And muffins on Saturday," he reminded me.

As we watched the movie, I stole long sideways glances at him and wondered what was preventing me from trusting him. Was it what Jasper had said after the backyard brawl, or maybe my own commitment issues? I had told myself that my past relationships ended because I had gotten tired of putting time and energy into something that had no future. But maybe the reason went deeper than that.

Those thoughts brought me right back around to Aunt Gracie and the question that seemed to have no answer: Why didn't she ever get married and have children? I understood that Aunt Gracie felt like Mama was her daughter and I was her granddaughter. But could she really have been satisfied with her adopted family, or did she never have one of her own because of the secret?

I was going in circles, and it was exhausting. In that very moment, I decided that whatever the secret was, it belonged in the past—maybe even in the grave with Aunt Gracie. It wasn't mine to find or to figure out. I loved her like a grandmother, and she loved me. That was all that was important. That did not mean I wasn't interested in knowing more about her past life—just not in chasing my tail wondering about it.

But what if this big secret is that the ghost in this house spreads mistrust among the women who live here? the pesky voice in my head asked.

I shivered at the idea, yet it had enough relevance to bear paying attention to.

"Cold?" Connor scooted over closer to me and pulled a crocheted throw from the back of the sofa to spread over both of us.

"Thank you," I muttered.

He slipped an arm around my shoulders but didn't take his eyes off the television. "I was getting a little chilly, too. I've always loved John Wayne. Moviemaking has sure come a long way from whenever this was made. I'd like to see it redone with today's technology."

"I'd go to the theater to see it, for sure," I said.

Redone today?

Those two words stuck in my mind. If Aunt Gracie had gone through that crisis today, would it be such a big thing? Or would social media blow it up for a day or two, then replace it with something even more spectacular, like what color nail polish or hair dye a famous person had used that very day?

"Happily ever after," Connor said when the movie ended. "Be nice if"—he paused and took a deep breath—"if people like you and me could overcome the obstacles life throws at them and find happiness."

"Well, that came out of left field. I'm not so sure I understand where you are going with this," I said.

"I'm a little bitter about getting discharged from the service, and you think I'm only trying to get this house and your land. Two big obstacles right there. I like you, Lila—a lot—but we've both got baggage."

"I like you, too, Connor, but like I said before, I need time to work out things in my mind."

He gently cupped my face in his hands. "Maybe we can both help each other through whatever is holding us back from commitment." His eyes locked with mine. "Think we might be more than friends?"

My heart raced. "It all depends."

"On what?"

"This first kiss." I threw caution to the wind and listened to my heart, even though I knew he might think it was out of the blue. I wrapped my arms around his neck and pulled his lips to mine.

The sparks I had felt before were nothing compared to the heat the kiss generated and I wished it would never end—but it did.

"Well?" Connor asked.

"I'd give it a five out of ten," I whispered.

"Then it didn't affect you like it did me," he groaned.

I kissed him on the cheek. "I'm teasing. I'd give it a fifteen out of ten."

"Then we can be more than friends," he asked.

"If we take it slow. We've only known each other thirteen days."

"But who's counting?" He grinned. "And besides, thirteen is my lucky number."

Chapter Fourteen

"I'm not going to no doctor," Jasper declared between coughs on Friday evening.

His favorite old gray sweater was hanging on the back of a kitchen chair. I grabbed it and draped it around his shoulders, where it hung just about the same. "You've been sick for a week, and you're getting worse. That cough sounds like a freight train engine. Either you will let me drive you or else I'm calling the ambulance. You lose your breath every time you cough, and in between, you are wheezing louder than Aunt Gracie's snores. Do you realize that whatever you have could go into pneumonia if it hasn't already? That would mean you would most likely have to stay in the hospital for days. And you know I'm not going to bring you food."

He folded his frail arms over his chest and glared at me. "Only doctor I ever been to in my life was the one who checked me out to go in the army, and another one when"—he had to stop and cough into the bandanna he'd pulled from the bib pocket on his overalls—"when I fell and hit my head on the sidewalk." He managed a weak chuckle. "I was pretty drunk that time. Had to have six stitches, but the nurse was right pretty."

I opened the door and stood beside it. "Me or the ambulance. Your choice."

"You are as stubborn as Gracie," he snapped.

"That's the best compliment I've had all day," I said.

"You can take me, but I'm not stayin' in that place. There's sick people in there, and I might catch something. I've got to live until my birthday, remember?" He stood up and shuffled outside.

I followed him out onto the porch. "It's cool out here this evening. Let's put your sweater on. And yes, Jasper, I remember that your birthday is coming up soon, right after fall strawberry season. If you don't get well, you might end up having to celebrate it in a nursing home."

He didn't argue when I helped him with his sweater, but he stopped before he took a step out into the yard. "Wait a minute! What about Sassy?"

"She'll be fine until we get back," I assured him. "And I can call Connor if we're late."

"How about we just go to one of them instant-care places?" he asked.

I looped my arm in his. "Do you mean *urgent* care?"

He grabbed his handkerchief and coughed into it. "Whatever it's called. They can check me out and give me a prescription I don't intend to fill. I'll come home and have my hot toddies until I get well."

"We are going to the emergency room, not urgent care." I hoped my tone left no more room for argument.

"I was wrong, Lila," he said as we headed around the house to where my SUV was parked.

"Oh, yeah." I walked slowly and made sure I kept him on the gravel driveway, which was more level than the grass. "Want to explain that?"

"You are more stubborn"—he stopped a minute to catch his breath—"and bullheaded than Gracie ever was."

"I had a good teacher." I opened the passenger door to my vehicle and settled him inside. "Matter of fact, I had three good teachers when it comes right down to it. You and Aunt Gracie, and Mama."

"Don't go layin' blame on me." He tried to chuckle, but it made him cough even more. "You are wastin' your time drivin' all the way to San Antonio. We got us one of the drive-through places in Poteet—what did you call it? Urgent care? It's closer than goin' all that distance."

I slid in under the steering wheel and started the engine. "San Antonio isn't that far. If you are good and don't cry if they have to give you a shot, then we'll stop for ice cream on the way back home."

"I'm not a child. You can't bribe me like that—and I'm not takin' a shot," he declared. "I don't like pills, but I hate needles."

"Then no ice cream," I said.

He lifted his chin up and looked down his long, thin nose at me. "I bet I can talk a pretty nurse into giving me a lollipop."

"You just proved my point." I backed out of the driveway and headed down the lane.

"What point?"

"That I got my stubborn streak from you," I answered.

"Hmmph!" he snorted, then coughed again.

Luck was with us that evening. The waiting room at the hospital was empty, and they took us right on back to a cubicle. A nurse that looked to be about Gina Lou's age pushed the curtain back, told Jasper to have a seat on the narrow bed, and asked him enough questions to exasperate him. She finally asked him to remove his sweater so that she could take his vital signs.

"I don't need to do that. I'm alive and kickin'. I just need you to give me some medicine so I can go home," he argued.

"Sorry, sir, but that's not the way this works." She winked at me. "We have to do a few tests and diagnose your problem so we know what kind of medicine to give you."

"I can tell you what my problem is," he snapped as he removed his sweater. "And if you wasn't hard of hearing, you would already know. I've got the croup."

She ran a thermometer over his forehead and behind his ear. "You might have the croup, but we have to be sure."

"Why did you do that?" Jasper asked.

"You have two degrees of temperature. That means you have a fever and an infection somewhere." She slipped a blood pressure cuff around his bony upper arm.

"You're about to cut all the circulation off," he barked at her when the cuff tightened, sending him into another cough.

"Just for a couple of seconds. See there, it's already loosening up. Blood pressure is fine. Someone will be in soon from the lab. Just sit tight."

"Can I put my sweater back on?" he asked.

"Yes, sir. Need some help?"

"I been dressin' myself since I was a little kid." He proved his independence by slipping his arms back into his sweater and buttoning it.

"What does the lab do?" he asked when she was gone.

"Someone will take blood from your arm," I answered honestly.

"Oh, no, they are not!" He started to stand up. "We are going home. I will not give my permission for anyone to put a needle in my arm."

"If you don't sit down and behave, I'll sell my place to Derrick, and he will plow under all the strawberries and plant marijuana. Do you want to smell skunk every time you walk outside to get a breath of fresh air? What about Sassy? What would that do to her?"

He sat down on the bed and focused on the wall ahead of him. "They keep it cold in these places to chill an old man's blood. If it was hot, we'd bleed to death when they stick a needle in us."

"Probably so." I shivered and wished I'd brought a jacket with me.

"I bet they don't put clocks in these places because they charge by the minute. I saw that woman write down the time with my vitals. Granny called that taking my temperature, but she did it with a thermometer under my tongue, like an honest woman," he whispered, then rolled his eyes toward the ceiling. "That thing has a hidden camera in it, and they are watching us. If I get off this bed and start toward the door, they will rush in here with needles to suck my lifeblood right out of me."

"That 'thing' is a smoke detector," I explained. "You've got one in your house. Insurance companies insist that we all have them."

"It might be, but that blinkin' red light means the camera is on and keeping watch on us. Maybe so they can see if we open up all of them cabinets over there"—he pointed to his left—"and steal stuff. Why else would they put people in here and trust them not to go snooping?"

"You've really never been in an emergency room before?" I asked.

His eyes darted around the room and finally went back to the ceiling. He waved and raised his voice. "No, I have not been in one of these rooms before. But I'm tellin' whoever is watching me on that camera—if you ain't here in five minutes, I'm leaving."

Within a minute, a lab tech arrived with a tote full of tubes and needles. "Hello, Mr. Carlson. I'm here to draw a little blood."

I glanced up at the smoke detector and wondered if he could be right.

"I ain't been called by my last name in more'n seventy years. I'm just Jasper," he told her. "You ain't old enough to be a nurse or a doctor."

"I'm not either one," she told him. "I'm a lab technician."

"That's a fancy name for a little bitty thing like you," he said. "I expect you'll want me to take off my sweater and roll up my sleeves?"

She lined all her equipment up on the stainless steel table. "Yes, sir."

I helped him with his sweater, but he rolled up his sleeve. He glared at me while she drew two vials of blood.

"Thank you," she said as she put the needle in a separate disposal container and the rest of what she'd used in the trash.

"I wish we still had party lines," he said.

"Why's that?"

"Because then I could call Gracie and tell her about all this."

"If she was still with us, you could do that on a landline or a cell phone," I reminded him.

He grimaced and sighed. "But if it was a party line, someone would be bound to listen in, and they would tell someone else, and pretty soon the news would be all over Ditto and Poteet."

"Why would you want everyone to know?" I asked.

"Then they'd know not to come here," he smarted off. "Them ain't even good nurses. Didn't neither one offer to give me a lollipop."

"If you've never been to a doctor, how do you know about lollipops?" I asked.

"I heard the kids at school talking about it."

We walked out of the hospital two hours later, and Jasper was still grumbling. "Are you happy now? I didn't need no dang doctor to tell me that I have the croup."

"Upper respiratory infection," I corrected him as I helped him back into my vehicle.

"Just a fancy new word for croup," he snapped.

I turned my phone back on when I was behind the wheel and wasn't surprised to find several missed calls from my mother and one from Connor. I laid the phone on the console between me and Jasper and called Mama first on speaker.

When she answered, I said, "Sorry, I missed your calls. I'm on the way home from San Antonio. I had to turn my phone off in the emergency room, but don't panic. Jasper just has an upper respiratory infection, not pneumonia, and we're on the way to the pharmacy to get his prescriptions."

"Which I am not taking," he protested loudly.

"Yes, you will!" Mama declared in her best no-nonsense tone. "I won't leave Texas on Monday if you aren't feeling better."

A rattly cough was all that kept Jasper from snorting. "One bossy woman is a cross to bear. Two is enough to drive a good man to drinking."

"Which reminds me," I said, "the doctor said no alcohol with your meds. That means two weeks at the least."

"What he don't know won't hurt him," Jasper groused.

"Quit your bellyachin' and listen to me," Mama said. "If I have to come stay with you every day until you are well, I'll do it. This vacation can come later."

He threw up his hands. "Okay, okay! I'll take the medicine."

"I'll see to it that he does, Mama. I'll take it all home with me and be sure he gets whatever he needs at the right times. And I'll steal all his liquor."

"Going to see Gracie and Davis is looking better by the minute," he fussed. "And you will not steal my whiskey. I promise to leave it alone until I'm well, but I trust hot toddies more than I do pills. Besides, that man wasn't old enough to be a real doctor. There wasn't no gray in his beard or his hair."

"If you don't do what you are supposed to do for the next two weeks and you die, I'm going to take Sassy to the pound," I threatened.

"And I'll drive her," Mama added.

He turned and stared out the side window. That's when I knew he was really sick, because he always wanted to get in the last word.

"Hey." Connor startled me when he called out from my back porch. "Anyone want to go into Poteet for a burger?"

Jasper shook his head. "Not me. I just ate a double dip of choco-late-almond ice cream, one for each time they stuck me with a needle the size of a tenpenny nail. I'm going to make myself a cup of good strong coffee and call it a night."

"Not until you get your first dose of medicine," I told him.

"Let's start that in the morning," he said as he carefully made it up the steps to his porch.

"We will start it as soon as I get in the house and read all the instructions," I fired back at him.

"If you'd had some ice cream, you might not be so bossy," he com-plained. "Don't take all night. I'm ready to settle back in my recliner and sleep through a Western movie or two."

"Is he sick?" Connor whispered when I was on the porch.

"Very." I opened the back door. "Come on in. I'll sort his medicine and take his first dose out to him. He's got that upper respiratory stuff that seems to be going around right now. At his age, it can be pretty bad. He's got to go to his primary in two weeks when he finishes all this stuff." I held up a paper bag. "And he says the only time he was ever at a doctor was when he went into the army and then when he had to get his head stitched. That would have been in"—I stopped and did the math in my head—"around 1947, and he hasn't seen a doctor since then."

Connor followed me inside. "I can ask Grandpa what local doctor he uses. He fussed going when Granny was alive, and he still does. But Granny made him go every six months for blood work and a visit, and he hates needles, too."

I pulled out a chair, sat down at the table, and poured out several bottles of pills and an inhaler with a sigh. "The next two weeks are not going to be fun."

"Nope, but I can help any way you need me to," Connor offered. "Did Gracie have any of those pill things that has the day of the week printed on them?"

"Yes, she did, and I almost threw them away." I got up and rustled through the junk drawer to the left of the sink, found a couple of pill organizers, and took them back to the table. "This one holds a week's worth of pills, four times a day."

"Looks like that's what you need, from what I'm reading on these labels," Connor said. "Are you going to let him be responsible for taking—"

I butted in before he could finish. "Nope. He'll throw this thing in a drawer and put the inhaler in the trash. I'll go out there four times a day to make sure he's doing what he's supposed to do." I popped open all the lids and started loading the sections with pills. Maybe I'd keep the pill stash at my house, just in case.

Connor pulled his phone from his pocket, then shook his head and put it back. "Is there a restaurant that delivers around here? I'm starving. Grandpa is having a steak dinner with some of his old cronies."

"I have no idea, and I'm not a gourmet," I said as I finished my job. "But I can make a mean omelet and the fluffiest pancakes you'll ever eat. Give me five minutes to take these out to Jasper, and I'll make both of us some supper."

"I thought you ate ice cream," Connor said.

"Jasper did, but it's way too messy for me to try to eat when I'm driving, so I'm pretty hungry, too."

The corners of Connor's mouth turned up, and his eyes sparkled. "I usually get breakfast the morning after, not the night before."

I put on my most innocent expression. "After what?"

"More than kisses," he said without hesitation.

"And how many after-breakfasts have you had?"

"More than four, less than a dozen," he answered. "How many guys have made you breakfast the morning after?"

"More than one, less than three." I poured that evening's pills into a small glass so all Jasper would have to do was throw them back. "I'm going out to Jasper's. Be back in a few minutes. Are you interested in just breakfast, not before or after more-than-kisses but merely food?"

"Yes, ma'am," he replied with a wide grin.

As I crossed the lawn out to Jasper's house, I could almost hear Aunt Gracie saying she was glad I had come back to Ditto. "You are welcome," I said under my breath. "I love him like a grandpa, but you sure put up with a lot out of that old codger."

I rapped on the door and went inside without waiting for Jasper to invite me in. He was sitting in his recliner with a cup of black coffee in his hands. "Run, Sassy, run. The bossy woman is here. Women like her are the reason this smart man never married. They take over your life whether you like it or not."

Sassy looked up at me with her crystal-clear blue eyes, and I swear the pup smiled.

"And we keep you alive," I smarted off. "Gracie left the job to me, so blame her for all this, not me."

He shot a dirty sideways look at me and then peeked into the glass, shook it around, and declared, "What are you giving me? I ain't takin' no green pills."

"Nothing green here. Mostly white ones, but I do see a yellow one. What have you got against green ones?"

"My granny's grandmother said poison is green. She would never give me anything that was that color." He threw back all the pills like a shot of bad whiskey.

"That's silly. It's probably just green dye."

"Then green dye is poison." He took another sip of his coffee. "Is that all?"

"You've got to use this inhaler three times a day for a week." I handed it to him and told him what to do with it. "I promise what comes out of it is not green."

He did what I asked, and immediately the wheezing stopped. "What was that stuff? Magic?" he asked.

"Yep. Looks like you won't have to smell skunk in your backyard after all, if you just use this magic thing three times a day and then when you need it after you get well."

He narrowed his old eyes until they were little more than slits. "Can I have my hot toddies with it?"

"We can ask the doctor when we go see him in two weeks," I replied.

He groaned. "Don't make me go back to that hospital."

"I'm not going to unless you get really sick again," I promised. "But we will find a primary doctor in Poteet to take care of you. You'll only have to go every six months if you stay well."

"I guess I can live with that," he said. "Reckon you could find one that makes house calls?"

"Not in this day and age." I wasn't about to tell him that some doctors did video appointments. Jasper was pushing a hundred years. It was way past time he got checked out twice a year.

"Man can walk on the moon, put machines up in space, and talk on a phone no bigger than a pack of cigarettes, and yet doctors can't make house calls. I'd like to go back to the good ol' days."

"So would I," I agreed, "but we can take comfort in knowing that we still grow and pick and sell strawberries the same way we have for years."

"God bless the strawberries," he said. "Now, get on back out there with your new boyfriend. Are you making breakfast in the morning, or is he?"

"He's not my boyfriend," I protested. "I'm making omelets and pancakes for supper, and he won't be staying all night. Would you like for me to bring you a plate?"

"Nope. I just want to finish my coffee and watch John Wayne teach them boys how to handle cattle."

I took a step toward the door. "I can come out here and make breakfast for you or make it at my house and bring it to you. Which one do you think will work better?"

"I usually just have a cup of coffee."

"Your medicine has to be taken with food."

"Then you can bring it to me. Not nothing big," he said. "You don't need to try to fatten me up."

"That ain't likely to ever happen. Good night, Jasper."

"'Night," he said.

Chapter Fifteen

Connor's deep country drawl singing the Alan Jackson song "Little Bitty" floated out across the yard when I left Jasper's house. I stopped at the back door and peeked inside to see him using a whisk for a microphone. I tapped my foot in time with the music and smiled when he traded the whisk for an imaginary guitar. Not a one of my previous boyfriends had liked country music, and the two serious ones had been so stiff that I couldn't imagine them ever belting any song out like Connor was doing. The lyrics sank deep into my soul and lay there like a warm blanket when the words said that it was all right to live in a little bitty town.

"Amen," I whispered as I eased the door open and slipped into the kitchen.

The song ended, and Travis Tritt started singing "It's a Great Day to be Alive." Connor turned around and grabbed me around the waist and two-stepped with me all around the room. My heart pounded so hard that I thought it would fly out of my chest and land on the linoleum. When the song ended, he flipped me back in true Hollywood fashion and brushed a soft kiss across my lips. The thumping of my heart got even harder, and my chest tightened. Lord have mercy! There was no way I could slam on the emotional brakes when it came to Connor Thurman.

"Thank you for the dance," I said when I could catch my breath.

"My pleasure," he said. "Mind if I leave the music on while we make supper?"

"Not one bit." I realized that the music and the energy made the empty house feel alive again. Was that the reason Aunt Gracie kept a radio going most of the time? Did she feel alone in this big place without some noise? I couldn't remember very many days in either this place or Mama's house when music wasn't playing—sometimes turned up to full volume, other times softly in the background, with Mama or Aunt Gracie humming along to whatever was on the radio.

"I'm willin' to make the omelets if you'll stir up the pancakes," Connor offered. "I make a mean open-face omelet or a really good frittata, but I'd have to buy a license to keep my pancakes in the house."

"Why?" I felt my brow furrow when I frowned.

"They could be used as deadly weapons if thrown at another human being," he chuckled. "What all do you want to put into the omelet?"

I took down a mixing bowl and headed to the pantry for all the ingredients. "Make a *gotta go* one."

"And that is?"

"Kind of like a meat lovers pizza. If you can find it in the fridge, then it's gotta go. Peppers, onions, ham, bacon, sausage, mushrooms . . . whatever bits and pieces you find in there. And of course, cheese on the top."

"Where did you come up with that *gotta go* phrase?" he asked.

I left the pantry carrying flour, baking powder, and cooking oil. "I didn't. Aunt Gracie did. We made *gotta go* soup, goulash, and omelets pretty often. She didn't believe in wasting anything."

"Neither did my granny, and my grandfather is the same way," he said as he opened a cabinet door and took out a bowl.

"How did you know where things—"

"Granny set up her cabinets for convenience. Glasses to the left of the sink. Plates and bowls to the right. She said that it made for an easy job when it was time to get them down or put them away. I figured that Miz Gracie might have done the same."

"Looks like you were right." I reached for the baking powder and bumped into Connor.

He bent over to get a skillet, and his hip touched my thigh.

"We need a bigger kitchen," I muttered.

"Why?" He raised up and laid a hand on my shoulder. "I'm rather enjoying this, and like that line in Alan's song, a little bitty house—or kitchen, for that matter—is all right."

"That all depends," I argued.

"On what?"

I thought of one of Jasper's lines and used it. "That's an explanation for another day."

He raised an eyebrow. "Because it makes for sparks?"

I stopped what I was doing and locked eyes with him. "So you felt them, too?"

"Yes, I did." He held my gaze. "From the first time I met you in that Dolly Parton shirt, there were sparks. If you felt them, then we need to decide what to do about them."

"Maybe it's only a passing thing and . . ."

"What if it is?" He finally blinked and poured eggs into the skillet on the stove.

"We'll get over it," I answered.

"How?"

"The same way I got over chicken pox when I was a little girl," I told him. "You weather through it."

"What if it doesn't go away?" he pressured.

"Then we can see if it's real or only a flash in the pan," I suggested.

"I think it's real," he said.

All this talk was making me as jittery as a wild turkey on Thanksgiving, and I almost burned the first four pancakes. "We are friends. We are neighbors. What about the consequences if it's not and we ruin what we already have?"

"Anything worth having is worth taking a risk," he assured me.

I set a platter of pancakes in the middle of the table. "I have commitment issues."

Connor brought over the skillet and set it on a hot pad beside the pancakes. "So do I." He poured melted butter and hot maple syrup on a stack of pancakes, took a bite, and rolled his eyes toward the ceiling. "You are right! These are the best pancakes I've ever eaten. What's the secret?"

"Whipping the egg whites and then folding them into the batter," I told him. "For your first try at a *gotta go* omelet, you did a mighty fine job."

"Maybe we should turn our backs on Ditto and put in a restaurant somewhere," he suggested.

"No, thank you! Running a café of any kind is at the top of my list of things that I do *not* want to do."

"Why?"

"Because I saw firsthand how much my mama's feet and back hurt when she came home from a shift. Standing on concrete for eight hours every day for a whole week does not appeal to me."

"I didn't think of the work, just the good food. I could enjoy your pancakes often," he said.

"I can make that happen without having to open up a café at five in the morning," I said. "You simply have to ask, and I will make pancakes. But I do not like to cook. I enjoy baking, mostly around the holidays, but making real food, like roasts and all that, it's not me."

He chuckled. "Well, darlin', I don't like you for your ability to make a roast."

"For a relationship to last past the . . ." I paused and thought about what I was about to say. "I was going to say past the lust stage, but I'm not sure we even had that. Which is really the reason my former relationships didn't last. There was no magic. In the end we were more like roommates instead of a couple. The breakups were actually kind of boring." I thought about Aunt Gracie's diary entry when she wondered if she could die of a broken heart.

"I hear you," Connor said with a nod. "Pretty much the story of my life, too. Do you know anyone who can honestly say that they have experienced the magic?"

"Mama did, even if my father didn't. I think Aunt Gracie did when she was very young, but whoever it was with ended up breaking her heart, and she never really got over it," I answered.

"How will you know if *you* find it?"

"I figure that once I've known that kind of love, then the mere thought of not having it will shatter my soul." I figured that he would make an excuse and never come back. This was some heavy conversation, but hey, if he wanted to run, the door wasn't locked. "If I don't feel like that, then there is no magic."

He finished off the last bite of pancakes and shifted two more from the platter in the middle of the table onto his plate. "I like that idea."

I laid it out there. "This is pretty heavy conversation for friends. But then, we did have one kiss, so maybe that gives us the right to talk about our feelings."

"I guess it does." He grinned.

The smell of coffee filled the whole downstairs the next morning. I made Jasper a stack of pancakes and fried several slices of bacon and carried a plate out to him, along with his morning medicine. He was sitting on the porch while Sassy chased a bee around the yard. The sun peeked over the treetops and threw a yellow glow on Jasper's face that morning.

"Did you make breakfast for Connor?" he asked.

"No, I did not. Old women are supposed to be the gossips, not old men," I scolded him. "Are you eating out here or in the house?"

He stood up and started inside. "Did he cook for you this morning?"

"No, but he's bringing me muffins."

Sassy ran up onto the porch and looked up at me with begging eyes. I picked up one piece of bacon and dropped it. She caught it before it hit the porch.

"Hey, now!" Jasper barked. "I was planning on saving back one bite for her."

"There's plenty enough that you can still feed her another piece." I set the plate on the table and poured him a cup of coffee. "Want water to take your pills with?"

"I can use the coffee. Let's do the breathing thing first. Pancakes look good."

I handed him the inhaler and waited to give him the pills until he was finished. Then I sat down at the table with him to be sure that he ate and didn't set the plate on the floor for Sassy to clean up.

"You don't have to stick around," Jasper said as he took the first bite. "This is just like Gracie used to make for us."

"Did y'all eat together every day?" I asked.

"Yep, three times a day, mostly after she retired. You should remember that," he said in between bites, then threw back the pills and washed them down with coffee. "It's tough to cook for two, but trying to fix for one is even harder."

"Why didn't you tell me that? I could have been bringing you food all this time."

"You got enough on your plate without trying to take care of me."

"Not anymore," I reminded him. "Right now I don't have a job, and other than getting the house and yard in shape, nothing else to do. I do remember that you ate with us when I was at her house. When I was little I thought you were my grandfather."

"I was," he said. "Don't take blood to make a family, and I was the only grandfather you knew." He took a couple of bites and then changed the subject. "Come January, you could have a strawberry farm to run."

"I don't know anything about that. I'm an accountant, not a farmer."

"You ain't stupid, Lila. You can learn anything, but it was probably a dumb idea."

"I'm going back to the house, and at noon, I'll bring you some lunch and more pills." The idea wasn't dumb. I owned the property, and the lease was up in January. Between now and then, I would have several months to learn what all was involved and even to get some hands-on experience. That would help me stay occupied while I figured out what to do with the rest of my life.

I was so busy thinking about strawberries that I forgot Connor was coming. I raced into the downstairs bathroom, brushed my hair one more time, and was busy applying a little lipstick when he knocked on the back door and poked his head inside. "The muffin man is here."

"Coffee is ready. Come on in. I'm on my way!" I yelled and checked my reflection in the downstairs-bathroom mirror one more time. I saw a tall red-haired woman who had to bend slightly even to see herself, and wondered why he had said I was beautiful the night before. Did he mean it, or was that one of his pickup lines?

The box of muffins was on the table, and he was filling two mugs with coffee when I made it into the kitchen. He looked up, smiled, and handed me my second cup of the morning. "You look lovely—but then, you always do. I smell bacon. Did you already have a first breakfast? Is this your second one?"

"No, I made Jasper some pancakes and bacon, but I haven't eaten yet. I was waiting for the muffins. Thank you for the compliment," I said and took a sip of the coffee. "And for the muffins. What are you doing today?"

He pulled out a chair for me. "I can only stay a little while. Grandpa wants me to work with the crew coming to work the strawberry plants. From fancy oil-executive meetings to farmer. Got to admit, none of it is bad work."

I sat down, more than a little envious and a lot disappointed. Connor seemed to have his life on track while I was still struggling, trying to get out of the thick woods. Talking to him had seemed to help me in my efforts to find a path, but there would be none of that today.

"So, what's on your agenda today?" he asked.

I opened the box and took out a muffin. "Gina Lou is moving in, but I'm not sure when. I may spend a little time in the room she'll be using—cleaning out the closets and dresser drawers, that kind of thing."

He sat down across the table from me. "Be careful. Today is March 15."

"Beware the Ides of March," I said in my best eerie voice. "Maybe it wasn't a good idea to have her move in today."

"Only if you are superstitious." He peeled the paper from a muffin and took a bite.

"My mama is. She doesn't even like to come in this house. Says that she feels ghosts in here." Saying that out loud to Connor didn't make me uncomfortable.

"I am pretty sure that any place that is still standing after a hundred years has a few skeletons hiding in the closets," he said.

"With that in mind, I should probably listen carefully for rattling bones or eerie sounds when I clean out the closet in Gina Lou's room," I teased.

"If you get scared, just call me, and I'll come running," Connor offered in a flirting tone.

"Keep your phone on," I told him.

"Always." He pushed his chair back, picked up his coffee mug, dropped a kiss on my forehead as he passed by, and headed out the back door.

I ate another muffin, had two more cups of coffee, and had started across the foyer when the house phone rang. I jogged back to the kitchen, picked up the receiver, and looked at the thing while it rang again before I realized there wouldn't be a name displayed.

"Hello?" I answered.

"Lila, this is Gina Lou. My car broke down last night. Just up and died and quit running when I was about a block from my trailer. Daddy says it's not worth fixing because the transmission is blown. I hate to ask, but can you come help me? My friend that was going to give me a ride had to take her grandmother to the hospital. Looks like she'll be there all day because they're admitting her granny." Her voice sounded like she was on the verge of tears. "I have to be out by noon because another person is moving in, and my dad is on his way to his job, and he can't be late . . ." She finally stopped for a breath.

"Slow down, girl. Of course I'll come help you. Just give me an address, and I'll be there in a few minutes."

"Thank you so, so much. The address is . . ." She rattled off a place I didn't recognize.

"Hold on just a minute. Now, repeat that address." I plugged it into the map app on my phone. "I've got it now, and we'll get you moved out long before noon. Looks like I can get there in ten minutes."

"I'm all packed and ready to go," she said. "I'll be waiting on the steps."

I picked up my purse, went out to Jasper's place, and told him where I was going, then got into my SUV. "Looks like the Ides of March is in full swing. WWAGD?"

What in the devil is that? the pesky voice in my head asked.

"What Would Aunt Gracie Do?" I said out loud, and then the answer came to me. She would let Gina Lou drive the SUV when she needed it. I could always drive the Ford in the garage.

"Whether I like it or not," I said as I made the turn toward Poteet.

Everything happens for a reason. Her voice was as clear as if she'd been sitting right beside me.

"I miss you so much," I whispered. "Sometimes the memories and the voices in my head aren't enough. I want to hug you, and sit at the table for breakfast with you, and make Christmas cookies with you."

Aunt Gracie had painted a vivid picture for me when she told me about the evening she went to bring Mama to Ditto. That memory went through my mind when I saw Gina Lou sitting on her porch with garbage bags all around her. She was moving to Ditto in about the same shape as my mother had been when Aunt Gracie rescued her.

The difference was that Mama didn't stay in Gracie's house very long. She went to her own place the very next day and made a home for me in the little four-room place.

I popped open the hatch and got out. "Is this all of it?"

"Every single bit, and I left the place clean, so I should get my deposit back."

"Where's your car?" I slid a box as far back as I possibly could.

"Daddy dragged it out to my folks' house last night with his vehicle. It's toast, but since I'll be living with you, I won't need it except . . ."

"Except when?" I asked.

"Annie's closes at three on Sunday, and I try to go to church with my folks that evening. Daddy picks up all the overtime he can, so they don't often get to go on Sunday morning," she answered. "It takes both of our vehicles to get us all to church, and now I don't have one."

"You can take my car anytime you need it," I told her. "How old are you?"

"Twenty-three."

"Lord, girl, I thought you had only been out of high school a year or two."

"Nope," she said with a smile. "I've been working for Annie since I was sixteen, and probably would be until I retire if she hadn't sold the café. I saved my money and bought my car when I was seventeen. That reminds me—I should drop the insurance on Monday. I can give that money to Mama to help with what my sister Stephanie needs for her high school graduation."

I'd never had to think about those kinds of things when I was her age. Aunt Gracie bought me a good used car when I was sixteen and paid the insurance until six months after I'd finished my education. I felt like I had entered the adult world when I traded that vehicle in for the SUV that I was still driving.

I didn't realize I had been woolgathering until it was time to turn down the lane to Aunt Gracie's house. Someday maybe I would be able to think of it as mine, but it had been hers my whole life and probably would be for a few more years.

"Do you have a list of things you want me to do when we get unloaded?" Gina Lou asked.

I parked in my usual spot and flung open the door. "Like I told you before, you've got the weekend to get settled in, and then we'll start to work on Monday."

"What are you going to do today?" she asked.

"First, I'm going to help you get all your stuff hauled upstairs. Then I'm going out to the strawberry fields." That was another impulsive thing, but maybe Jasper had been right. I could learn the business by January and then make up my mind if I wanted to stay with it.

"What's going on out there?" she asked as she got out of the SUV and grabbed two bags from the back.

I stacked one box on top of the other and picked them both up. "I have no idea, but I'm going to learn."

"Why?"

"If I don't figure out what I want to do with my life by January, then I'll be a strawberry farmer. To be one of those, I need to know everything about the business."

"Kind of like going to college, right?" she said as she followed me into the house.

"That's right. Who knows? I might love strawberry work." I started up the stairs with her right behind me.

"This place is even bigger than it looks from the outside," she whispered as she tried to take everything in with one glance.

"Yes, it is, and that's why I need help getting it put into shape," I told her.

"My mama loves the vintage look. Maybe someday I could bring her here for a tour?"

"Anytime," I said when we reached the top of the stairs, and nodded to the left. "That is Gracie's room. I was using the next one for an office. This one"—I turned my head to the right—"is my room, and the next one will be yours. Linen closet and bathroom are at the end of the hallway."

"When you own something like this, why would you want to be a farmer?" she asked.

"I have to have *something* to do. I need to feel like I am being productive."

Was I grasping at something—anything—to give my life purpose? Or was I just making an excuse to spend the day with Connor?

"If you need to go see what's going on in the fields, I can finish unloading. Just show me my room," she said.

"Sounds good to me." I opened the door and dropped the boxes on the floor. "This room probably hasn't been cleaned or used in thirty or more years. If there's anything in the closet or the drawers, just put it all in garbage bags. You'll find clean sheets and bedding in the hall closets if you need them. That bed probably needs to be remade."

"That thing"—she pointed toward the four-poster king bed—"looks like it covers ten acres."

"Not quite, but you will have plenty of room to stretch out." I opened a closet door to find it totally empty; same with all the dresser drawers. "I'd planned to have this closet cleared out for you, but it looks like you won't have to deal with musty old clothing."

Gina Lou dropped her bags and rushed over to wrap me up in a fierce bear hug. "Has anyone ever told you that you are an angel?"

I hugged her back and said, "No, they have not. I've been called a lot of things in my lifetime, but no one ever thought I had wings or a halo. I'm not even sure angels have red hair."

"In my book, they do," Gina Lou said with a sigh. "Where are the cleaning supplies and the washing machine?"

"Both are in the utility room. Cleaning stuff, broom, and vacuum are in the closet to the right of the washer," I replied. "I can show you when we go downstairs."

"You need to get out there to your Strawberry 101 class. Professor Connor might dock you a letter grade if you are late," she said with a smile. "I'll be fine. No, that's not right. I'll be *great* right here. While you are learning to grow the berries, you might think about making strawberry wine as a side job. Mama and Daddy have a little patch at the end of our garden, and she gathers them for making jelly to sell to folks at the festival each year. She also makes a few bottles of wine every year for us to toast with on New Year's Day and for other special occasions. The little kids get strawberry juice mixed with lemon-lime soda to give it a little fizz."

Blessings come in strange places.

That was another of Aunt Gracie's sayings. The memory of Jasper telling that story about him and Davis and Gracie making wine came to my mind. He'd mentioned that there was a cookbook somewhere in the house with a recipe. Then I thought of the wine that Connor had brought. Thinking of Aunt Gracie put a smile on my face. The feeling I had when Connor had fed me filled me with warmth.

"Good luck finding a cookbook in all this mess," I muttered, shaking away the thoughts.

"What was that?" Gina Lou asked.

"I was just thinking out loud. Working at home with no one else around for months on end makes a person do that."

"I hear you," she said. "During those horrible months when we had to close the dining room in the restaurant and just do home deliveries, I missed the folks coming in and visiting with us. But I did have my family and thank goodness the whole bunch of us stayed healthy through it all."

"Amen to that." I followed her down the stairs. That's when the door to the basement caught my eye. In the past, I had only been brave enough to walk down those creaky steps if Aunt Gracie was with me. I figured that if ghosts were really in the house, they hid out behind all the boxes of stuff that were stored down there, and the place still had a strange smell to it.

One time, I asked Aunt Gracie what was in the boxes, and she told me that the past was down there and packed away where it all belonged.

According to her, you couldn't ever get rid of the past, but you didn't have to drag it out and let it ruin the future.

The door squeaked loudly when I pushed it open, testifying that it had been a while—probably not since the last time the exterminator sprayed the house—since anyone had forced it open. I groped blindly until my hand found a wooden thread spool attached to the end of a string and pulled hard, turning on a bare bulb that was so dusty it only threw off a dim excuse for light. Shelves on one wall held jars and jars of canned food, but the rest of the place had not changed in the past decades. A shiver chased down my spine when I thought of going through all the boxes that were stacked up higher than my head. I would have to clean out the whole place if I was going to store my first batch of strawberry wine next spring.

Chapter Sixteen

Aunt Gracie's big floppy hat hung on the rack beside the back door, along with a couple of her aprons and a heavy coat. I put the hat on and tied the strings under my chin. Hopefully that would keep the sun from making a million new freckles.

"Hey, where are you off to?" Jasper called from his front porch.

"To the strawberry fields." I stopped to talk to him. "You look like you are feeling better."

"I am, a little, so I guess them pills are helping, but I don't want you or nobody else fussin' over me," he declared. "I'm out here to let the sunshine have a chance to work some magic."

Sassy followed me out to the gate and whined when I wouldn't let her go with me. "I'll be back by noon to give you another dose, and I'll even bring you some soup and sandwiches."

Jasper threw up a palm. "I've got a can of bean-and-bacon soup that I'm going to heat up and some ice cream sandwiches for dessert. You just bring the pills and that sucking thing that opens up my lungs."

I slipped through the gate and closed it behind me. "Will do. I've got my cell phone if you need me; just call. I won't be far away."

"Has Gina Lou moved in?" he asked.

"She's workin' on it right now."

The buzz of conversations among dozens of men reached me before I rounded the last curve and made it to the strawberry fields. Everyone, including Connor, had a garbage bag tied to their belt and was bent over, carefully pulling plants out of the ground. They moved up and down the beds like bees, talking while they worked.

Everything went so quiet that I could hear the birds flapping their wings above me. Connor finally noticed me and raised up. "Hey, everyone, this is Lila Matthews, the new owner of this place."

Those within hearing distance doffed their straw hats and nodded. The one closest to me shoved his hat back on his head and said, "Are you going to continue to lease this to Mr. Everett?"

"I haven't decided," I said, "but I'm here to work today. Whether I enjoy being outside will determine whether I want to be a strawberry farmer." I laughed to kill the tension.

His frown furrowed his broad brow. "If you are the boss, why would you want to pull weeds?"

"Got to learn the business if I'm going to run it," I replied.

He chuckled and went back to work.

"What are you really doing out here?" A wide smile broke across Connor's face. "Did you come to tell me that you are making this whole crew sandwiches like you did when we were selling the berries to folks? If so, you are too late. We all brought sack lunches."

"I'm really here to take my first class in strawberry growing," I said. "Why are they pulling up the plants? Is that a pruning process?"

He removed his cowboy hat and fanned his sweaty face. "We are carefully pulling up weeds. *Carefully* being the key word. If there are any seeds on the weeds, they could get loose and propagate into more of the same. Grandpa likes to have the after-harvest job done in the first two weeks, or it's too late to mow and we have to hand-prune all the plants. Are you serious about learning this business with me?"

"You've never done it before, either?" I asked.

"Not in the spring. I helped with it last fall, but the system is a little different this time of year. These guys all know what they're doing, and they are teaching me—*us*, if you are serious," he answered.

"Well, then show me what weeds look like and where the bags are, and I'll try to keep up."

He pulled a bag from a roll lying not far from him and handed it to me. "Anything that's not a strawberry plant is a weed."

I tied the bag to my belt loop and pulled my first weed. When I reached for my second one, Connor handed me a pair of gloves. "You'll need these or else your hands will be ruined. Grandpa told me to bring extra in case I got a hole in one. Some of the weeds are real demons to pull up. Tell me again, why do you want to learn this business?"

"Richie mentioned wanting to buy the place as a hobby farm. Maybe that's exactly what I need. Something to keep me busy part of the time but then giving me a chance to do something else when there's no work here to be done. I have until January when your grandpa's lease runs out to make my decision. And . . ."

Connor raised his head and locked eyes with me. "And what else?"

"You'll think I'm crazy, but I might make strawberry wine as a side business," I blurted out.

"Sounds like a plan to me," he said with a shrug. "There's water bottles in that cooler over there under the pecan tree."

I appreciated him more than ever when he didn't laugh at me. "Do I hear a *but* when I told you about my new plan?"

"Yes, you did. But . . ." He paused for a second. "Both of us may be ready to run for the hills after we pull weeds all day in this twenty acres. And the bad part is that we won't be done. We'll come back on Monday and Tuesday and Wednesday to get the job finished. Thank goodness we have a big crew, or we'd be out here for weeks."

"After we get all of it weeded, what happens?" I asked, figuring I would be spending Thursday in the bathtub, trying to soak the ache out of my back.

"When we finish weeding each section, we remove the straw bedding; then we mow all the plants down to the ground and fertilize," he explained. "In the fall, we straw the plants before the first crowns show up and then do a lot of praying that hail or locusts don't ruin the crop. This is a lot like picking season. There's no rest for the weary until it is finished."

"How do you know all this?"

He carefully tossed a handful of weeds into his garbage bag. "Like I said, I was here for the winter preparation last time around. The rest I've learned from the guys on the crew and Grandpa," he chuckled. "And the internet."

"I'm going to start researching everything I can about this business."

"What made you even think about doing this?" he asked.

"Jasper reminded me that I could," I told him. "It's an impulse thing, like quitting my job on a whim to help Mama and Annie. I've never done anything on the spur of the moment in my whole life. I don't even buy magazines or candy by the grocery store checkout counters. I had a plan to become an accountant when I was in high school. I focused on that and didn't look back. Then I come to Ditto and started making rash decisions. I think there's something in the water here that causes problems."

"Could be. Or fate might be pointing you in the direction you should go. Does accounting make you happy?"

I took time to stand up and stretch my back. "I've always believed that we make our own fate, and I thought I liked my job. But looking back, maybe it was just a placeholder for something better."

"Sometimes our choices determine our fate. Sometimes we just follow where we are led and are amazed when we find happiness," Connor said.

"I thought you were a soldier, not a philosopher," I teased.

"Granny's words, not mine. Another thing she said was that to get to know someone, you should work with them for a few days. Think we'll be better acquainted with each other any better at the end of this job?" he asked.

"From working from daylight to dark, we just might."

"Eight to six," he corrected me. "We take an hour off from noon to one to have a bite of lunch and take a power nap under the shade tree. We also break for fifteen minutes midmorning and midafternoon."

"What if it rains?"

"Weatherman says sunny days until the weekend. We're hoping to have everything done by Wednesday, and then it can storm all it wants. Ever gone outside and played in the rain?"

"Yep, with Aunt Gracie, and then we had hot chocolate and cookies." I kept working while we talked.

"If it wasn't lightning, Granny would let me go outside and get wet while I caught raindrops on my tongue," he said.

"That was the rule for me, too. I got a late start this morning, but when we break at noon, you could come to the house and eat with me and Gina Lou. I have to give Jasper his medicine, but it won't take long to make sandwiches."

"Thank you, but I packed a lunch," he said. "Already tired of this new plan?"

I straightened up and worked the kinks out of my back. "Nope, just realizing that I won't need to go to the gym after days like this."

"You go to the gym?" He sounded totally astonished.

"Hey, now!" I shot a mean look his way. "Are you saying that I'm too out of shape to have ever gone to a gym?"

"No, ma'am. You are perfect," he said quickly.

I laughed. "You covered that well."

"I hope so," he said with a smile.

"I worked out in Austin. Not really in a gym but a workout room in my apartment complex. After sitting most of the day, I needed to have a little exercise routine. How about you?"

"Didn't need to when I was in the army. We had regular workouts, but Grandpa has kept me busy since I got home with physical labor like this."

The roar of a mower cutting all the plants back to ground level started up. The noise kept conversations at a bare minimum the rest of the morning, giving me time to really think about the second rash decision I had made when I decided to be a farmer. Learning how to take care of strawberries, and even how to make wine, wasn't something I couldn't conquer. But I was an accountant, with six years' experience.

If I'd wanted to pull weeds, mow, and fertilize, why had I even gone to college? And how was I helping people like Aunt Gracie did by sweating in a strawberry field?

Those poor hired hands had worked four hours, and I had only been bent over in the sun for half that time when noon finally arrived. My back and neck actually creaked when I straightened up, but my bag was half-full of weeds, so I considered it a good morning. Connor and the rest of the guys went to their vehicles and carried brown paper bags over to a shade tree. I envied them as I walked to the house. They could eat in a hurry and have time for a power nap before attacking the weeds and running a loud mower for another five hours.

I opened the gate into the yard and Jasper waved. "So, are you ready to give up on that silly idea?"

"Have you been sitting there all morning?" I asked.

"Nope." He shook his head and coughed. "Went in to get an early lunch about thirty minutes ago."

"Why did you do that?" I fussed at him. "You are supposed to have your medicine with food."

"There's still part of a bologna sandwich in my stomach," he protested.

"Well, you are going to have to eat a little more." I rushed across the yard to Aunt Gracie's house. I still couldn't see it as mine.

"Yes, ma'am, Miz Bossy Britches!" he yelled.

I dragged myself up the porch steps and into the kitchen, where Gina Lou was pouring sweet tea in a couple of glasses filled with ice. I would have as soon put the ice down my shirt as have cold tea.

"Hey, my room is all clean," Gina Lou said. "The bedding is in the dryer."

"That's great. I've got to get Jasper's noon meds out to him," I said as I got his pills ready.

"Can I help?" she asked.

"No, it's only for two weeks, but thanks for the offer." I poured the noon pills into the small glass and picked up a bottle of water and his inhaler on the way out.

When he saw me coming across the yard, he started singing, *"Here she comes, Miz Bossy Britches."*

"Hush!" I scolded as I twisted the lid off the water and handed it to him along with the pills. "Next time, wait for me to get here before you eat. The instructions say to take them with food, not thirty or forty minutes afterwards."

He threw them all back and washed them down with a few swallows of water and handed the bottle back to me. "Go get me another ice cream sandwich. That should keep the pill police from putting handcuffs on me."

I put the lid back on and set the bottle on the stump. "You are a smarty-pants today, so you must be feeling better. The doctor said lots of liquid, so you need to drink at least three bottles of water today."

"I'll drink coffee or tea—or even apple juice—but water gags me," he protested.

"Lots of apple juice, then. See you later." By the time I made it back to my house, twenty minutes of my hour was gone. I was surprised to see a sandwich, chips, and a pickle spear on a plate and sitting on the table.

"Thank you," I whispered as I sank into a chair.

"You are so welcome." Gina Lou carried the sweet tea to the table and sat down. "I figured if you were going to make it back out there in an hour, you would be pushed for time to eat."

"You are so right," I said as I bit into the best bologna sandwich I'd ever eaten. "Just the way I like it—mustard, lettuce, tomatoes, and cheese."

"I didn't know what time you would be here, so I ate when I was hungry, about fifteen minutes ago," she answered. "I can't just sit around all afternoon. Tell me where to start cleaning."

"Whole house needs done, so choose your place—maybe the upstairs, but not Aunt Gracie's room. I'm still working on that," I said in between bites.

"How will I know which is her room?"

"Red panties are on the bed. I cleaned out her dresser drawers and haven't had time to do anything with them," I said.

Gina Lou slapped a hand over her mouth. "Are you kidding me? Miz Gracie wore red panties?"

"Yes, she did." The diary entry came back to my mind, and since I hadn't found anything but red in her underwear drawer, I wondered if she was buried in them. If she was, I bet her dear mother flipped over in her own grave half a dozen times.

Gina Lou's giggles were infectious, and soon we were both laughing out loud. She finally wiped her eyes on a paper napkin and hiccupped. "So, Miz Gracie had a wild side to her. Mama told me there was some big secret about this house. I never figured it would be red panties. I wonder if she hung them on the clothesline."

"Probably not in her day. She would have washed them by hand and dried them in the bathroom, or maybe in a spare bedroom or . . ." I remembered seeing one of those expandable wooden drying racks in the basement.

"Or what?" Gina Lou asked.

"In the basement," I finished the sentence.

"This place has a basement?" Her eyes widened, big as saucers. "Can I go see it?"

"We'll do that when I come home this evening. I want to clean it out and use it for storing my strawberry wine—if I decide to do that," I told her.

"Can I just peek down there now?"

"Sure, but don't move anything until I get back this evening. I'll need to go through the gazillion boxes to see if I can find a particular cookbook that has a strawberry-wine recipe in it." I finished the last bite of my pickle.

"If you can't find it, Mama has one that I'm sure she'll be glad to share with you," Gina Lou said. "There is a muffin in the box over there on the counter. There were two, but I ate one. Want it for dessert?"

"No, I've had enough for now." I stopped speaking when I saw a red cardinal land on the windowsill outside the kitchen. My aunt always said that meant someone who had passed was coming back to visit. The cardinal sang his song and then flew off, and a feeling of comfort filled my heart. Aunt Gracie had just put her seal of approval on Gina Lou being in the house.

"I could make some chicken teriyaki for supper and have it ready to put on the table when you get here," she suggested.

"Yes! Please! Do you need to go to town to get anything?"

She shook her head. "Nope, I found everything to make it in the pantry and freezer."

"You don't have work today, and you sure don't have to fix meals for me," I told her as I carried my plate to the sink. "But keep track of your hours, and I'll pay you time and a half for anything over forty hours a week."

She shook her head a second time. "Today doesn't go on any time sheet. You came and rescued me, and you have no idea how much I love this house. There's a feeling of . . ."

"Peace?" I finished for her.

"More than just peace. Kind of like serenity. Like I've gone to heaven."

"I understand completely." I smiled as I headed out the back door. "See you a little after six."

My muscles and back were screaming loudly when the day ended, but at least a fourth of the job was done. The sound of all the vehicles leaving the place filled the air, and then everything was quiet, and I heard crickets chirping and Sassy barking as I walked from the fields back to the house.

"We made it through day one," Connor said from behind me. "Only three more to go, but we have tomorrow to talk ourselves into coming back out here on Monday."

"I thought you were already gone."

"I had to check the water situation," he explained. "We're down to the last ten bottles, so Monday I will bring another case or two and another bag of ice. I'm sure glad that we don't have to do this job in the middle of July."

"Amen to that," I agreed. "We'd have to get us one of those hats that frat boys use to suck down beer."

"Only we'd be drinking water and running to the port-a-potty all day," he said.

I glanced over my shoulder. "Is there one out there? Where is it?"

"At the other end of the field. It's green, so it kind of blends in with the tree leaves." He pointed in that direction. "It's just as close for you to go back to your house as it is to walk all the way down there."

"Is it always there, or do you rent one in the spring and fall?"

"We rent it," he replied. "That's one more little lesson for us in how to do this job next spring if you decide not to renew Grandpa's lease."

"What's this 'us' business that you are talking about?" I was surprised I had the energy to tease.

"One never knows about the future," he flirted right back. "I'll ask Grandpa what company he uses to rent the toilets on wheels. Seems kind of strange to be joking around about our future and talking about toilets at the same time."

"I never thought I would have a good-looking guy flirt with me and say he'll find out where to rent a toilet in the same breath, either. Which reminds me, where did you find the work crew?" I asked.

"Several folks around these parts use them, and Grandpa has hired them for years. The crops come off different all over this part of the state. The reason we worked Saturday is that they have another job that starts on Thursday of next week, and they wanted a day to get ahead."

"But it's supposed to rain after this week," I reminded him. "Do they work in the rain?"

"It's only going to rain here, not where they'll be working," Connor said. "If you decide to be a farmer, I'm sure they'll be glad to work for you twice a year. They'll be on the calendar for the fall and then in January to start getting the field ready for the plants to grow again."

"After that, I'll have to do my own hiring, right?"

He removed his hat and wiped his forehead with his shirtsleeve. "Yes, ma'am, you will, but after what you are doing now, and will most likely do in the fall, there won't be a problem with them working for you."

"Why do you say that?"

Connor opened the gate for me. "Because they respect you for sweating right along with them today. See you Monday, if not before."

"Make it *before* if you can."

"Do my best," he said with a tired grin.

Now why had I said that? Sure, I wanted to see him again, but would it truly be wise to encourage whatever was between us?

Sassy met me at the gate and followed me to the porch. She grabbed a toy snake and shook it so hard that it was nothing but a blur. When I rapped on Jasper's door and then stuck my head inside, she tossed the toy in the air and dashed inside.

"I'm done for the day. I'll bring your supper and meds"—I covered a yawn with the back of my hand—"in a few minutes."

"Just the medicine," he said. "Gina Lou already brought me a plate. It looks good and smells even better, but I'm not taking a single bite until you get back with them pills. I don't like the look on your face when you are mad."

"That's a good thing." I tried to smile, but it took too much energy. "If you are hungry, that's a good sign."

"My appetite never did leave me," he argued. "I was coughing so much that it was a pain in my butt to try to eat. But I'm all better now. You can throw the rest of them pills in the trash. They have done cured me."

I shook my finger at him and then groaned at the spiky sensation. "You are going to take all of your medicine."

"Maybe *you* ought to take them pills since you're so sore that you can't even wiggle your finger without hurtin'," he suggested and then chuckled. "Hard work is tougher than sitting in front of a computer all day, ain't it?"

"Yes, it is, but I didn't quit. I'll be back in five minutes—and anyway, what you're taking doesn't cure muscle aches from weeding strawberries all day. It's for upper respiratory problems."

He shook his finger at me. "It don't need no fancy name. It's the croup. And, young lady, you don't need to be out there in the sun doing that kind of work. You will be the boss lady if you decide to really do this, girl. Do you see Everett out there pulling weeds and mowing?"

"A good boss knows the business from the ground up," I smarted off on my way outside.

He raised his voice as he repeated what he had told me for years. "As long as you are alive, Gracie will never be dead."

"Thank you so much!" I yelled over my shoulder.

I groaned again when I started up the back-porch steps. I was determined to make it through the process until Thursday, and then I'd have lots of time to go through the stuff in the basement. But for now, I planned to eat supper, spend a couple of hours riffling through boxes, and then take a long, soaking bath.

Gina Lou was busy setting the table when I came in the house. "Supper is ready, and I already took a plate to Jasper."

I dumped another dose of pills into the little glass. "Thank you for that. He says that it smells wonderful, and he's ready to eat. I'll take his medicine out to him and be right back."

"I could do that for you," she said.

"Thanks, but I'll have to do it. He thinks because he's starting to feel better that he doesn't need to take pills anymore. He'd try to hoodwink you, but he's afraid to pull any stunts on me."

"I would be, too." Gina Lou's tone was dead serious.

I chuckled on my way outside. Jasper used his inhaler and downed the pills with a swallow of sweet tea and then took a bite of the stir-fry. "This tastes a lot like the summer goulash my Granny used to make of fresh garden vegetables."

"I'll tell Gina Lou that you like it. See you about nine with the rest of today's medicine," I said, but a tiny little part of me was jealous that Gina Lou cooked and I didn't.

You are being childish, the voice in my head barked. *He might like Gina Lou and her cooking, but he loves you like a granddaughter.*

"Don't be late. Me and Sassy like to call it a day by nine thirty. Do I have to eat then, too?"

"Yes, you do. Want me to bring you a muffin?" I asked.

"I'd rather have another ice cream sandwich," he said in between bites.

"Okay, then." I made a mental note to pick up a couple of boxes of ice cream sandwiches when Mama and I went for lunch the next day.

I used to wonder what Aunt Gracie meant when she said she was dog-tired, but I knew now. Never in my life had I felt like I did that evening. Still, I stopped to admire the sky, which was lit up in a whole array of pastel colors by the last rays of sun. Today was almost finished. Tomorrow I could rest up and then Monday, start all over again. Somehow I felt so much better, even with all the stiffness and pain, than I did at the end of a working day in front of a computer. I had pulled weeds, and Connor said I did a good job of not spreading the seeds. The work crew had even talked to me when we all had our afternoon break.

Gina Lou made a motion toward the table. "Chicken stir-fry and sliced pineapple. A woman who works as hard as you did today needs a good hot meal."

I didn't have to be asked a second time, even though I was almost too tired to chew. I sat down and loaded up my plate. "I really don't like to cook. I'm fair at baking, and I make really good pancakes and french toast, but making a meal has always seemed like too much work for just one person. So, how did your first day go? Did you get your things all unpacked?"

"It went great." She passed the chicken to me.

"Please, help yourself first," I told her.

She nodded and said, "I peeked in Miz Gracie's room and got tickled all over again when I saw those red panties. I called Mama and told her that the big secret out here was that Miz Gracie had a wild side. I hope that was all right."

For a second, a burst of anger shot up from inside me, but then a small voice whispered in my head and told me that whatever the real issue was—if there even was one—wasn't anyone's business but Gracie's. Like Jasper had said, if she had wanted me to know, she would have told me.

"It was just fine for you to tell your mama," I said. "Aunt Gracie wasn't ashamed of her decisions. Red was her favorite color, as you can tell by her car. Evidently, she liked silk panties better than the old white cotton ones that grannies wear."

"Oh. My. Lord!" Gina Lou gasped. "Look at that beautiful sunset. Not even a professional painter could create something that gorgeous. What a way to end my first day here."

"Well, that was an abrupt change of subject."

"Sometimes my mind jumps around," Gina Lou explained. "I *had* to focus on orders and what folks were kin to each other in the café. I didn't want to offend someone by calling them by someone else's name. You know small towns. Someone is always mad at someone else for something. But cleaning house and cooking is a natural thing, so I don't have to concentrate."

"Think you could focus if you went to college to be a teacher?" I asked.

If she didn't leave, I could kind of adopt her like Aunt Gracie did me. Only she was a full-grown woman, not a baby, and it would be selfish of me not to let her follow her dreams. After all, the aches and pains in my body were proof that I was following a whim that could become my own dream. Gina Lou deserved to at least have the opportunity to do the same.

"I really do. I got a scholarship and had applied for student loans. Then Daddy got sick and couldn't work for a few months, so I had to help out the family," she said with a sad smile. "But Mama says everything happens for a reason."

"So did Aunt Gracie," I said. "I hope in five years we look back on this time and find out they were both right." I covered another yawn and moaned at simply raising my hand.

"If you are too tired to check out the basement, I understand."

"No, ma'am," I protested. "We're going to spend a little while down there, and then I'm going to have an hour-long bath and watch some television in my bedroom until I fall asleep."

"Maybe you should have that bath before we tackle the basement," she suggested.

"I'm already stinky and sweaty, so we'll sort through a few boxes first," I told her. "And, Gina Lou, you could easily put in your own restaurant. This food is delicious." I thought about Mama and all those years she sacrificed to raise me. I was beginning to understand what she had drilled into me: *Every choice has a consequence.*

"Lila, that takes a lot of money," she said. "And I'm hoping to save up enough money in a year or so to go to college. I really would like to be a teacher."

Chapter Seventeen

My mind flitted from one memory of Aunt Gracie to another, and among them all, I couldn't recollect a single bad one. She'd always showered me with love. Maybe all the reminiscences about the good times we had was what kept me from demanding answers from God as to why He took her away from me. I so wanted her to live to be a hundred, or maybe even more. I wanted her to rock my babies like we did the dolls in her bedroom when I was a little girl, and to hear her sing to them.

Among all the other memories, I remembered attending a funeral with Mama and Aunt Gracie when I was about five years old. The preacher had said that we were all born with an expiration date, and Miz Loretta Garrison had found hers and was now in the arms of Jesus. I wondered if the elderly lady with gray hair up there in that white casket with pink roses on the top of it wanted to be hugged up with Jesus forever and ever. Seemed like when there were streets of gold to be wandering up and down, and old friends to catch up with, that she might like for Jesus to let her go so she could go check out the rest of the place.

Afterward, we had gone to a family dinner at the church. The parents of my friends hadn't brought them to the funeral. We had talked about the funeral the next day at Sunday school, and they'd had dozens of questions that I tried to answer. I told them about the preacher talking about an expiration date, and we all checked to see if we could find one somewhere on our bodies. I even looked at the bottom of my feet, but none of us could find anything. I figured that would be a good thing to know if I could find it.

Gina Lou broke into my thoughts. "I'll clean up while you take your bath."

"Okay, and thank you." I wondered if that preacher had been right after all, and if so, then shouldn't I live my life in a way that brought me happiness? I wasn't going to die until a date that was written somewhere in the universe or maybe in invisible ink on my birth certificate—seemed only fitting since the birth date was there that my expiration would be on the same paper.

"What are you thinking about?" Gina Lou asked. "Did I do something wrong?"

"Oh, no." I laid my hand on her arm to reassure her. "You've already proven that hiring you was the smartest move I could ever make. What do you say that we go see that basement?"

Gina Lou and I pushed back our chairs and stood up at the same time. "What were you thinking about so hard?" she asked. "One minute, you were smiling, and then your expression turned like you were trying to get someone to answer a question."

"Thinking about Aunt Gracie, for the most part." I opened the squeaky door, and a heavy musty odor slapped me in the face.

"She was a great lady," Gina Lou said.

"Yes, she was," I agreed, shaking my head to dispel the fumes.

"This place smells like Miz Josie's old cellar, where we go when the tornado siren blows," Gina Lou said with an identical shake. "I can't find the light switch, Lila."

"There isn't one. Like the rest of the house, you have to pull the string." I found the thread spool and lit up the place—dim as it was. "There's a cellar on Mama's property, and it smells like this but not as bad. I figure it's all the clothing or mothballs in those boxes that makes it so strong."

As we descended the stairs, the air got heavier and heavier, as if there wasn't quite enough of it. I thought I should bring a fan from upstairs to at least keep things stirred up a little.

Gina Lou grimaced. "This place is a mess. You sure you want to make wine down here?"

"Not make it; just store it. Once we have it all cleaned out, I don't think it will be so stinky."

I thought of the old barn that a tornado had destroyed, the place where Aunt Gracie and the boys had gotten drunk on their own home-made wine. Maybe I could have one built at the edge of my twenty acres and, with a little persuasion, get Mama and Annie, and maybe even Gina Lou's mama, to help me in the wine-making process. That would be a part-time job for Mama and Annie, and they could still travel.

Gina Lou made her way through the maze of wooden and cardboard boxes over to the shelves lining three walls and wiped the dust off a quart jar. "If this is the newest of the lot, then we should get rid of all of them. This one is dated 1974. But that's your decision. I've been here less than a day . . ."

I held up a palm and shook my head. "I'm always open to suggestions, and you might know more about some of this stuff than I do. Let's leave the shelves alone until we get everything else cleared out. Then we won't be stumbling over boxes while we're taking jars upstairs to clean them out."

Gina Lou twisted her blonde hair up into a messy bun and held it there with a clamp she had had attached to the bottom of her T-shirt. "Where do we start? Back or front?"

"Let's start closest to the stairs. We can each take a load up to sort." I picked up the first two to carry them to the foyer. "I feel like I'm suffocating down here." I wasn't sure if it was the smell or if it was psychosomatic from all the ghosts I imagined hiding inside the boxes.

Gina Lou came right behind me with one in her arms. "Me too. This box is pretty light, and it's not marked like the ones you are taking up. I wonder what's in it."

I set my two on the floor and brushed the dust off the tops. One said "Clarence's coats." The other said "Betty's clothing."

"Why didn't they get rid of these things years ago?" I wondered out loud, then remembered the outfits in Aunt Gracie's closet. She had had her reasons for keeping those things, so maybe her parents had theirs.

"Maybe whoever worked here back then packed them all up and stored them in the basement. Miz Gracie might not have even realized what was down there," Gina Lou answered. "Hey, if the red panties aren't the big secret, we might find a clue tucked away in all this stuff. Looks like someone in the family wore long oat-colored underwear, but I'd say this is all trash since there's holes and patches on every single one."

"According to what Aunt Gracie told me, for a long time after the Depression years, no one ever threw away anything, not even a foot-long piece of thread." I pulled out a long gray coat with a plaid scarf still tucked around the collar. Both were dotted with moth holes. I wondered why whoever had packed them away didn't at least throw in a handful of mothballs. Then I remembered that passage in Aunt Gracie's diary about being so angry with her father.

She had never told me that the bedroom Gina Lou was using had once belonged to her father and mother, but it made sense. The closets and dresser had been cleaned out, and since she hadn't forgiven him for whatever he did, then she wouldn't have cared if his things were well preserved or not.

"Looks like what's in this one goes to the trash, too. I'm glad we've got a big dumpster and not one of those little poly-cart things," I said as I shoved the box to one side and opened the next one to find the same thing: woolen skirts and vests with holes eaten in them. "Let's just carry these outside and bring up one more load. I'm tired and already feeling downright grimy from pulling weeds most of the day. I'm in desperate need of a long bubble bath."

"I'm not as tired, but I am looking forward to sinking down in that big old claw-foot tub near my room and then climbing into that heavenly bed with a book." Gina Lou headed out the back door with her box in her arms. "Do you think that this is what we'll probably find in most of what's down there? Not much of a treasure trove, is it?"

"Nope," I agreed.

"What are y'all doin'?" Jasper asked.

"Throwin' out stuff that should've been tossed years ago," I replied.

"How are you feelin'?" Gina Lou asked.

"Better than yesterday at this time. What's in them boxes?" he asked.

"Moth-eaten coats and long-handled underwear with holes and patches," I told him. "And there'll most likely be more of the same. We are cleaning out the basement."

"Why?" Jasper asked.

I kept walking toward the gate. "I'm going into the strawberry business, and I'm going to store my strawberry wine down there."

"Can I come live in the basement?" he teased.

"No, but I might bring you a bottle for your hundredth birthday."

"Then I guess I'm going to have to live a while longer," he said with a big grin. "I wouldn't want to miss out on that. Did I tell you about the time me and Gracie and Davis made wine?"

"You did." I was suddenly worried about his memory. I could never put Jasper in a nursing home, but I wasn't sure I could care for him if he had dementia.

"Well, remind me to tell you again sometime. I like to remember them days," he said. "When I tell them stories, it's like Gracie and Davis are still with me and we are having fun."

"You haven't told me," Gina Lou said, "so I'll remind you later."

"I'll hold you to that," Jasper told her.

The next boxes we brought up were filled with clothing that seemed to be even older than the first three and in even worse condition. Jasper was still on his porch even though it was beginning to get dark.

"What's in those?" he asked.

"Looks like stuff from long before Aunt Gracie was born. There's long dresses with ruffles everywhere."

"Her grandparents built this place back in the late 1800s. Clarence was born in that house, and so was Gracie. And they both died there," he said with a long sigh. "It's stood up to a lot of stuff, with arguing and lovin' on the inside and bad weather on the outside."

I stopped and said, "Tell me those stories."

"That's something for another day. Right now I'm going inside to watch my shows. Y'all don't work too hard." He stood up and disappeared into his house.

"So, is that it for this day?" Gina Lou asked.

"My muscles and body are telling me to go get into a nice warm bath," I moaned. "So yes, this is it for today. And the car keys are hanging on a rack inside the back door if you want to take the SUV to church tomorrow morning. I plan to sleep late."

She held the door open for me. "Don't forget Jasper's last dose of medicine for today."

"Thanks for the reminder." I made my way up the stairs and into the bathroom, where I adjusted the water in the tub and peeled out of my sweaty clothing. I poured in both bubble bath and salts and sank down into the warm water with a groan. Thank goodness tomorrow was Sunday.

"Why didn't they just wait to start the work until Monday?"

I was half-asleep when a squeaky step about halfway up the stairs warned me that someone was on the way. Figuring it was Gina Lou, I adjusted the rolled-up towel at the back of my neck and closed my eyes.

"Lila, are you up here?"

The sound of Mama's voice startled me so badly that my eyes popped wide open and I sat up. The towel at my neck fell over the back of the tub, and I couldn't reach it even with my long arms.

"Mama?" Surely I was imagining things. She didn't come into the house unless it was absolutely necessary. At best, she would make it into the kitchen, and even then she couldn't wait to get back outside.

After spending a while in the basement, I wasn't so sure anymore that she wasn't right.

She opened the door, peeked inside, and then came on into the bathroom. "What is this I hear about you going to be a strawberry farmer?" She picked up my towel from the ladder-back chair sitting beside the tub, laid it on the edge of the sink, and sat down.

"Who told you?" I sank down so that bubbles covered me all the way to my neck.

"I called to ask Jasper how he was feeling, and he said you pulled weeds all day and then came home and started cleaning out the basement so you'd have a place to store wine. What has gotten into you, girl? You've got a good education. If you think you need a job, you can find one at a bank or at a firm in San Antonio. The commute isn't bad, and—"

I pulled a hand up out of the water in a gesture to shush her and then butted in before she could really get riled up on a rant. "Mama, you know I've never done a single impulsive thing in my life."

"Except quitting your job on a whim to help me," Mama said. "And don't you shush me with an arm that looks like it's been dipped in meringue. Your steadfastness is one of the things I've always admired about you."

"I got that from you, Mama—and I can use my education to manage the estate that Aunt Gracie left me, but I'm not sure I want to spend every waking day behind a desk again. I'm tired tonight, but it's a good tired. My muscles ache, and the sun probably produced another hundred freckles on my face. People can take me or leave me when it comes to my looks or my choice of jobs. I sweated off all my makeup, and the weeds didn't care. Connor and the work crew were sweating as much as me, so they didn't care, either." I finally stopped for a breath.

She eyed me and set her mouth in that firm line she always did just before I got a heavy lecture about life. Then her whole expression changed, and she giggled. "I guess I did teach you to fight for what you want. But be honest with me: Is this because you are seriously thinking of not renewing Everett's lease in January or because you want to spend time with Connor?"

"Maybe some of both, but, Mama . . ." I threw a handful of bubbles at her. "I feel free tonight, as if a weight has been lifted from my shoulders. I figured out something today. You know those old black party line phones that are still in the house?"

She brushed the bubbles off her shirt with the side of her hand. "What about them?"

"They are obsolete, and I'm getting rid of them, but I thought of them today. In their day, folks listened in on gossip and then spread it all over town—over backyard fences, behind those church fans with Jesus holding a baby lamb on one side and an advertisement for a funeral home on the other, or in hushed whispers in aisle three in the grocery store."

"Why aisle three?" she asked.

"That's where the feminine products are kept. No man would ever be caught there, so they couldn't accuse their wives of spreading rumors," I explained.

That made her giggle. "And what's so different today?"

"We have cell phones, and a few folks still have landlines, like what's in this house. But party lines are a thing of the past. Today, social media takes the place of party lines, and that's the way that gossip gets spread all over town."

"What has that got to do with Connor, or with anything else?" she asked.

"The things that were heard by eavesdroppers on the party lines in their day are probably most likely the same as what creates a good gossip session today. Only now it's spread over social media for a day or two, and then something better comes along to take its place."

"I'm still confused," Mama scowled.

"What I'm trying to say is that I don't care what people think or gossip about. I'm going to make myself happy." I took a deep breath.

"If getting into a relationship with Connor Thurman makes me happy, then that's what I'm going to do."

"I love that," Mama said with a smile, "but I still can't figure out what party lines have to do with it."

"Probably nothing, but I believe that this 'big secret' thing started when Aunt Gracie overheard something on one of them," I replied. "I don't want to let anything other people think—even if it turns out to be something that's whispered about for decades—keep me from living my life."

"Okay, then," she said. "I was also wondering if you're stirring up other trouble. What's this I hear about Gracie's red panties?"

Not even sucking on a lemon could have kept the smile off my face. "Don't you think those panties are a big enough thing to keep the few folks here in Ditto talking for a few weeks? Which reminds me . . . When you took her clothing to the funeral home—"

"Yes, I took red silk panties and a red pantsuit and told the funeral director not to put shoes on her. She loved the feel of the green grass on her feet. I bet that sorry sucker started the rumor." She narrowed her eyes and set her mouth in a firm line.

"Nope, Gina Lou did the honors when she told her mother," I told her. "I don't think there's a funeral home–confidentiality thing like with lawyers and doctors, but he probably just gasped and did what you told him to do. You told me that she died right here at home. I was so shaken up and so busy I didn't ask questions. Tell me more about that evening."

"Jasper called me." Mama shivered. "I was here when the ambulance arrived. They took her to the hospital, but it was too late. She'd been diagnosed a month before with congestive heart failure, and the doctor said she probably had a year to live. I wanted her to turn the downstairs office into a bedroom."

"Why? Had it become hard for her to go up and down the stairs?" I asked.

"Yes, it had, but she was as stubborn as . . ." She narrowed her eyes and shot a look over my way. "As stubborn as you are."

"I've heard that before."

"Anyway, the doctor at the hospital ruled that she died of a heart attack," Mama said.

No wonder Mama felt like there were ghosts in the house. Something akin to a cold chill chased down my spine.

She stood up and placed the towel back on the chair. "I'm going now. I'm trying really hard not to let the eerie feeling in this place keep me from coming to see you, but I've got to admit, I'm glad I'm leaving on Monday. This is all I can handle for a while. Will you come help me pack tomorrow?"

"Why don't we go for burgers at the Dairy Queen and then spend the afternoon together?" I suggested.

"I'd like that," she said. "Are we going to church?"

"Let's play hooky. Jasper won't feel like getting out yet. I'll pick you up at eleven thirty so we can beat the church crowd to the café."

"I'll be ready," she said and hurried out the door.

I could hear her footsteps practically jogging down the stairs.

"Bless her heart," I whispered and ducked my head under the water.

I came up for air, washed my hair, and rinsed it. Then I stayed in the tub until the water was stone cold and the bubbles had gone flat. When I pulled the plug and stepped out onto the rug beside the tub, my skin was almost as wrinkled as Aunt Gracie's had been when I saw her the last time. I wrapped a towel around my head turban-style and another one around my body and padded barefoot to my bedroom.

I thought about Aunt Gracie drawing her first breath in the room a few feet across the wide hallway from my bedroom and then taking her last one in that same room. I pulled on a pair of pink bikini under-wear and a nightshirt that had been worn so much that it was soft and comfortable.

I heard the bathroom door open and then close, and then Gina began to sing. I've never been musical, either in playing an instrument or in singing, so I couldn't be a good judge, but she sure sounded like

Miranda Lambert of the Pistol Annies when she belted out "Hell On Heels."

"Yep, we are hell on heels, and even though we might not be looking for a sugar daddy like the song says, we aren't going to let anyone else tell us what to do or how to live our lives," I said, then headed downstairs for a glass of sweet tea.

I forgot all about what I was doing when I passed by the door to the basement. Before I knew it, I was turning on the light and easing down the rough wood steps in my bare feet. When I got to the bottom, I glanced around the room and my eyes landed on a shoebox sitting over to my left on one of the shelves. "Gracie's Stuff" was written on the end. How could I have overlooked that when we were down there earlier?

Without even thinking about the dust on the floor or my bare feet, I walked across the room and picked it up. Not wanting to share the contents with Gina Lou, I hurried back up to my bedroom and wiped my feet on the damp towel I'd wrapped around my head. Then I used the other one to clean the outside of the box before I crawled up in the middle of my bed and set it down in front of me.

Rather than being taped, the box was tied with a faded-red satin ribbon. I pulled on the string, and the bow let go. I eased the top off and found at least a dozen dried roses covering an old wine bottle with a note stuffed inside. I tried to shake it out. That didn't work, but I didn't give up. Tweezers from the manicure set Aunt Gracie gave me for my birthday was what finally rescued the piece of paper.

I carefully unrolled it and read: *These are the roses that Davis gave me for my birthday, and this is one of the wine bottles that we used to make our own strawberry wine. I don't ever want to forget the days we had. It seemed that we only had a minute together before he was killed, but it was a precious one. I loved him, and he was taken from me.*

I sighed as I put the lid back on the box. Her red panties weren't the secret at all, but her love for Davis. I wondered why they couldn't be together. Had her parents forbidden it because he was the help? Had her father paid his mother—what was her name?

"Rita!" I snapped my fingers. "That was her name. Did Gracie's daddy pay her to break up a budding young romance? Why didn't they rebel when they graduated from high school? Had he been made to believe that he wasn't good enough for her?"

The answers to my questions were at the cemetery with Gracie. That was probably where they belonged because, as Jasper had said many times, "If she had wanted you to know, she would have told you."

Chapter Eighteen

"What's the matter?" Mama asked as we went into the Dairy Queen.

"Nothing." I looked up at the menu above the counter while we waited behind a couple of bikers in leather, chains, and gray beards.

"Are you thinking about me being gone?" she pressed on with a worried expression.

"Honest, nothing is wrong. I'm over-the-moon happy that you are taking a vacation, as long as"—I leaned over and whispered in her ear—"you and Annie don't take up with bikers and become road-queen mamas."

"We make no promises and have no shame. What happens on a road trip does not come back to Ditto," she said out the side of her mouth. "We might go *hog* wild while we are away."

"So you might come home with another secret that no one can figure out?"

Mama smiled back, and we stepped up to the counter.

A middle-aged woman with short gray hair dried her hands on a paper towel and hurried over to the counter. "Hey, Sarah, I hear you and Annie done retired and that you are about to go on a trip to Nashville. I've always wanted to go there. Think you'll get to see George Strait?"

"That would be nice," Mama said. "When are you going to retire, Miz Brenda?"

"Never." She frowned. "The boss doesn't get to take days off, much less retire. Not with as tough as it is to keep good help these days. You want a job when you get back from your vacation? I'll let you pick your hours. Or . . . ." She leaned over the counter and whispered, "I'll sell this place to you."

"Thanks, but no thanks," Mama said. "I don't know what I want to do, but I know it's not café work. We'd like a couple of burger baskets. Mustard, no onions, on both burgers. French fries on one and onion rings on the other and make that to go. And we'll need another one with fries, too, for Jasper."

"We'll get that right out." Brenda glanced over at me. "Lila, do you want a job?"

"I've got one," I assured her. "I'm learning the strawberry business."

"I heard that you were out there working in the fields yesterday." Brenda hung the order on a round rack, just like I'd seen Mama do so many times where she worked, and then set two empty cups on the counter. "Are you really not going to renew Everett's lease?"

"I don't have to make a definite decision until January."

Mama picked up the cups and headed to the drink fountain.

"But who would have ever guessed that you would come home and take over the strawberry business? Or that the big secret is just that Miz Gracie had a wild side?"

"Not me, for sure," I declared. "And where did you hear about Aunt Gracie?" My voice had an edge to it. Even though I knew there were rumors, it still angered me that folks had heard about her red underwear.

"Gossip travels fast in small towns," Brenda said and lowered her voice. "I would have never thought such a thing from a prim and proper lady like her."

"Who truly knows another person? Now that the secret is out, will folks stop talking about it?" I wanted to ask her what color *her* panties were, but I kept my mouth shut.

"Oh, no, honey," Brenda chuckled. "Now we want to know who she was wild with. Was it Jasper or some other man in these parts?"

"Not Jasper, for sure." I would do my best to divert any rumors away from him.

"Why would you say that?" Brenda asked.

"Just a feeling I have. Did you know that he was in the emergency room with an upper respiratory infection?" I said, trying to change the subject.

Brenda nodded. "I heard about that. Poor old darlin'. I'm glad you moved back here to help take care of him. That takes a load off Sarah's shoulders."

"Order up!" the cook yelled, even though she was only ten feet from us.

Brenda held up a finger. She brought a sack back and set it on the counter. "Here you go, and if either of you change your mind, just let me know." She nodded toward the parking lot, where folks were getting out of half a dozen cars. "Looks like church has let out. We're about to get swamped."

"Thank you, Jesus," I muttered on my way out to the vehicle, where Mama was waiting.

I slid in behind the steering wheel and set the bag on the back seat. "We didn't order Jasper anything to drink?"

"When I called him, he said he already had tea made up," Mama said. "I'm just glad we decided to eat with him on his porch and not in the restaurant. Brenda had more questions than a four-year-old can conjure up."

"Now everyone is trying to figure out who Aunt Gracie wore her red panties for." I started the engine and backed out of the parking lot.

"Bless their hearts—and I do not mean that in a nice way," Mama whispered. "When will people learn to stop gossiping?"

"When they're laid out in the cemetery, I guess. Maybe there's a special little area in heaven for the ones who can't wait to tell what they know. It's got barbed wire fences all around it so they can't be a hindrance to the other folks up there."

"You could be right," Mama giggled. "Lila, I've got to admit, I'm so excited about this trip. I keep waiting for something to come up to prevent us from going."

"Not if I can help it." I drove through town and turned onto Highway 16, then made a left onto the road to Ditto a few minutes later. "Do you think this secret stuff will ever completely die down?"

"Someday," she said. "The next generation won't be interested in something that old any more than they are interested in their grandmother's crystal and silver. They probably won't even know who George Strait is. They'll be too lazy to pick strawberries, and the big wine companies and jelly businesses will be the ones who are buying the berries."

I parked the Ford in front of the house. "No secret . . . no Strait . . . That's too depressing to even think about."

She got out of the car and carried our drinks around the side of the house. "Instant gratification is what children are being taught, and they'll teach their kids the same. Picking strawberries is tedious work. Young folks today are too lazy to do hard work, and they'll teach the next generation by example."

Jasper held on to Sassy's collar while we went through the gate and turned her loose the moment we locked it behind us. "I told her that company was coming, so she got all excited. Let's eat before y'all play with her. I been lookin' forward to a big old juicy hamburger all morning."

Mama set the two drinks down beside his tea on the stump. "It's good that you've got an appetite. I see you've already brought out another chair. We could have done that."

"I keep tellin' Lila that I've got my strength back and don't need no more medicine," he said.

"And that rattle in your chest when you cough says otherwise." I took the food from the bag and set his burger and fries on the edge of the stump. "You go ahead and start eating. I'll get your medicine and be right back."

"Gracie didn't just leave her the house and land," Jasper told Mama. "She also left Lila enough bossiness for half a dozen women."

"That, she did," Mama agreed.

"And I love it!" I yelled from my back porch.

Gina Lou was still gone when I came home from helping Mama pack, but Connor was sitting on the front-porch swing. I sat down beside him and set the swing in motion with my foot before pulling both feet up and wrapping my arms around my legs.

"Did you get Sarah all packed up and ready to go?" he asked.

"I did. Where are my manners? Can I get you a glass of sweet tea or a beer?"

He leaned over and picked up a six-pack of sweating bottles. "I chilled them before I came over. Are you ready to get busy picking weeds tomorrow, or would you rather mow?"

"I don't know nothin' about no 'chinery," I said in the heaviest fake southern accent I could muster up. "Let me pick weeds. That's more my speed."

Connor chuckled and then laughed. "Have you ever mowed a lawn?"

"Oh, yeah, lots of times before I moved to the big city."

He twisted the top off a bottle of beer and handed it to me. "It's no different than that. The commercial mowers they use are the width of a strawberry bed, so your job is just to keep it steady. Why don't you give it a try? You said you wanted to know the business from the ground up, and this year will be your only chance. Next year, you'll just turn it over to the supervisor of the crew."

I took a long drink of the cold beer. "This tastes wonderful. I suppose if I mess up, I can always go back to pulling weeds."

"That's the spirit," he said. "So, how is Gina Lou working out?"

"Fantastic. I'm going to hate to see her leave in the fall."

"Why would she leave?" He turned up his beer and downed a third of it.

That old advertisement came to mind. *Beer: ten dollars. Finding Connor on my porch: free. Sitting beside him: priceless.*

"Earth to Lila," he whispered.

"Sorry, I crawled into a time machine." I reminded him about my plan to offer college tuition to Gina Lou. "I already told you that Aunt Gracie helped several young women follow their dreams. I want to pay that forward."

He held the beer in his left hand and slipped his right one around my shoulders. "So you are still serious about that idea."

"Yes, I am," I said.

"You are an amazing woman, Lila Matthews."

"No, I'm not," I protested. "I'm only doing what I can to empower other women, like Aunt Gracie and Mama did for me all from the time I was a little girl."

"Well, whatever they did, it made you who you are, and I like you. Please don't ever change." He held his bottle toward me.

I touched mine to his. "I like you, too, Connor Thurman."

Not even the cold beer could put out the heat inside my body right then. I changed the subject to something that didn't have me thinking about taking his hand and leading him upstairs to my bedroom. "Have your muscles stopped aching?"

"Almost. Yours?"

"Same."

"Okay, enough small talk," Connor said. "Let's talk about us."

"You go first," I told him.

He set his bottle on the porch, scooted over, and cupped my cheeks in both his hands. "I really, really like you," he said in a low voice that sent more delicious little shivers down my spine.

I barely had time to close my eyes before his lips pressed to mine. My arms wrapped around him; I leaned into the kiss and didn't even try to stop my hands when they found their way up his neck and pulled him closer for another.

I reminded myself that this wasn't the movies. I didn't make out with a guy and then fall backward onto a bed and pull him down on top of me, but that sure didn't keep me from wanting to take the session upstairs. My heart might have won over my good sense if Gina Lou hadn't driven up.

"Hey, y'all, what's goin' on?" she asked as she got out of the SUV.

"You want to tell her, or should I?" Connor chuckled.

"Neither one," I whispered.

He raised his voice. "Want a beer?"

"Love one," she replied and sat down on the porch step.

"How was your day at home with the family?" I asked.

"I had a fantastic day with my family. We went to church and then went back to the house for dinner. Mama fried chicken, and we all pitched in to help. Then we played board games. They were still at it when I left."

"I love fried chicken," I said, trying to turn the conversation to food rather than answering her question about what was going on.

Connor opened a bottle and handed it to her. "It should still be cold. Sounds like you really enjoyed your Sunday."

"I did, and Mama is so excited about my job here. She even said"— she paused and took a long drink—"that if I ever quit, she's applying for the job. Of course, she wouldn't live here, but she'd be a good employee. Not that I'm even thinking about turning in my resignation. Not until I have enough money saved up for a semester of college. You've made me think that I can do anything, Lila."

Connor gave my shoulder a gentle squeeze. "She's good at that, isn't she?"

"You bet she is," Gina Lou said. "I'm going to take this in the house and finish it off in a long, hot bath. I just love that claw-foot tub." She paused as she turned. "Sorry, I didn't mean to butt into whatever y'all were talking about."

"You didn't," Connor said. "We've got a tub like that at Grandpa's place, and it is pretty great when you need to soak tired muscles."

Gina Lou slid a long sly wink at me as she went inside the house. "See y'all later."

"Did that kiss affect you like it did me?" he asked.

"I wouldn't know, since I'm not you. But if it curled your toes, then the answer is yes. I'm still feelin' it."

"Have you always been this blunt?" he asked.

I snuggled down against him and laid my hand on his chest. His heart was pounding almost as hard as mine still was. "Yes, I have. I inherited that trait from Aunt Gracie. Jasper says I'm as bossy as she was, too. Which reminds me, I have to go take him some supper and medicine."

"And I have to go home. Grandpa wants me to drive him to Sunday-night church service since we missed this morning." He kissed me on the forehead and stood up.

"That's all I get?" I teased.

"One more little make-out session like we just had, and I would be begging to spend the night," he flirted right back. "See you in the strawberry field tomorrow morning."

"Eight o'clock," I said as I pushed up out of the swing. "I'll be the one in the floppy hat."

Chapter Nineteen

I fell into bed on Monday night even more exhausted than I'd been on Saturday, and Tuesday wasn't any better. The only two things that kept me going were the memory of that make-out session with Connor on Sunday and that on Wednesday we would be finished until fall.

On Wednesday morning, I woke up early and almost hit the snooze button, but there was no way I was going to let the weeds get the best of me. I would survive one more day. Still, I groaned when my feet hit the floor. "There's a reason not to do anything stupid on March 15, like make a decision to learn the strawberry business."

The mirror in the bathroom gave a loud testimony that I had grown at least a hundred new freckles. My eyes had bags under them, and my lips stayed dry no matter how much ChapStick I used. "If Connor tells me I'm beautiful today, I will know that he's feeding me a line of pure crap."

The wonderful smell of coffee wafted up the stairs and put a little extra spring in my step. Then I got a whiff of cinnamon, and my mouth started watering. "You cooked breakfast again. Bless your heart—and I mean that in the best possible way," I said when I entered the kitchen.

Gina Lou piled french toast onto a platter. "Well, your boyfriend could have made it, but he hasn't been around since Sunday. I'm a grown woman, Lila. Connor doesn't have to leave before daylight because I live here. It won't embarrass me if he stays over and has breakfast with us."

"Thank you for that, but we haven't taken that step yet. We've only kissed a few times," I admitted as I loaded my plate with toast and scrambled eggs. And people called *me* blunt! How could someone younger than me be so direct about relationships?

Refreshing, isn't it? Aunt Gracie was back again.

My phone rang, and when I saw it was Mama I put her on speaker. Gina Lou turned to face me and popped both hands on her hips. "Hot dang, girl! What are you waiting for? Christmas?"

Before I could reply or even say hello, Mama asked, "Who's waiting for Christmas?"

"Where are y'all?"

"On the road, but I miss you already—but what's this about Christmas?" she asked.

"I was wondering if we'll put up a tree at Christmas," Gina Lou answered.

Thank you, Gina Lou, I thought. *Mama doesn't need to worry on her trip about whether Connor and I are getting serious.*

"Of course you will. Aunt Gracie loved her trees. She usually had about four scattered about the house. A big one in the living room. A little one on the dining room table and one in her bedroom. Then there was a tall skinny one at the end of the credenza in the foyer. She still uses—*used*—the ornaments that Lila made in elementary school." Mama took a deep breath and let it out slowly. "Okay, I should probably hang up."

"Call me every night when y'all get checked into the hotel, and send lots of pictures." I remembered the last thing Mama always said before I went back to school after a holiday: *Call or text me as soon as you are home safe.*

"I will," she promised.

I hung up the phone and sat down at the table. "Thanks for covering for me. Connor and I have just figured out that we like each other. We don't want to rush into anything."

Gina Lou brought her plate to the table. "I wish I'd been that smart when it came to Derrick. He charmed me right into bed and then dumped me when the going got tough. Next time, I'm going to follow your lead."

"Oh, honey, don't be doing that," I argued. "I'm not exactly the poster child for long-term relationships."

If Connor hadn't been there to encourage me, and if I hadn't had a stubborn streak that wouldn't let me give up, I would have never reached the end of Wednesday. Looking back that evening, over what looked to me like a massive field now stripped of all the strawberry plants, I felt a sense of pride that I had endured the tough times.

The crew members loaded up their equipment into trailers and drove away. Connor and I slowly walked back toward the shade tree. I grabbed two bottles of cold water, handed one to him, and sat down with my back against the trunk.

"Are you still going to go into the business?" he asked.

I gulped down a third of the water. "Yes, I am. It's hard to believe that I've made so many hasty decisions in the past few weeks."

He removed his hat and fanned my face with it first and then his own. "I'm rowing in the same canoe. I was angry at the army and floundering when I first came to Ditto. Grandpa told me that hard work would help with both."

"What did you do?"

"He put me to chopping firewood the first two weeks," he said. "That took the anger out, and then he started teaching me how to run all the pies he has a finger in, and before long, I felt like I had a home and was putting down some roots in one place. Which is strange, considering my upbringing." He reached across the distance and took my hand in his. "Have *you* found a home yet?"

"Yes, I have. Every day I find something new that assures me that this is where I belong."

He gave my hand a gentle squeeze. "Me too, and even though it's been backbreaking, sweaty work, I've enjoyed our time this week. Would you go to dinner with me tomorrow evening?"

"Are you asking me on a real date?"

"I am."

"Yes, I would love to, but it'll have to be after five because I'm still giving Jasper his medicine," I told him. "And we'll have to be home before nine thirty because that's his bedtime. He believes in that thing about *early to bed and early to rise*."

Connor's grin was tired, but it lit up his eyes. "Maybe we would all live to be almost a hundred if we obeyed his rules and lived as simply as he does. I'll pick you up right after five and have you home before Jasper's bedtime."

I moaned when I stood up. "I'll be ready, but for now, I should get to the house and take his supper and meds out to him. I'm glad I'll be the boss next year."

He leaned on the tree for a few seconds when he got to his feet. "Leg still gives me fits after a hard day's work."

"But it sure doesn't slow you down, does it?"

"No, ma'am, but it lets me know I'm damaged goods."

"Aren't we all," I whispered.

Gina Lou was removing a cast-iron skillet from the oven when I made it to the kitchen. "Hey, you're home half an hour early—but soup is ready, and corn bread has just finished baking."

"I told you that you don't have to cook," I said. "I hired you to clean and maybe do some yard work."

"I put the soup on to simmer right after lunch and mowed the lawn while it cooked," she said. "I'm like Oprah. I can multitask. The yard could have waited, but I want to help you clean the basement completely out the next couple of days. I'll get Jasper's supper ready while you get his meds together."

I gave her a quick side hug and then washed up in the kitchen sink. "Thank you so much. Connor asked me to go to dinner with him tomorrow night," I blurted out.

"Well, it's about time," Gina Lou declared as she filled a bowl with soup and put it on a tray. "But I'm not sure you should go. I can figure out a really good excuse for you." She handed me a dish towel for my hands.

"Why not?"

"Because he's slow-witted. You've been in Ditto for three weeks, and he's just now getting around to asking you out," she giggled. "I'll take care of Jasper for you so you don't have to rush home. Maybe"—she winked at me—"he'll even cook breakfast in the morning. You said he makes a really good omelet."

I added the medicine to the tray. "Life is not dull or boring with you around."

"I try," she said dramatically and placed a hand over her heart.

She opened the door for me, and I carried the tray outside. Jasper was waiting on the porch and waved when I started over that way. He eased up out of his chair, whistled for Sassy, and headed into the house. The dog ran from the far corner of the fenced-in yard and beat him inside when he opened the door.

"What do you have there?" he asked when I set the tray on the table.

"Soup, corn bread, and medicine. I'll pour you a glass of iced tea."

"Smells and looks great, but I'll sure be glad when I can have a beer in the evenings instead of pills," he bellyached.

"They'll all be gone a week from tomorrow," I assured him. "On Friday of next week, you can celebrate being well with a beer or a hot toddy."

He sat down and changed the subject. "Are you done with that fool notion of being a strawberry farmer? Accountants don't exactly grow on plants around here."

I set the glass of tea on the table and sat down beside him. "No, I'm even more determined to do it. It's exactly what I need, and I'm going to talk Mama and Annie into helping me with the wine part of the business. I'm going to name the wine Strawberry Grace."

Jasper swallowed his pills with a sip of tea. "She'd like that, and she'd love that you are doing this, but make sure it's more than a whim. I miss her so much, Lila. The last few years, we were together from breakfast to bedtime. Sometimes she drove us into Poteet to the Senior Citizen Center for lunch. We would play dominoes or cards all afternoon and visit with the youngsters."

"Youngsters?" I frowned.

"Honey, we are done past ninety. Them other folks were at least twenty years behind us, so yes, they were babies to us. We were already either runnin' a business or else in the army when they was in diapers."

"Either me or Gina Lou will be glad to drive you into town every day if you want to go spend some time there. You just have to take your meds before you leave and be home in time for supper," I told him.

"Hmmph," he snorted. "I don't need a curfew. Besides, by four o'clock all of them folks is ready to go home and get a nap anyway. But thank you for the offer. I might take you up on it come Monday, if you don't think that's too soon to start socializin' since Gracie's passing."

"I don't think so. Folks in this day and time don't pay much attention to those old rules," I said as I started to leave. "Besides, you and Gracie did things your way and didn't let other people's opinions matter."

"I s'pose. Tell Gina Lou thanks for the supper," he said.

"Will do," I nodded.

I was almost across the yard when the ringtone on my phone let me know Mama was calling. I sat down on the top step and hit the accept button. "Are we there yet?"

She giggled and said, "We are in Nashville, right here in a hotel on the strip. We stayed in Montgomery, Alabama, on our way, and we saw the grave site where Hank Williams was put to rest and went through his museum, and it was absolutely awesome, Lila, and"—she stopped for a breath—"tonight we're going to walk down the strip and listen to the music in a couple of bars. Everything is within walking distance. We went to some of the places Connor mentioned, and we can't wait to be in the Ryman. It's all too much to even describe in words, and we aren't even unpacked yet. Tell me what's going on at home. I'm having the time of my life, but I got to admit, I'm a little homesick."

"Catch your breath, Mama," I said with half a chuckle. "We finished up the strawberry fields today, and Connor asked me for a date tomorrow night. Jasper is getting well and seems to be resigned about taking his medicine. We've been taking his meals out to him, and Gina Lou is a fantastic cook."

"What did you say?" she asked.

"About which one?"

"A date with Connor, and where is he taking you?" Mama's tone wasn't as excited as it had been a few minutes before.

"I have no idea. We're going out for dinner. Are you upset about that?"

"He might recommend good honky-tonks, but he better take my daughter out to a nice public restaurant with cloth napkins. If he gets a six-pack of beer and a couple of bologna sandwiches and drives out to the river, then I might have a problem with it," she said.

"Are you speaking from experience?" I asked.

"I am, and you need to learn from my mistakes. Your father never took me anywhere but the river," she said with a long sigh. "I want more for you than what I got."

"Mama, you were seventeen," I reminded her. "I'm almost thirty."

"Age makes no difference when it comes to lust."

I could hear the worry in her voice. "Mama, stop fretting and enjoy your time away. Tell me where y'all are going first."

"Tonight, we're going to Tootsie's Orchid Lounge, and tomorrow night, the Ryman, for whatever show is playing there. I hope it's a bluegrass event." Excitement had returned to her voice.

I heard a door open and then Annie's voice. "Are you talking to Lila? Did you tell her that we're going home through Memphis so we can go to Graceland?"

"Not yet," Mama answered, "and we're also going to go tour Loretta Lynn's place and eat in her kitchen in Hurricane Mills, Tennessee, on the way back. It would take a month to see everything here."

"Please don't stay away that long," I begged.

"We won't," Annie said, "but we are already planning a trip to Las Vegas. And maybe one to the beach in Florida in November."

"And maybe a cruise in July," Mama piped up.

Gina Lou opened the door and raised an eyebrow. I held up a finger and mouthed, "My mama."

She nodded and disappeared back into the house.

"Sounds like y'all have the travel bug. You will be home for Christmas, won't you?"

"Why?" Annie and Mama asked in unison.

"You know that I've wanted a Christmas wedding since I was a little girl, and it just wouldn't be the same without you walking me down the aisle. Since Aunt Gracie's favorite color was red, it seems fitting, doesn't it? I may cut a little piece of her red underwear, make a rose out of it, and stick it in my bouquet," I teased.

"Sweet Lord!" Mama gasped. "Please tell me you are kidding."

"Gotcha!" I giggled out loud. "Y'all go on and check out Tootsie's. Take more pictures, and maybe don't lean out of the car and do it while you're driving. I wasn't quite sure *where* you were. See you in a couple of weeks. Love you—and, Mama, you don't have a thing to worry about." I ended the call before either of them could say anything else.

Chapter Twenty

Five outfits, from jeans and a T-shirt to the fancy dress I wore to the company Christmas party the year before, cluttered my bed. If I wore jeans for my date and Connor took me to a bougie restaurant in San Antonio, that would be a disaster. If I wore the little black dress with sequins scattered on the bodice and we went to the Dairy Queen in Poteet, that would almost be worse.

Gina Lou knocked on my open door and peeked inside. "All right if I borrow the car this evening? I've got a hot date with Jasper."

"No problem. Thank you for taking him for a ride. Where are y'all going?" I turned my back on all the clothing.

"We are going to my folks' house for ice cream. Daddy is hand-churning some, and if Jasper's not too tired when we come home, we are going to watch an episode or two of the first prequel to *Yellowstone* on television. I haven't ever seen it, and Jasper says the only way to appreciate the series is to start from the beginning." She nodded toward the bed.

"I've never seen that series, either, but I know Jasper will love having a night out." I glanced over at the clothes on the bed. "I wish Connor would have told me where we were going." I sighed. "When in doubt, don't."

"What's that supposed to mean?"

"Mama used to tell me that all the time when I was a teenager," I said. "It means if you have doubts or if you're fighting with yourself, then you better take a step back and figure things out before you jump headfirst into the water."

"Or the frying pan. Mama told me that Derrick was nothing but a scalding-hot skillet. Sweet as strawberry wine one minute and mean as a snake the next. But I wouldn't listen." She pointed at an emerald green sundress. "Wear that one. No matter where you go, it'll be fine. The night could turn out chilly, so take a cardigan or your cute little denim jacket with you."

"Great idea. You and Jasper have a good time. I'll be back by nine to give him his last dose of medicine." I removed my robe and slipped the dress over my head. "It's been so long since I've been out on a real date that I'm acting like a sixteen-year-old."

"You must really like him. There's a full moon out tonight. You know what that means?"

"That I can see better in the dark?" I asked.

She grinned. "No, it means you might get lucky."

"I'm not superstitious." I frowned. "All that old moon will do is light up my freckles even more."

"I'd take those freckles any day of the week if I could have your height to go with them."

I checked my reflection in the mirror and brushed out my hair one more time. "I'd give you both if it was possible."

Gina Lou cocked her head to one side. "I hear a truck pulling up in the driveway."

I grabbed my sweater and purse and started out of the room. Gina shook her head and pointed to my bare feet. "Might be best if you wear shoes."

I slipped my feet into a pair of flats. "Yep, I'm more wound up than I was when I went on my first date." Connor was taller than me, but heels would put me right at eye level with him, and I enjoyed the rare feeling of being short.

"Did you get lucky that night?" Gina Lou giggled.

I gasped. "I did not!"

"Well, you can make up for it tonight," she teased as she hurried down the stairs and headed toward the kitchen.

The back door slammed seconds before Connor knocked. I opened the door and motioned for him to come inside. "You are right on time."

"Grandpa and the army taught me that. You are stunning, Lila." He scanned me from my toes to my eyebrows. "Are you ready?"

"I am, and you look pretty nice tonight, too."

He held his arm out for me. "But I pale in comparison to you, darlin'."

"That is a bit clichéd, but thank you," I told him.

"I'm not much of a romantic," he said on the way to his truck, "but I was speaking the truth."

He looked sexy that evening in his T-shirt, which stretched over his chest and defined every ripped ab and muscle. From that and the fact that his boots weren't polished and his jeans weren't creased, I guessed that we would be eating dinner in Poteet. Annie's Café had reopened sometime early in the week with a different name—the Ambrosia. That sounded pretty fancy for a café in Poteet, Texas. I wondered what the menu would offer. Somehow it didn't seem like they would have sausage gravy and biscuits.

"Are you listening to me, Lila?" he asked.

"Yes," I nodded. "I heard every word. I was just admiring your body."

He shuffled his feet like a little boy flirting with a girl on the school playground. "I won't ever have to worry about you not telling me the truth, will I?"

"No, you will not!" I declared. "I'll be truthful with you every time. When I was a little girl, Aunt Gracie told me that I might hide things from people, but I could never hide anything from God—not even a little white lie. So do the same for me. If I ask you if a dress or my hair or any other thing about me looks all right, tell me the truth, not what you think I want to hear. That way, when I ask you something really important, I'll have confidence that you aren't lying to me."

"Yes, ma'am, I can do that." He slipped my free hand into his. "But what if it causes a big fight between us?"

"Then we'll argue, settle it, and go to the bedroom to make up," I said.

He chuckled. "What if I start a fight just so we can do that?"

"What if *I* start the fight?" I was flirting and it felt so good.

"Lady, you are going to be a handful," he said as he opened the passenger door for me.

"You wouldn't want me to be any other way, would you?"

"No, I would not." He closed the door and whistled all the way around the front of the vehicle and slid in behind the wheel.

"Is that fried chicken I smell?" I asked.

"Busted," he grinned. "I thought I could keep our destination a secret until we arrived. We're having a picnic by the river. I wanted us to have an evening all alone."

Mama's words about where Connor and I would go on our first date came back to my mind: *If he gets a six-pack of beer and a couple of bologna sandwiches and drives out to the river . . .*

Is fried chicken a step up from bologna sandwiches? I wondered as he drove toward the Atascosa River. Driving time was a little less than seven minutes. I knew because more than once, a bunch of us high school kids had driven down to the river to party. My weekend curfew was eleven o'clock, so I could leave ten minutes before the hour and make it home on time.

I'm not a high school senior, I reminded myself. *And this is not an adult dinner date, no matter how good that chicken is.*

He parked the truck near an enormous oak tree with roots as big as my waist running on top of the ground. I looked around for the picnic table, but apparently either a bunch of kids had stolen it or else the wood had rotted and it had been washed away by one of the floods in the last twelve years. Connor opened the door for me and gave me his hand to help me out of the truck.

"Grandpa and I have fished right here ever since I was a little boy," he said as he opened the back door.

When I saw that he had a real picnic basket, a quilt, and a tote bag, I figured that maybe—just maybe—Mama wouldn't think history was repeating itself.

"I'll carry the tote bag." I picked it up and followed him near the tree.

His memories were different from mine. I had had my first beer, my first kiss, and my very first dance with a boy right here under that big tree. Some of the kids I'd partied with shucked all their clothes and dove right in, not caring if the water often looked like thin chocolate milk. I wondered if my parents had ever skinny-dipped in the river.

He spread the quilt out on a grassy area just a few feet from the tree roots and put the basket in the middle. I set the tote bag off to the side, and he dropped down on his knees. "Turn around and don't look until I get everything set up," he said.

The sound of tinkling glass and what sounded like a match being struck added to the duets the tree frogs and locusts were performing. I'd never been fishing in my entire life, but when a couple of fish flopped out there in the water, creating little ripples all the way back to the shoreline, I wondered if Aunt Gracie, Davis, and Jasper had ever come down there. I made a mental note to ask Jasper about it when I took him his evening meds.

"Okay, you can turn around now," Connor said.

It looked like something out of a movie set: Two places set with real plates, wineglasses, and cloth napkins. Twinkle lights all around the quilt and a bouquet of yellow roses in a crystal vase right in the middle.

I gasped. "How did you . . ."

"I wanted you all to myself tonight, but you deserve a special first date." Connor stood up and took me by the hand. "Welcome to Café River. Please come in and be seated."

Mama, there's cloth napkins and flowers. Does that count as a fancy place?

"Would it be all right if I take a picture of the café before we mess it up with food?" I asked.

Connor led me the half a dozen steps to the quilt. "Are you one of those people who post food pictures on Facebook?"

"Nope." I shot half a dozen photos with my cell phone. "But this is so beautiful I want to send a picture of it to my mama. And, Connor, don't kid yourself. You are definitely a romantic."

"Thank you, ma'am. Lila, you are a breath of fresh air to this drowning man," he said.

I wanted to lay my hand on my chest and sigh.

"No comment or smart remark about that being a lame pickup line?" he asked.

"No, I'm enjoying letting it sink into my heart. That is even more romantic than all this is. Whoever told you that you weren't romantic should be exiled from the human race."

"What I said was the truth. Every time I'm around you, it's like the world lights up in Technicolor." He motioned to a place setting.

I truly felt like I was in one of those old romantic movies when I sat down. "Thank you for this beautiful date."

He sat down and leaned across the space and kissed me. "I've ordered a shooting star for you. I hope the company doesn't run out of them before you get yours."

"If they do, we'll have to do this all over again," I whispered.

"Anytime, darlin'. Anytime. Now, there's not a big selection on the menu, but we don't have to wait for it to be cooked and served."

"It's got my favorite food of all time on the menu: fried chicken," I told him.

He passed the container of chicken over to me. "You mentioned that when Gina Lou said they had had it at her folks' house last Sunday."

Yep, a whole lot better than a bologna sandwich and then a romp in the back seat of an old car.

"You pick up on so much. What was it like to be a military kid? Is that part of it?"

"I usually lived on a base with other kids—some younger, some older, and lots in between. I made friends, and then some of them moved, new ones came in, and finally I was the one who moved. We were usually in one place a year, or maybe two. How about you? What was it like to live in Ditto your whole life?"

"Like you said, it was life." I shrugged. "Same friends until I left."

"Do you still keep up with them?"

"Not really." I gave another shrug. I hesitated and bit into a chicken leg, chewed, swallowed, and then took a sip of wine. "I was kind of a loner. I had lots of acquaintances but not many close friends. And those girls all moved away. Facebook doesn't keep people that close in touch."

He took a long sip of his wine. "I liked it here when I came to visit Grandpa in the summers. Which reminds me, I wonder why we never met during those times."

"You were a boy," I whispered.

"So?" he asked.

"Neither Aunt Gracie nor Mama let me have playdates with boys. They were evil little critters," I answered, a laugh escaping.

"Did they tell you that?" Connor's tone was full of pure shock.

"No, but when I made a guy-type friend in kindergarten, they made all kinds of excuses why I couldn't invite him to ride the bus home with me after school. I figured out a few years later why Mama didn't want me to be friends with boys, but I never quite understood Aunt Gracie, since Jasper was her best friend."

"Life is complicated," Connor replied and then leaned over and kissed me on the cheek. "But tonight, I'm sure glad I'm a boy."

"Me too."

Gina Lou was sitting in the dark living room when I got home that evening. I'd already taken a couple of steps toward the kitchen when I heard her whisper, "Well, how did it go? Did he take you somewhere fancy? Is he cooking breakfast?"

"What . . . Why . . ." I stammered.

"Look—I didn't want to cause a problem if Connor was going to stay the night. I had turned off the lights and was going up to my room when I heard y'all drive up. I wasn't spying on you, I promise."

"I've got to take meds out to Jasper. Come on into the kitchen, and we'll talk when I get back."

She followed me and sat down at the table when I flipped on the lights. "So, you're not going to fire me?"

"What are you thinking? Of course not!" I declared and handed her my phone. "Here, look at these pictures while I get things ready to take out to Jasper."

She gasped. "Oh. My. Sweet. Lord! That is the most romantic thing I've ever seen."

"That's just the beginning. Go on through them since you like sunsets and sunrises so well." I had this medicine thing down to an art: pills in the glass, inhaler tucked into the pocket of my sundress.

Jasper frowned at me and pointed at the clock when I stepped inside his house. "You almost broke curfew, young lady."

"It is nine fifteen, and you don't go to bed until nine thirty," I reminded him.

"That's right, but I'm old, and it takes me a while to get into my pajamas and brush my teeth," he smarted off. "I suppose I have to eat something now, too. That will take even more time."

"Quit your fussin' and get busy, then," I told him, refusing to let him take the shine off my evening.

"Get me a couple of cookies and half a glass of milk," he ordered.

"Yes, sir, Captain Jasper."

He narrowed his eyes until they were little more than slits. "Don't you get sassy with me, Lila Grace." His expression changed from anger to a smile. "I miss Gracie so much. She would argue with me just like you do."

I got three cookies from the jar and filled a glass with milk. "Here you go—and I miss her, too, Jasper."

"I know you do, baby girl," he said with an extra-long sigh.

He hadn't called me by that nickname since I was a little girl. When I started to kindergarten, I fussed at him for calling me a baby. Was he getting dementia and thinking that I was still a child? Maybe I should have the doctor check him for that on the next visit. He ate the cookies and swallowed the pills with the last of his milk.

"How was the big date? Did he take you somewhere fancy up in San Antonio?" he asked.

I pointed at the clock. "It's ten minutes past your bedtime. I'll tell you all about it tomorrow at breakfast."

"I'll hold you to that," he said.

I took a couple of steps toward the door. "I promise I will, and I even have pictures to show you."

Had Aunt Gracie felt the same shot of pure passion when Davis kissed her that time like I did with Connor?

"Get on out of here, then, so I can go to sleep. I'll look at them pictures tomorrow." He shooed me out of the house.

I looked up at the star-dotted sky, and there was that falling star Connor had promised.

Chapter Twenty-One

"What kind of name is the Ambrosia?" Jasper's tone matched his expression on Sunday morning—downright grouchy. But I was determined not to let him bring me down off the pretty white cloud I had been floating on since my date with Connor.

"Evidently, the new owner thought it was cute," I said as we walked across the church parking lot to Aunt Gracie's Ford after service that morning. "I'm so glad you felt like going to church today."

"I didn't plan on it, but when I woke up, God told me to get my sorry, skinny butt out of bed and go to church," Jasper declared. "I tried to bargain with Him, but He wouldn't have none of it. He sent Sassy to whine at the edge of my bed. I got up to let her out and figured I might as well fix myself a cup of coffee and stay up."

"God speaks to you?" I asked.

"He don't speak to you?" he fired right back.

"Not audibly."

"Well, I hear His voice in my ear. Like He's sitting right here." Jasper tapped his shoulder with his bony hand.

I couldn't argue, since Aunt Gracie seemed to sit on my shoulder and whisper in my ear more often since she had passed away than ever before. I helped him get settled in the passenger seat. "So, did you get a message out of the sermon this morning?"

He folded his arms over his chest and nodded. "I got the message, but I don't like it. Don't tell me that you did."

I slid into the car and started the engine. "I might have, but my mind kept jumping track and wandering off to pick wildflowers."

"In other words, you were thinking about Connor and that date you had down by the river," Jasper snapped. "You're supposed to go to church to get a message to your soul, not sit there and relive a date."

I drove from the church to the new café. "Maybe that *was* God's message to me."

"Hmmph," Jasper snorted, then coughed. "God don't bring a person to church for them to think about their boyfriend. You're supposed to listen to His word when you're sitting on the pew."

"I guess I just applied His word differently than you did. The message I got was to trust and not have doubts," I said with half a giggle. "What did you get?"

"I don't want to talk about it right now." He looked out the side window. "I hope that this new place didn't throw out Annie's menu and we can get chicken and dressing today."

Annie's Café always had a full parking lot as soon as church services were over, but that morning, I only counted six vehicles. "Looks like we won't have any trouble getting a table."

"Empty parking lot. Poor food and service. I bet they even use instant tea," Jasper muttered, and was out of the car before I made it around to help him.

"If they do, we won't come back." I looped my arm through his to steady him. His croup—as he still called it—had left him a little wobbly.

"If the food ain't no good, we'll go to the Dairy Queen and have a burger next week," he said, loud enough the angels in heaven heard it.

"Jasper!" I scolded.

"I'm making a vow to God. He is not only speaking today but He's listening, because I sure heard Him loud and clear this morning," he said.

The inside of the restaurant was the same as it had been when Annie owned and ran it, except all the old pictures of Poteet had been taken down, leaving white spots on the light brown walls.

"You guys can sit anywhere you want," a waitress called out from a table across the room. "We haven't gotten the place fully remodeled and all the decorations up yet, but we're in business."

"She ain't from around here," Jasper whispered.

I led him to a booth near the back of the dining area and slid into the seat across the table from him. "How do you know that?"

Two of his fingers shot up. "One is that she didn't say *y'all*, and the other is that she ain't got no accent."

The lady hurried right over to us when she finished getting the orders from the other folks. She laid a menu in front of each of us. "My name is Kiki. We are offering our basic burgers all the time, but starting on Sunday, the rest of the menu changes each week. That way no one gets bored with the same old menu all the time. We also have vegetarian options."

"Pleased to meet you, Kiki. We like our bacon and our chicken-fried steaks, so we aren't interested in a vegetarian menu," Jasper said. "You ain't from around these parts, are you?"

Kiki tucked a strand of her brown hair behind her ear. "No, sir, I am not. I grew up in a little town outside of Pittsburgh, Pennsylvania. What can I get you guys to drink?"

"Sweet tea?" Jasper asked.

"We only have unsweet, but I can bring you some sugar packets," she said.

"Then I'll have a root beer." From the set of his jaw, I could tell that we would be going to Dairy Queen next week.

"Same here," I said and then studied the menu. For the next six days we had a choice of three different kinds of soup, six sandwiches or wraps, and salads. And of course, several different burgers, all with cute little names.

In only a few minutes, she brought a glass of ice and a can of root beer for each of us. "Ready to order?"

"I'll have the soup and sandwich—club and baked-potato soup." I handed her the menu.

"I want a burger and fries," Jasper said.

"Which burger?" Kiki asked. "The top three are made with hamburger. The last are black bean burgers."

Jasper rolled his eyes. "I want meat in mine."

"Then do you want the brunch burger with meat, eggs, and cheese; the one with mushrooms and slathered with brown gravy; or the standard one with mayo, lettuce, and tomatoes?" she asked.

"The last one, only I want mustard and pickles."

"We always put a pickle on the side with our sandwiches," Kiki told him.

"I want dill pickle slices on the burger." His voice left no doubt this would be our last visit to this place.

"Sorry, sir, we don't do that with our burgers," Kiki said with a big smile. "But they do come with potato chips."

"Are you open seven days a week?" he asked.

"No, sir, closed on Mondays and Tuesdays. My sister, Deanna, is now the owner of the former Madge's Diner, which is now Pastalicious, and she will be open on those days and closed on the weekends. She's serving up pasta and different kinds of sauces, plus an assortment of salads and flavored teas."

"Like chicken-fried steak?" Jasper asked.

Kiki's smile seemed forced. "No, but she is also open for breakfast and offering bagels with lox and cream cheese, and her pasta and salads for lunch. My hours are eleven to six Wednesday through Sunday. I'll get your order right out. Oh, I forgot to ask how you want that burger cooked. Rare, medium, well done?"

"Well done," I answered for him.

"Dairy Queen next week?" I whispered when Kiki was out of hearing distance.

"I'd walk all the way to San Antonio to eat Sunday dinner before I would come back here," he said out the corner of his mouth. "A steak is mighty fine with pink in the middle, but not a burger."

My sandwich and soup were pretty much the same as what I'd gotten at a lunch place in Austin. But Jasper's burger was open-faced, with a lettuce leaf, a slice of tomato, and a pickle spear on the side, along with a package of mustard. An individual bag of potato chips was on the other side of the fancy oblong plate.

"Enjoy," Kiki said and rushed away to wait on another group coming inside.

"Do I get a discount for building this thing myself?" Jasper asked. "The bun hasn't even been toasted, much less put on the grill until it's nice and brown. We need to send Gina Lou down here to teach these people to cook."

"Next time maybe you should order a cold sandwich and hot soup," I suggested and got his noon pills out of my purse.

Jasper swallowed the pills with a sip of root beer. "There won't be a next time. This is the first and last. Can we go get ice cream at the Dairy Queen after we eat this?"

"Yes, we surely can," I said with a nod. "I've got a question."

"About?"

"Why didn't Aunt Gracie and Mama ever want me to have little friends that were boys?"

"Well . . ." He set about putting his burger together.

I could almost see the little wheels churning in his head with some kind of answer about the weather or Sassy.

He shifted his eyes to the right and then to the left. "It's a bit of a story, and not to be told in a café where there's other folks. Let's go see Gracie and Davis after we eat and then come back to the Dairy Queen for ice cream."

"Whatever you want," I agreed.

"Well, I *wanted* a big old greasy burger, fries, and sweet tea," he huffed. "Experience is what we get when we didn't get what we wanted."

"Who told you that?"

He opened the bag and shook the potato chips out onto his fancy plate. "My granny did, and it's the gospel truth about this place. I can't believe that we aren't ever goin' to have chicken and dressin' again." He sighed and took a bite of his burger.

"I could ask Gina Lou to make it for us at least once a month," I offered.

"I can live with that, but every two weeks would be better," he said.

"Consider it done, but you can't just make a little bit of chicken' and dressin', so you might have to eat leftovers for a few days."

"You'll get no complaints from me," he declared. "The burger ain't bad, but Dairy Queen's are a dang-sight better and a heck of a lot cheaper."

I didn't care about the food. What I couldn't hardly wait for was the answer to my question. I wasn't sure why Jasper wanted to tell me about it in the cemetery, but I wasn't going to even say a word about the *why* or where he wanted to talk.

Jasper sat flat down on the ground and leaned back against Gracie's gray granite tombstone. He patted the place next to him, and I eased down beside him. "She didn't like to be hot, so I'm glad she's resting beneath this shade tree."

A flash of red flew past us and lit on a low limb.

"I was about to ask God for a sign, and He's delivered it," he said. "That bird is telling me that the time has come, and I imagine that Gracie has told God not to let me come to heaven without me doin' what she told me to do."

"What are you talking about?" I asked, but I liked the idea of Gracie watching over us.

"You know what a cardinal means," Jasper said, then went on to tell me again. "It means someone that has gone on to eternity is thinking about you. Gracie is telling me everything is going to be all right. Her spirit is here among us. You asked me about why Gracie and Sarah never wanted you to have boys as friends. Well, the answer is that Gracie was hurt once very badly, and she never trusted men or boys again. Same with your mother. But you've got to understand that Sarah was barely eighteen, and Gracie was only fourteen when she got hurt."

"But you are a guy, and you were her very best friend," I argued.

"Me and Davis both were," he nodded. "I was ready to die when you hauled me to the hospital. Do you have any idea why I got well?"

There he went, changing the subject again. I wasn't going to get any answers from him today.

"Good medicine, rest, and food." I watched the cardinal sit there and stare at us with his beady little black eyes.

"No," he disagreed. "It was because I made a vow to Gracie that I would answer your questions before I died. I want to get this life over with so I can go on to heaven and see my two best friends again, but it was so hard to come out with. You idolized her."

"I love my mama and Aunt Gracie, so there's no tarnishing," I said.

"There isn't just one secret," he whispered and looked all around.

"Jasper! This is turning into something out of *Dynasty*, and boy, did Aunt Gracie like that one." I nudged him with my shoulder.

"Fine. But you got to understand the past to be able to look forward to the future. Gracie was born November 11, and Davis came along a week later and me at the end, right after Thanksgiving. Granny said there was a big party to welcome Gracie into the world when she was about a month old. People came from miles around to see the new baby girl that would one day run Clarence's estate."

He stopped and seemed to be trying to gather his thoughts. "When Davis and I were born, there were no parties. My mama left me with my grandmother a week after I came into this world, and we never saw her again. So, anyway, my granny took me to work with her every day from the time I was a week old. She was nanny to Gracie as well as cook and housekeeper until Davis's mama, Rita, recovered from giving birth to him. Then all three of us babies were in the house together every single day."

"I kind of figured that out on my own," I told him.

He nodded and pointed at the cardinal. "Gracie is giving me the sign to keep talking. So get comfortable because this is not a short story.

"I remember the day that we went to first grade. Rita held Davis's hand, and Granny held mine and Gracie's, and we all five marched into the room to meet our teacher."

He was taking me so far back that we could still be sitting in the front of that tombstone until the cardinal found a mate.

He coughed and went on. "I cried and didn't want to be left behind, but Gracie and Davis did no such thing. They waved at Granny and Rita and went right over in the corner and started whispering to each other. I didn't want to be left out, so I let go of Granny's hand and joined them. We were inseparable from that time on. Not that we hadn't been before, but that day seemed to be a turning point."

"I figured all that out, too," I said.

"Aren't you sassy? Just let me tell this in my own way. I want you to understand that there was a bond between us, but the one between Davis and Gracie went even deeper. I think they might have fallen in love when we were all still crawling around on the kitchen floor."

"Really?" I didn't dare tell him that I had snooped through her diary.

"Yep. Now, fast-forward—as you kids say these days—to that summer before we were fourteen. That was when we got drunk on the strawberry wine and when Davis and Gracie went about holding hands and staring into each other's eyes. Always seemed to me that they could talk to each other without words."

"Did that make you feel left out?" I asked.

"Not in the least. We were all together every day, and we didn't keep secrets from each other. I knew the minute that they admitted they had feelings for each other, and I wasn't a bit jealous of Davis. Seemed like it had been written in the stars even when they were just babies that someday they would be together," he told me.

"Then he got killed, right?"

"No, that came after . . ." He sucked in as much fresh air as his lungs could hold and didn't cough when he let it all out.

"After what?" I expected him to tell me that it was time for us to go get ice cream and go home.

"The party line thing," he whispered. "She always kept those two old phones in the house to remind her of what she heard that night when Davis kissed her for the first time. She said that they were a constant reminder to never trust a man again."

"Did Davis hurt her that badly?" I asked.

Jasper shook his head. "Wasn't Davis that caused her to go to her room for a whole week. Did I tell you why he was named Davis?"

"No, why?"

"His mama was Rita Poteet, and her mama's maiden name was Davis. Her daddy was Billy Poteet."

That part of history didn't mean anything to me. I figured Jasper was rambling, but I kept quiet because I wanted to hear the rest of the story.

"Was he a part of the family that founded the town?" I was confused. Why would Rita be cleaning houses if she came from the county's royalty?

"Yes, he was a cousin to them, but when he married Rita's mama . . ." He stopped and scratched his head, then grinned. "I remember now. Her name was Esther. Anyway, the family blacklisted him because she was kind of what we used to call 'loose legged.' He wound up working as a truck driver and drinking up whatever money he made on the weekends. I got sidetracked with my story. Betty—that would be Gracie's mama—hired Rita to help my granny in the house. Rita was a beautiful young woman, maybe about nineteen when Miz Betty hired her. And about a year later, all of us babies were born. Davis was a family name on Rita's side of the family, so when she gave birth to a baby with no father, that's what she named him.

Folks said that she was just a chip off her worthless father's shoulder. Back then, having babies out of wedlock was a bigger deal than it is these days, and Rita and my mama were paddling the same canoe."

I really didn't want to hear the background of every woman who ever strolled down the streets of Poteet, but suddenly I understood—or thought I did. Gracie's folks were the upper class, and they didn't want their only child tangled up with an illegitimate son.

He glanced up at the cardinal, who was still sitting on the tree limb right above us. "Things kind of rocked on until the night of Gracie's fourteenth birthday, and us being kids, we thought the world was perfect. Except that Gracie was the queen, and me and Davis were the fatherless kids of the help. Davis wanted to do something special for Gracie, but neither one of us had much money. I suggested that he pick the last roses of summer from the bushes beside Rita's house—that would be the one where I live now—and if there wasn't enough to make a bouquet, I would bring some from Granny's old place. He thought that was a romantic idea, and together we fixed it up and tied it with a red ribbon."

I laid a hand on his shoulder. "I found a shoebox tied with a red ribbon down in the basement. Inside was a bunch of dried roses and a wine bottle."

"Probably the same one," Jasper said. "This next part is hard, mainly because it reminds me of Gracie's broken heart and Davis's anger."

"Was he upset because her parents didn't want her tangled up with the help?"

"Well, there was that, and if it hadn't been for the bigger issue, I imagine they would have sent her off to boarding school to get her away from him."

"Bigger issue?" I whispered.

"That night, after her birthday dinner with her folks, she climbed out her window and met Davis in the backyard. He gave her the roses and kissed her. They thought that it was late enough no one would see, but Rita did, and the next morning she called Clarence on the party

224

line that three people shared—my granny, Rita, and Gracie's folks. Miz Betty had the phones put in so that if she wanted Rita or Granny in the middle of the night, she could get a hold of them."

"And Gracie listened in on the conversation, right?" I asked.

Jasper nodded, his face turning very, very serious. "Gracie stormed downstairs and confronted Clarence right in front of Betty."

"What had she heard that upset her so badly?"

"That, darlin' girl, is the big bad secret," Jasper said softly, as if he couldn't say it out loud. "She overheard Rita telling Clarence that they either had to tell the kids the truth or he had to help her move. Clarence said it was for the best and said he would set her up in a nice place in Poteet because he didn't want to stop seeing her."

"What was the truth?" I was all ears by then.

There was a long, pregnant silence that seemed like the air just before a tornado hit. Finally, Jasper broke through the thick, heavy stillness.

"That Davis was Gracie's brother."

That almost took my breath right out of my chest. My poor Aunt Gracie. No . . . poor Davis, who had been shunned and treated like the help.

The world stopped turning, and I sat there in stunned silence, unable to think. Tightness filled my chest, and tears rolled down my cheeks.

"Are you going to faint?" Jasper asked.

"No, but that doesn't mean I'm not shocked and sad for Gracie and Davis," I whispered. "Go on with the story, please."

"The story that Gracie told us was that she stormed down to the living room and confronted her father with a big fight. Betty heard it all, and the two of them had a screaming match right in front of their daughter. Clarence accused Miz Betty right to her face of being cold in the bedroom. Then, in a fit of anger, he said that all she had produced was a daughter, and he couldn't even acknowledge his son because he was married to *her*. Back then, divorce was a pretty big deal—not as huge as fatherless boys, but still it wasn't accepted like it is today. Gracie went back up to her bedroom. She told me and Davis in between sobs that she would never forgive her father for abandoning him or for not telling her that Davis was her brother."

"What happened then?" I asked around a baseball-sized lump in my throat.

"Miz Rita moved into a house in Poteet. We still saw each other at school. 'Course we didn't talk about those things there, and then me and Davis went to the army, and you know the rest. It wasn't long until Miz Betty left. She tried to get Gracie to go with her, but there was no way she would leave me and Davis. I expect, although I do not know for sure, that Clarence kept seeing Rita until the day she died. And now you know the secret of the house."

"Why did Gracie want me to know?" I asked.

"You can ask her when you get to heaven," he said. "She just told me to tell you. What do you intend to do about it?"

"Not one thing," I replied. "For all I care, everyone can think that she had a little wild streak because she wore red panties. If she had wanted the whole state of Texas to know, she would have put it in the *Dallas Morning News* or maybe went on *Oprah* and told it on live television. I have no idea why she's trusted me with it, but she has."

"What about Connor? You going to tell him?" Jasper asked.

"Not even Connor," I vowed. "What's in the past should stay there. It's Gracie's secret, and I can't pass it on."

"That's good," Jasper said. "She never loved another boy, and as far as I know, she never even kissed another one. I would have just as soon taken the story to the grave with me, but she wanted you to know."

"Probably because I was always a nosy little brat." I tried to laugh, but it came out more like a snort.

"She told me that you would find things in the house that would make you wonder. She had pinned notes to her clothing in case she got that forgetful disease. She wanted to remember the past, especially after you came into her life. She always said you were a little piece of heaven on Earth and had brought light back into her heart," Jasper said.

Tears began to stream down my cheeks and drip onto my olive green shirt. Swiping them away was useless because more kept taking their place. "That's quite a thing to have to live up to."

Jasper put his arm around my shoulders. "Let it out, Lila. You haven't had a really good cry since Gracie died. You've had to be strong for your mama and for me, but it's time for me to be a rock for you now. And like I said, that's not the only secret I have to tell you."

"I'm not sure I can handle much more today." My tears left wet circles on his suit coat.

His whole wrinkled face changed to be even more serious than it had been. "Well, you have to, because I'm not going to live forever, and someday I might need some help like she did."

My breath caught somewhere in my chest, and I couldn't make myself exhale. "What are you talking about?" I asked, even though I pretty well knew what the answer was.

"She never forgave Clarence for what he did or her mother for leaving her, but she did sit beside her father's bedside the last two weeks of his life. He had congestive heart failure, and he refused to give up his cigarettes or his liquor. Then he got lung cancer, and he died a hard death, gasping for every breath. He wanted to die at home, so she granted him that wish. He begged her to forgive him, but she couldn't do it, not until a few minutes before he passed."

"I'm not so sure I could have forgiven him, either. I'm glad I didn't have to meet my own father," I said in a low voice.

"She finally said the words that let him go in peace. I didn't ask if she meant it or if she was just too tired to argue anymore. His last words were 'Davis, I am so sorry I didn't do the right thing by you.' Then he was gone."

"Is that the second secret? That she forgave her father?" I asked.

"No, ma'am. The second one is that last year, the doctor told her she had congestive heart failure and spots on her lungs that should be biopsied for cancer. She told him no on the biopsy thing and that she was too danged old for any of that chemo crap. She and I had a good year together knowing that it was our last one."

"Hey, now, how did she know that?" I argued.

"No one could ever tell Gracie Evans that she would finish this life on anyone's terms but her own or that anyone else could set her expiration date. We decided on a time, and I tried to back out, but she wouldn't have none of it. The cough had gotten worse, and she was in pain. Going up the stairs took three or four tries, and she would be exhausted at the top." Now tears were rolling down his thin cheeks, settling in the deep wrinkles.

We both simply sat there for a few minutes. I was sure I knew what was coming next, but I didn't want to hear it. The cardinal left his perch on the tree limb and flitted down the cemetery a ways until it came to rest on Davis's tombstone.

"I guess that's my second sign," Jasper finally said. "So, to get to the end of this story, the date came that she had marked on her calendar. She had the pills ready, and all I had to do was crawl up in the bed with her and hold her until she went to sleep. She warned me that if I called 911 or Sarah before she quit breathing that she wouldn't let Saint Peter open heaven's gates for me. She told me she loved me and that I'd been the best friend a woman could ever want, and that she was going home to be with Davis. Her last words were 'I loved him so much.' And then she went to sleep. I held her until she stopped breathing. It was so peaceful, sitting there in her bedroom with her in my arms. I was with her when her dad died, and her passing was nothing like when we watched Clarence take his last breath."

"Then you called 911 and Mama?" I sobbed.

He handed me the blue bandanna from his pocket. "That's right, and if a doctor tells me that I've got maybe a year or two to live if I don't get treatment, I will be doing the same thing she did. Promise me you'll be the one who sits by my side until my soul has gone to be with Gracie and Davis."

"I promise," I whispered and hoped that I wouldn't have to make good on it for a long time.

"Good, and now would you look at that? The cardinal has flown away. Gracie is at peace at last. Help me up, Lila. It's time for us to go get our ice cream."

Chapter Twenty-Two

I was glad that the house was empty when I got home that evening. I really, really liked Connor. Maybe I was even falling in love with him. And Gina Lou had fast become a good friend. Still, I needed time to process what Jasper had told me. I went from room to room and mourned Aunt Gracie like I had not done at her funeral, or even since. I cried for the love she never had, for the way she must have felt when she found out Davis was her brother. But most of all I wept for the guilt she would have experienced knowing that she had been the princess and he was treated like a stable hand. He had lived in a tiny house in the backyard, and she'd had all the luxuries that money could buy.

I made my way up to her bedroom, shoved the panties off onto the floor, and stretched out on her bed. She hadn't left all those little clues for me, but for herself in case she ever got dementia. The diary had been shoved into a drawer to rest beneath her underwear—panties that her mother had forbidden her to wear—so that she didn't have to look at it and remember that horrible day when she lost respect for her father and also lost the love of her life at the same time. I wondered why it hadn't been relegated to the shoebox with the dried roses and wine bottle, but I was sure she had her reasons.

I knew the big secret now, and I had vowed that I would never tell anyone, not even Connor. When Jasper had joined his precious Gracie and good friend Davis in eternity, the secret would be safe with me. I focused on the pink floral wallpaper and muttered, "But why did you even want him to tell me? Why not my mother? That would have put her mind at ease about ghosts in the house."

"Lila, are you there?" Mama's voice echoed off the walls of the room. "Answer me. Are you all right?"

"I'm fine," I whispered. Maybe there were ghosts in the house after all. If Mama could answer my questions from a thousand miles away, then there had to be something strange going on.

"Your voice sounds muffled!" Mama yelled.

That's when I realized I had butt-dialed my mother on my cell phone. I fished it out of my pocket and took it off speaker mode. "Is that better?"

"Yes, I was about to call the Poteet sheriff and send them out to Ditto for a wellness call." Her tone sounded frantic. "All kinds of things shot through my mind. I heard you talking about ghosts, and a shiver went down my back."

"I didn't mean to call you. My phone was in the pocket of my skirt, and I must've rolled over on it and hit redial," I told her.

"Where are you right now, this minute?" she demanded.

"I'm at home, in Aunt Gracie's room." I hopped off the bed and picked up all her underwear. "I'm doing a little straightening up in here and got tired, so I stretched out on her bed for a few minutes. Where are you?"

"We're still in Nashville." Mama's tone told me she was excited. "We're going to the Belle Meade Plantation today—that shows up in so many of the stories I've read. Did you and Jasper go to church this morning?"

"Yes, and then we went to Annie's—I mean . . . the Ambrosia, for lunch. Jasper declares it's a one-and-done experience. I agree with him. The whole menu is changed, and they serve burgers on cold buns."

Mama snorted with laughter. "I bet that went over like a lead balloon."

"Yep, it did for Jasper," I agreed and laughed with her.

"Did you take him to the cemetery after lunch?" Her voice sounded like it had a touch of homesickness in it.

"Yes," I said, "and then to the Dairy Queen for ice cream after that. We've only been home a little while. He's feeling so much better that he should be well by the end of the week when he takes his last medication."

"Thank you," Mama said and then sighed.

"For what?"

"Aunt Gracie made me promise not to talk you into moving back to Ditto. It had to be your choice. But if you decided to stay in Austin, then I had to give her my word that I would look after Jasper," she explained. "Now that you are there, I can travel and do things I've always thought would never be possible."

"Family takes care of family," I told her. "Jasper is as much my grandpa as Everett is Connor's. You don't have to have the same DNA to be family."

"What about Connor?" she asked. "I was so excited about the Grand Ole Opry that I didn't ask where he took you on your date."

I slapped my forehead. I'd been so careful not to bring up Connor's name. Now that I had accidently let the cat out of the bag, I might as well feed the thing.

"I'll send you pictures right now so you can see. I clean forgot to send them. We went to the river, but we didn't have bologna sandwiches. And, Mama, he came over the last two evenings. We sat on the porch and talked for hours. Here they come . . ."

"Oh. My. Goodness!" she gasped. "Do I really see cloth napkins?"

"You do, and a bottle of very good wine."

"I hear something in your voice, Delilah Grace. Are you falling in love with him?"

"Yes, I am," I admitted. "I asked him outright if he was only interested in me so he could sweet-talk me out of my house and land. He assures me that he is not, and I believe him. Even if we ever did get married, this place is mine and will be forever."

"Are you still not going to renew Everett's lease on the strawberries?" she asked.

"I need something to keep me busy and so I will feel productive," I replied, "so yes, ma'am, I'm going to be a strawberry farmer. I might even start going to the meetings of all the growers in this area. I want to talk to you and Annie about working for me part-time when I start making strawberry wine."

"Annie is back from her workout in the little gym here in the hotel," Mama said. "We'll talk more later—and, honey, be careful with all your decisions."

"Will do," I said, "and y'all have a good time."

I shoved the phone back into my pocket and started down to the kitchen to get a glass of tea when I heard, "Lila!"

There was no mistaking that the voice was Connor's, but how had I accidently called him? I jerked the phone out, but the screen was dark.

"Lila, are you home?" he called out again.

I realized that he was yelling from the front porch and picked up my pace. "I'm on my way down. Come on in."

We met in the foyer, and he wrapped me up in his arms. "I know I just saw you last night, but this has been a very long day. I missed you so much." He tipped up my chin with his fist and kissed me—long, lingering, and hotter than the tip of the devil's little forked tail. My arms snaked up around his neck, and I leaned into his body. Chest against chest. Heartbeats in unison.

I wished I could stay right there forever in our own little bubble, where the world and all the people in it disappeared, but he finally took a step back and gave me one final kiss on the forehead.

"I might live now," he said and took my hand in his and led me into the kitchen.

Something had changed in the house when he kissed me that time. It felt like one of those musicals that is shown on television when the music at the end is playing as the credits roll. The happily ever after has been reached after obstacles and loops have been overcome, and the couple are together. No more ghosts, no more eerie feelings—just pure old unadulterated joy filled the house.

"Was that as good for you as it was for me?" he teased.

"Well, darlin', I don't know whether to drink the iced tea I'm about to fix for us or pour it down my shirt. Does that answer your question?"

"Perfectly. Can I help?"

Ice cubes clinked against the tall glasses and then crackled when I poured the tea in on top of them. "Nope, but let's take our tea out to the porch, and I'll tell you all about the new café."

"Why not the back porch?" he asked.

"Jasper is taking his nap, and if Sassy hears someone talking, she might wake him up," I explained.

"Front porch, it is," he agreed and carried the two glasses through the foyer and outside.

He waited for me to be seated and then handed me the tea. Then he took a seat and a long drink before he said, "I meant it when I said I missed you. This morning it seemed like the minister was never going to end his sermon, and then he called on Hoot McGeady to deliver the benediction. Hoot thanked God for everything from the day dirt was created and for the rainbow that appeared in the sky after the great flood to the food that we would be partaking of this day and at least four of his previous meals."

"Compared to that, we had a very good service," I chuckled.

"Then Grandpa had heard that neither of the two new cafés had chicken and dressing or even chicken-fried steaks on the menu. We stopped at the Dairy Queen, but it was jam-packed, so we ended up driving up to San Antonio for lunch," he said. "I would have gladly had a bologna sandwich or a can of soup with you rather than the steak that took forever to cook and bring to our table."

I reached up and patted his cheek. "Poor baby. Did this day just plumb test the Jesus in you?"

"It sure did, but I'm here now, and being with you makes me happy." He leaned over and kissed me.

"Sweet tea sure tastes better when mixed with a kiss than it does when it's coming out of the glass," I told him.

"I'm not so sure about that," he said as he leaned in for another.

I was practically panting when the kiss ended. A whole gallon of sweet tea wouldn't be able to cool me down. "Well?"

"Still not sure." He picked me up like I was no heavier than a snow-flake and set me on his lap. "Let's give it one more try."

Fifteen minutes later, I wiggled free of his embrace, set the tea on the porch, took him by the hand, and led him inside. "Slow just stopped," I whispered.

"What does that mean?" he asked.

"I know we said we were going to take it slow, but . . ." I started up the stairs and had only made it to the second step when he scooped me up and carried me to the top.

"Which room is yours?" he asked.

I pointed to the open door. "I have to give Jasper his medicine at nine."

"That gives us three hours," he whispered, "and then the rest of the night to make up for the time you are gone."

"I like that idea." I closed the door with my foot as we went inside.

Chapter Twenty-Three

"You could stay the night," I suggested at nine o'clock when I made my weak knees get up out of the bed and get dressed.

"We're taking things slow, remember?" Connor teased as he jerked on his jeans. "We'll take the sleep-over step on down the road, but tonight was amazing, Lila." He circled around the bed and kissed me.

"Yes, it was," I agreed.

If only Jasper didn't still need medicine, I thought.

Then a little voice inside my head reminded me that Connor and I had just spent some fantastic time together—with no phone calls. One miracle a day was all anyone could ever ask for.

We started down the stairs, and halfway down he brought me close to his body and kissed me again. Two steps more and he did the same. My whole body was humming by the time we reached the foyer. He walked me backward to the door, and one steamy hot kiss led to another one. I was pinned against the wall—with no complaints—when the door opened and Gina Lou interrupted us.

"Good night, Lila," Connor whispered softly, his warm breath on my neck every bit as hot as his kisses. "Evenin', Gina Lou."

"I guess this means you aren't making breakfast?" she teased.

"Not this time." He grinned and disappeared out into the darkness.

The wall was still supporting me because if I took one step, my wobbly knees were sure to fail me. "Did you . . ." I panted. ". . . have a—"

"I had a wonderful day, but it looks like you had a better one. Let's go get out the leftover peach crisp and the milk and talk. I'll go first to give you time to catch your breath. Derrick goes to our church, and he cornered me tonight out in the parking lot." She headed toward the kitchen.

My heart slowed down enough that I could take a few steps, then a few more until I sank down into a chair. A roller coaster of emotions and questions flooded my mind. Connor had proven more than once that evening that he was a man, so why didn't he want to spend the night? Why wait when we had taken down the stop sign when it came to going slow?

Then it dawned on me what Gina Lou had said, and I gasped. "Wait, Derrick?" I screeched.

"Yep, the sorry sucker asked me out on a real date. I almost caved, Lila." She set two bowls of peach crisp on the table and a glass of milk before me. "I probably deserve a gold star or a shot of Jim Beam, but this will have to do for tonight," she said and took a drink of her milk.

"Did you say yes?" I asked.

"I did not!" Her voice went up a couple of octaves. "Burn me once, shame on you. Burn me twice, shame on me."

"Isn't that *fool* me once?"

"Same difference. Besides, why would he want to date me now? He made it clear I was beneath him when I was a waitress. Now I clean houses and mow lawns—which reminds me, I'm doing yard work tomorrow to work off some of this anger," she said through gritted teeth.

"You did the right thing," I assured her and pushed back my chair.

She held up both palms. "Hey, you can't leave. We haven't talked about that scalding-hot scene I disturbed. Sorry if it was the prelude to y'all leaving your clothing strung from the foyer to your bedroom."

"I'm not leaving, and there wasn't any bras or shirts on the staircase," I said as I dipped up another helping of peach crisp and poured myself a second glass of milk.

"You must've worked up quite an appetite," she said.

I sat back down at the table. "Yes, I did, but I don't kiss and tell the details."

Gina Lou finished off the last of her milk. "You really don't have to. You are flushed and your lips are bee-stung, and sucking on a green persimmon couldn't wipe that smile off your face. Have you ever felt this way about anyone else?"

I shook my head.

"Then you've found your gold mine. I thought Derrick was mine, but I found out he was just fool's gold. Pretty and shiny, and worth nothing."

So, Connor was a gold mine, was he? I couldn't think of a single comeback for that one because I agreed with Gina Lou wholeheartedly.

Gina Lou found time to put a chicken in the slow cooker before she went outside to work on the lawn on Monday. I spent the morning in San Antonio with the lawyer who had always handled Aunt Gracie's affairs. Sending both Gina Lou and her sister to college in the fall would be no financial burden with all the money that had been left to me, and if I wanted to build a place to make my strawberry wine, that was totally feasible. That afternoon, I wandered through a shopping mall and wound up buying new red underwear from Victoria's Secret.

Tuesday evening, Gina asked for the car to go take her mother for groceries. Jasper's pill bottles were almost empty. Only three more days to go, and he would be free of taking medicine. I took his supper—meat loaf and mashed potatoes—out to him and sat on the porch with him while he scarfed down every bite.

"Man could get real spoiled to having food brought out to him three times a day, but after I get done with all them pills, you don't have to do this, Lila," he said.

"Even after Gina Lou leaves us, I have to eat, and it's much easier to make food for two than it is for one," I told him. "Or I might just hire someone to cook for us."

"So, she's leaving us in the fall?" he asked.

"I talked to the lawyer yesterday. I have control of the estate, but I wanted his advice," I said with a sigh. "And he thought it was putting the money to good use."

"That's good," Jasper said. "Now, what about Connor? I hear his truck leaving about nine o'clock every night. Does that mean you aren't having breakfast together?"

"Not yet."

Jasper patted his lap, and Sassy jumped up onto it. "You kids today have it better in some ways than me and Gracie did when we were your age. Folks might get frisky out behind the barn, but they did not ever move in together."

"You just want to see me settled and having grandbabies for you to rock," I teased.

"That's right, and Sassy wants a baby to protect," Jasper said. "But I want to talk about something else. Now that a couple of days have gone by since I told you what I did, how are you feeling?"

"Strangely enough, more at peace than ever before. The house seems to have a new energy to it, like it's alive after being in a coma for years and years."

"Granny told me that Clarence and Betty were the golden couple of this area from the time they were in high school until whatever happened that fall when Rita moved to Poteet. She never knew what caused them to change, but she figured it was because Betty and Rita had words. They were both pretty high strung in those days. I let her think that even though I knew better."

"How long after that did Betty leave?"

Jasper frowned as if he couldn't quite remember. "It was kind of a gradual thing. She had friends that she'd known in school. One in particular that she went up to Oklahoma City to spend time with."

"Didn't she hate to be away from Gracie?"

"Granny was still alive in those days. Gracie was a teenager, so she didn't need much looking after," Jasper said. "Clarence tried to get back on her good side, but Gracie wasn't having none of that. I reckon he was still seeing Rita on the sly even then. He loved Betty, but Rita was like a magnet for him."

I handed him his pills and he swallowed them with a sip of tea. "How do you know all that?"

"I don't for sure, but I'm speaking from experience. I loved one woman in my life, but there were others that I was drawn to," he admitted.

"Was it Gracie?" I asked.

"Yep, but she was in love with Davis from the time we were babies. There was something indescribable between them. I couldn't have her, so I was quiet about my feelings. But I've had what you kids call 'flings' through the years with others. They were loves of the mind and body, not of the heart. Which one is Connor?"

The question caught me so much by surprise that for a minute I couldn't form a single thought to answer his question. Finally, I said, "The heart."

"Good, then it will last. Connor should be here soon. You go on and get freshened up to see him. Don't drag your feet and let a good thing slip through your fingers," Jasper said.

I kissed him on the forehead. "Connor and Everett have something they have to take care of in San Antonio. Dinner with some oil executives. He won't be by tonight, but he promised that we'd go out tomorrow evening for burgers. See you at nine."

"I'll be right here or else in the house. Sassy likes to watch shows with me in the evenings, so we go on inside pretty early. Thanks again for bringing her to me. She sure is a lot of company," Jasper said.

"I'm glad," I told him as I headed out across the yard, with intentions of going over the books for the estate.

On Wednesday morning, I was awakened by my mother's voice. "Lila, are you awake?"

In my half-asleep state, I figured I had butt-dialed her again, and I checked under the sheets for a few seconds before I heard actual footsteps on the stairs. She eased open the door and peeked inside. Wide eyed, I glanced over at the pillow with Connor's head indention still on it and shoved it off onto the floor. I rubbed my eyes and blinked several times to be sure I wasn't dreaming.

She picked up the pillow, laid it back where it belonged, and gave me a quick hug. Then she sat down in the wooden rocking chair at the end of the bed. "Annie and I got a little homesick and came home late last night. Something has changed in this place, Lila. That eerie feeling is gone. What happened? Did you burn white sage or something while I was away?"

"Ghosts want someone to release them to go rest in peace," I told her. "Gina Lou and I've been cleaning out the place, and we tossed everything that might have had a lingering spirit in the trash. Plus, I've been filling the place up with love."

"Connor?" she asked and sniffed the air. "He's spent time in this room. I can smell his cologne."

"Yes, Connor, and yes, he has been in this room."

"Does it look like there might be a future?" she asked.

I smiled. "Yes, ma'am. But he hasn't spent the night. We're taking it slow."

"You look happy," she said.

"I am, Mama. Do you and Annie want to help me make wine? It would be a great part-time job for y'all."

"Maybe so," she said with a smile. "I'll talk to Annie about it. We've got plans for some more traveling, but we'll have until next spring to make up our minds, right?"

I threw back the covers, got out of bed, and gave her another hug. "Absolutely. Now, I'm going to take a quick shower, and then we'll go have some breakfast. Gina Lou will have it ready by then. She's been wonderful. I'll miss her in the fall, and we'll talk about that while we eat."

"Good mornin'," Gina Lou called out as she walked past the open door. "Hello, Sarah! Good to see that you are back home."

"Glad to be here," Mama said.

The smell of coffee and the buzz of conversation reached me when I left the bathroom. Mama's voice was higher pitched, and the Texas accent was stronger than Gina Lou's. I stood in the shadows outside the kitchen and listened to Mama talk about her trip. Excitement oozed with every word, and I was so glad she had made so many good memories.

"Hey, why didn't you wait for me?" I asked as I entered the room and went straight for the coffeepot.

"I don't mind telling my stories over and over again," Mama declared, and went straight into describing the Hank Williams Museum again. "Aunt Gracie loved him so much. She said when he died she was twenty-three years old, and she cried for a week. I wished that she could have been there to see his car and watch the old reels of him when he played on the Grand Ole Opry stage."

I sat down beside her and covered her hand with mine. "Remember what you told me about going to the beach so she could see it through your eyes? Well, I reckon she saw the museum through you as well. She would be so happy that you are going places she wanted to see and that the mother and daughter bond y'all had lets her visit them, too."

Mama swiped her wet cheeks with a paper napkin. "Maybe that's why the weird aura in this house is gone. She is getting to do some things that she never did through me."

"Probably so," I said.

Gina Lou grabbed a napkin and dabbed at her eyes. "That is a beautiful thing."

"Yes, it is, and I've got something else to tell you that I hope you think is as wonderful. This fall Aunt Gracie wants to give you and your sister both a scholarship to go to college," I told her.

Her eyebrows drew down. "How can Gracie give me anything? She's gone."

"She left a certain amount for scholarships . . ." It wasn't a lie. She did have a fund set up while she was alive to help women in need. "And since I'm the one who takes care of the estate, I'm giving you and Stephanie funds for books, tuition, dorm fees, and a cafeteria card. You can save what you make this summer for spending money."

"Are you serious?" Gina Lou plopped down in a chair.

"Yes, I am," I told her. "All you have to do to keep the scholarship from one semester to the next is pass all your courses. Same for your sister."

"I'm dreaming, right?" she whispered.

"No, darlin', you are wide awake," I replied.

"Can I tell Stephanie?"

"Why don't we make a party of it and invite your family to dinner tomorrow night? Lila can announce it then," Mama suggested. "Annie and I will help cook and organize. It's been a long time since a party has been held in this house."

"And we can ask Jasper and Connor, too?" Gina Lou asked.

"Of course." Mama shot a look at me. "I need to get to know Connor. He could very well be the father of my grandchildren someday."

"Mama!"

"Well, I'm right and that's the truth," she said. "I'm a new person since I've traveled outside of Texas. I'm not going to judge all men by your biological father anymore. There are a few good guys out there. Take George Strait, for an example. He's been married for more than fifty years, and I've never seen any rumors on him in those trashy magazines."

"The hero of Poteet, Texas, wouldn't dare," I said in mock horror. "Aunt Gracie would have given him a talkin' to if she'd seen his face on one of those things. And nobody would want her to be angry with them."

Mama's eyes darted around the room. "She's not here anymore."

Gina Lou got up from the table and brought a pan of hot cinnamon rolls out of the oven. "Breakfast is served—and, Miz Sarah, I do believe that Gracie decided to stay behind in Nashville for a few more days. You don't have to worry about her coming back to this house. She's done with it."

"Thank you," I mouthed.

Gina Lou glazed the rolls and set the pan in the middle of the table. "I love the idea of a party tomorrow evening. I'll tell Mama that the family is coming to tour the house. What are we serving? Is it going to be a sit-down meal?"

"Let's do it up right with Aunt Gracie's good dishes," Mama suggested. "We can make a ham and have all the trimmings. I'll do the hot rolls."

My phone rang. I fished it out of my back pocket and okayed the FaceTime call.

"Good morning, Connor," I said. "Mama came home a day early. I'm having cinnamon rolls and coffee with her and Gina Lou. Want to come over and share?"

"Can't. Grandpa and I have another meeting today, and we'll be late getting out of it, but I might be able to come by about seven," he said.

"That sounds great, and tomorrow night we're having a little dinner party for Gina Lou's folks. Can you come to that?" I asked, and then added, "And bring Everett with you."

"Wouldn't miss it for the world," he said. "Y'all enjoy your breakfast."

Chapter Twenty-Four

The dining room table would accommodate fifteen people, and every seat was full when we all sat down for supper. Maybe Mama had been right about ghosts being in the house, because I could feel Aunt Gracie hovering around. In my imagination she had a big smile on her face when she looked at Gina Lou's parents—Rachel and John—and her six siblings. At one time I swear I saw her even wink at me and give me a nod of approval.

Connor nudged me with his shoulder. "What are you thinking about?"

"How nice it is to have a full table," I whispered.

"Connor tells me that you are thinking about running the strawberry farm when my lease is up," Everett said.

"Yes, I am, and maybe even making strawberry wine." I noticed that John had finished the last of his hot roll, so I passed them around the table.

"I can't ever remember a time when this table has been full," Mama said. "It feels good."

"Amen," I agreed. "And Gina Lou has an announcement to make while we are here together, but before she does . . ." I raised a glass. "To many more times like this."

Connor clicked his glass against mine. "Hear, hear!"

Jasper touched his to Everett's and then John's. "I hope that folks in heaven can look down on us, because if they can, Gracie will be so proud to see this."

Gina Lou pushed back her chair and stood up. "I can't do this without crying, so, Lila, you're going to have to tell them."

I got to my feet. "I'm not sure I can, but I'll give it my best try. Mama says that Aunt Gracie was an early proponent of women empowering other women, and I want to keep that legacy alive. She gave several young women scholarships to go to college. She helped others open a small business or helped them be productive in many other ways. So I am giving Gina Lou and Stephanie both scholarships to the college of their choice. The funds will go toward books and tuition, also for dorm and meal fees—or if Gina Lou and Stephanie would rather share an apartment and cook their own food, that's an option."

The only sound in the whole room was the rustle of my dress on the wooden chair seat when I sat back down. Stephanie's eyes were as big as saucers. Tears dripped off Gina Lou's and Rachel's cheeks.

John cleared his throat twice and then said, "You've done so much for Gina Lou, giving her a job and letting her live here and"—he paused and wiped his eyes with his napkin—"and even letting her borrow your vehicle. We can't accept something this big."

"It's Gracie's money that is doing this," Jasper said. "So I guess you'll have to argue with her, and that's going to be a tough job."

"I still think I'm dreaming," Gina Lou said.

"Thank you," Stephanie whispered.

"*Thank you* is hardly enough," Rachel said. "What can we do to repay you?"

"Well . . ." I paused. "I've given this a lot of thought, and maybe y'all won't even be interested in what I've got in mind. I sure don't want to make Brenda at the Dairy Queen mad at me for poaching her help, but when Gina Lou leaves, I could use someone to clean house and cook. And, John, I don't know what you're doing now, but I'm going to need someone to oversee the strawberry crops. I'm learning how they regrow in the fall and spring, but someone who understands all the business would be great."

Grow. That word stuck in my head. Just a short while ago, I had met Connor, and look how much our relationship had grown.

"Gina Lou tells me that y'all grow some for your own use, so I reckon you'll know what to do, even if it is a bigger operation," I went on. "And, Rachel, I plan to use a lot of my strawberries for making wine, so you could also help Annie and Mama in the winery I'm going to build. They haven't agreed to help me, either, but none of you have to decide today. You've got all summer to think about it."

"We'll talk it over," John said. "And I'll add my thanks to the girls'. Like Gina Lou said, this is a dream come true for them."

"And like Jasper said, you can thank Aunt Gracie." I smiled.

"Speaking of possible and definite changes . . . ," Everett said. "Connor?"

"Now?" he asked.

Everett smiled. "No time like the present."

"You deliver the news," Connor said.

"Okay, then," Everett said with a nod. "I'm retiring and moving to one of my rental properties here in Ditto—the little house next to Sarah's place. I'm not waiting around for Connor to hear my will read. He's young and more than able to take over my businesses. Except for the strawberries. I'm breaking my lease, Lila, and turning that over to you as of right now."

"What are you going to do? Take up knitting?" Jasper asked.

"No, I'm taking a page from Sarah's book," Everett said. "I've always wanted to travel, but my wife was a homebody. The first thing on my agenda is that I'm going on an Alaskan cruise for senior citizens at the end of May. Then I'm going to fly down to the Bahamas and spend a few days with my son. If I like the cruise thing, I may do a long one to see more of the world. You want to go with me, Jasper?"

"No, sir!" he declared and shook his head. "I'm a homebody, too, and them cruises probably wouldn't let me bring Sassy with me. I'll just stay right here in Ditto, and you can tell me all about your adventures when you come home."

I leaned over toward Connor and laid my head on his shoulder. "Change is good, right?"

"We're fixin' to find out!"

Everyone had left after the party except for Gina Lou and Stephanie. In my mind I pictured them in Gina Lou's bedroom with their phones out and their thumbs working overtime to find what beginning classes they would take in the fall at the University of Texas in San Antonio.

Connor and I finally had a minute to ourselves, and took a couple of cold beers to the front porch. We sat down on the porch swing, and he cupped my face in his hands. "I've been wanting to do this all evening." His lips closed on mine, and once again we were in our own little bubble. When he pulled away, I laid my head on his shoulder and my hand on his chest.

"I love to feel your heartbeat," I said.

He kissed me on the top of my head. "If it ever quits beating, you'll have to take the blame for breaking it."

"I would never, ever . . . ," I promised.

"Then you aren't upset that I didn't tell you earlier that Grandpa was retiring and I was stepping into his shoes?" he asked.

I leaned back so I could see his eyes. "Darlin', we've both been testing each other to be sure that we're ready to commit."

The corners of his mouth turned up in a smile. "You really do speak your mind."

"You've known that from the beginning. Look!" I pointed to the sky. "What?"

"A falling star," I said.

"Then we get to make a wish, right?" he asked. "I'll go first. I wish that when Gina Lou leaves in August, we could move in together. You can choose which house we live in."

I snuggled in closer to him. "I thought we were taking things slow."

"We are," he assured me with a kiss on the forehead. "I love you, and I'm ready to commit, but there have been so many changes in our lives to get used to that we don't need to try to live together with someone else in the house. How about September 1?"

"Why that date?" I asked.

"Because that's six months from the day we met." His thumb made little circles on my arm and turned up my internal heat to the scalding-hot level. "And then maybe we'll have a Christmas wedding? We can't get married in October because we'll be knee deep in your first harvest. November won't work, since we'll be planning Jasper's birthday party."

"I'm not easy to live with. I speak my mind and I don't like to cook," I whispered, and then gasped. "Did you just ask me to marry you?"

"No, ma'am, I did not," he answered. "When I do, you won't have to wonder about whether I did or not. I just said that maybe we would have a December wedding."

"Can you tell me two reasons why you want to marry me or even live with me?" I asked.

He held up one finger. "Because I've fallen in love with you." Another finger joined the first one. "And two, because I've fallen in love with you, Lila Matthews. Now, you tell me two reasons why you would say yes to living with me or marrying me."

"One, because you make me happy, and two, because I love you."

Epilogue

A conversation in the next aisle of the grocery store stopped me in my tracks on the Saturday morning before Easter. Two ladies were talking about which wine to buy for dinner the next day.

The one with a nasal twang said, "Well, I'm picking up three bottles of Strawberry Grace. It sells out within days of them stocking it here."

"Can I help you ladies?" a stock boy asked.

"We were just talking about this strawberry wine," the one with a smoker's voice said.

"I just put out a case this morning," he said. "That was twelve bottles, and there's only six left."

"Not anymore," Smoker said. "I'm taking the last three. You best go get another case."

"Can't." His voice faded as he walked away, but I heard, "We could only get one this season. The big cities have found it, and they preorder as much as they can get."

"Mama, why did you stop?" my nine-year-old daughter asked. "Daddy will be waiting for us."

I tucked her red hair behind her ear. "I was thinking about how neat it is that your daddy and daughter dance next weekend is right at the end of the spring strawberry season."

She seemed to float on air as she walked along beside me. "I'm so happy that he's going shopping with us to find my dress. Jasper is jealous because I get Daddy all to myself, and he can't go."

"Your little brother can stay home with me." I set all my items on the cash register conveyor belt. "We'll have a mama-and-son night and watch a movie."

Grace popped her hands on her hips. "Is he going to get to invite his friend Thomas to come over?"

"No, but if he did, you get the night with your dad, right?"

"Yes, but . . ."

"Grace Thurman, you can't be selfish," I scolded. "You are going to get to go shopping and buy a new dress for the dance, and your daddy is spending the whole evening with you."

Her grin reminded me of Aunt Gracie's. "Yep, and I will have the most handsomest daddy there."

"Yes, you will," I agreed.

"I want a red dress," she declared. "And will you do my nails with red polish?"

"I suppose you want red shoes, too?" I asked.

"Yes, ma'am!"

Connor chuckled when Grace chose a bright red dress for the dance. "We marked our baby girl, didn't we?"

I kissed him on the cheek. "Oh, yes, but then we couldn't expect anything else. We made Grace's room into a nursery for her. Then we named her Grace and have raised her to be independent."

"I'm glad that Jasper and Grandpa got to spend some time with her. I wish they could have lived long enough to know that we named our son Jasper Everett after both of them," Connor said with a sigh.

I slipped my arm around his waist as we made our way to the checkout counter. "They know. If we were to have a third child and it was a boy, would we name him Davis?"

"Are you trying to tell me something?" he asked.

"Well, we do have one empty bedroom in our house," I teased.

"It does seem a shame to leave that room empty, doesn't it?"

"What room?" Grace asked. "Are you going to do something with the guest room?"

"Not for a little while," I told her. "We need to stop by the store that sells fingernail polish and let you pick out the right red color."

"You do realize that you aren't going to be able to redirect her to another subject very much longer, don't you?" Connor whispered.

I nodded and gave him another kiss on the cheek. "Got to take advantage of that little trick as long as I can."

"Yuck! Y'all ain't 'posed to do that in the store," Grace fussed.

"Yes, ma'am," Connor said and then leaned over and whispered for my ears only, "If we *do* have another boy, I agree on the name Davis. Maybe we can rewrite history a little bit, and they'll all grow up with no secrets."

I don't think about the big secret very often anymore, but the idea of it is still alive and well in Atascosa County. Pretty often someone will make a comment or ask me about it, and my answer has always been the same: *Aunt Gracie didn't tell me anything.*

Acknowledgments

Sometimes I'm asked where the ideas come from for my stories. They can come from anywhere—a young cowboy waiting in line at the burger shop, a little boy's eyes when his teacher brings the class into an ice cream shop, or even two people arguing over a barbed wire fence. For the book you are holding in your hands today, the idea came from many years ago when I spent a lot of time at my friend Janice Davis's house.

Her parents lived in the country and were on a party line. We used to try to lift the phone receiver so carefully that the folks who were talking wouldn't hear the click. We failed too many times to count, but it led me to playing a game of *what if.*

What if we heard something that would break our young hearts? What if it was something so horrible that it defined the rest of our lives? Out of those questions, this story was formed. I hope you all enjoy it.

As I've said many times before, it takes a village to bring a book from a very rough idea to a finished product. I would like to take a minute to thank all those in my village: Folio Literary Management and my agent, Erin Niumata, for continuing to represent me. Amazon/Montlake and my editor, Anh Schluep, for believing in me. Krista Stroever, my developmental editor, who makes diamonds out of lumps of coal. All my family, friends, readers, and fans. The list could go on and on because my village is very large.

Happy reading to all y'all!

Until next time,
Carolyn Brown

About the Author

Photo © 2015 Charles Brown

Carolyn Brown is a *New York Times, USA Today, Washington Post, Wall Street Journal,* and *Publishers Weekly* bestselling author and RITA finalist with more than 130 published books. She has written women's fiction, historical and contemporary romance, and cowboys-and-country-music novels. She lives in the small town of Davis, Oklahoma, where everyone knows everyone else, knows what they are doing and when, and reads the local newspaper on Wednesday to see who got caught. She and her late husband, Mr. B, are parents to three grown children and too many grandchildren and great-grandchildren to count on the fingers and toes of one person. For more information, visit www.carolynbrownbooks.com.